# SILVER BELLS

PALISADES CONTEMPORARY ROMANCE

# SILVER BELLS

## WISH LIST
### LISA TAWN BERGREN

## MYSTERY AT CHRISTMAS
### LAURA KRAUSE

## THE BEST MAN
### SHARI MACDONALD

SILVER BELLS
published by Palisades
a division of Multnomah Publishers, Inc.

Wish List © 1997 by Lisa Tawn Bergren
Mystery at Christmas © 1997 by Laura Krause
The Best Man © 1997 by Shari MacDonald

International Standard Book Number: 1-57673-119-7

Cover illustration by Paul Bachem
Design by Brenda McGee

Printed in the United States of America

For information:
MULTNOMAH PUBLISHERS, INC.
POST OFFICE BOX 1720
SISTERS, OREGON 97759

LIBRARY OF CONGRESS CATALOGING-IN-PUBLICATION DATA:
Silver Bells.       p. cm.         ISBN 1-57673-119-7 (alk. paper)
   Contents: Wish list/ by Lisa Bergren–Mystery at Christmas/by Laura
      Krause–The best man/by Shari MacDonald.
   1. Christmas stories.  I. Bergren, Lisa Tawn. Wish list. II. Krause, Laura.
Mystery at Christmas. III. MacDonald, Shari. Best man.
PS648.C45S58    1997                          97-18326
813'.0108334–dc21                               CIP

97 98 99 00 01 02 03 — 10 9 8 7 6 5 4 3 2 1

# WISH LIST

## LISA TAWN BERGREN

# ONE

ome on, Lia." Noel Stevens waved a makeup brush in what she hoped was an enticing manner. "Let me do your eyes again. I'm bored out of my mind." Scarcely ten customers had come through Sundstrom's department store since her shift began, and none of them had wanted any cosmetics or skin-care products from the Jean Van Dorne counter.

"Oh, Noel." Lia grumbled under her breath, but allowed herself to be led to the tall white chair. She sat, carefully smoothing out the folds of her uniform—a white lab coat identical to Noel's.

"Thanks. Just one more time and I'll leave you alone. I promise," Noel said. She quickly doused a cotton ball with makeup remover and began to clean off her friend's face before Lia could voice any further protests. "We both need to get to know these new colors. And I can't try them on myself. You know they'd never work on me."

Lia closed her blue eyes in resignation. "Oh, for a real customer," she sighed.

"They'll come," Noel said confidently as she perused the tray of eyeliner samples. "In droves. More than we want to see. Hmm, I think we'll go for the sixties look. All very pale except for liner."

Lia's eyes snapped open. "You know I hate that look."

"I know." Noel ignored the objection and continued to fish the colors she wanted out of the bin: Icy Danube for Lia's eyelids, Frosted Atlantic as a highlighter. "But we'll have fifty high school girls at the color seminar next week, and they're all going to want it, at least as a freebie. Think ahead. Think marketing. If we're prepared, we can sell them a whole boatload of makeup." She grinned. "After all, nobody with any sense would already have these colors in their drawer."

Lia giggled, then relaxed under Noel's professional touch. As Noel worked, she brushed away a strand of dark brown hair that kept falling into her eyes. "I always wanted to be a beautiful blonde, you know. These colors would look awful on me."

Lia picked up a hand mirror and surveyed her reflection. "Um, sorry to break this to you, Noel, but they look pretty bad on me, too."

Noel studied her critically, then smiled. "You know what? You're right. They're ugly. Really ugly. And we're supposed to sell this stuff?"

"Yes," came a cool voice from behind her. "And quite a lot of it, too."

Noel felt the blood drain from her face. She froze in place as a feeling of horror crept over her. After months of working on the retail floor, trying to prove her worthiness to management, had she really just made the ultimate faux pas—publicly criticizing their product—in front of her prospective boss? Lia stared over Noel's shoulder, her colorful eyes growing bigger, confirming Noel's fears.

Taking a breath, Noel turned and found herself looking up into the disapproving face of Margaret "Mamie" Sundstrom, vice president of marketing for the Sundstrom chain.

"Hello, Mamie," Noel began, thinking fast. Maybe there was still some way to turn this fiasco to her advantage. This, despite the fact that she suddenly felt very small, in more ways than one. At five-foot-three, she stood a full six inches shorter than the statuesque, beautiful, and completely composed executive before her. She forced herself to meet Mamie's steady gaze. "Now you know the truth. I belong in the back office, working on marketing materials, not up front selling mascara and lipstick. Please," she urged, using her most conciliatory tone, "I've done my six months. Can we talk about a prospective move date now?"

Mamie shook her head almost imperceptibly, a faint look of disappointment registering on her features. "Noel, your assignment is not some form of punishment. This is not about 'doing time.' This is about understanding the heart of our business and knowing the customer. I'm sorry to say it appears your six months haven't been nearly enough." The words were spoken gently but firmly. "We'll talk again." She nodded at each woman in turn. "Ms. Ashton. Noel."

Stunned, Noel watched as Mamie spun on her heel and walked away, carrying herself with the poise of a fashion model. "There goes my future," she murmured. "I've been condemned to sell perfume for the rest of my life."

Lia bristled. "Some of us like this work, you know. We don't all have a master's degree in marketing that makes us blind to the good parts of our job." She hopped off the stool. "Besides, it could be worse. You could be working in Shoes."

Despite her bleak situation, Noel smiled at the thought. In some ways, she pitied the poor shoe department interns who were required to run three flights of stairs in the back of the store, pulling shoe boxes for salespeople. It was tough, exhausting work. But at least they weren't consigned to work within a two-by-six-foot corridor like she and Lia. Noel stared at the wall of fragrance samplers behind the counter, envisioning herself wearing sweats and no makeup as she jogged up and down those stairs. It wouldn't be so bad. And she wouldn't have to go home to do time on her NordicTrack, either.

A soft cough interrupted her reverie, and she lazily glanced to her right. There, leaning over the counter, stood a well-dressed, attractive man with light blue eyes and sandy brown hair, obviously trying to catch her attention. Cute, she thought absently. Then, as understanding dawned on her, she uttered a startled "Oh!" realizing with embarrassment that she had practically fallen asleep at her post. She shook her head to clear it of its wayward thoughts and moved to help her customer.

"May I help you?" she said, sounding as professional as she could for a woman who had just been caught daydreaming.

"I hope so," the man said warmly. He seemed unrattled by her sloppy sales approach. Thank goodness. The last thing she needed now was to have a customer lodge a complaint against her. "I'm looking for the right perfume for a special lady," he said in a confident baritone.

For one brief moment, Noel felt a flicker of dismay. Of course all the attractive, normal-looking guys were already taken. But the feeling of regret was fleeting, and her marketing side quickly kicked in.

"I see," she said, adopting her most businesslike tone. "Does she have a favorite fragrance?"

He pursed his lips and shook his head. "I don't think so. Not that I know of."

"Tell me a little bit about her, then. What's she like—what sort of personality?"

The man's forehead furrowed into wrinkles as he thought. "I guess you could say she's pretty straitlaced. She's not your typical woman, doesn't like froufrou flowers and such. She's one who knows what she wants. A take-charge sort of person, but still very feminine."

Noel threw her customer a sidelong glance, trying to size him up. It irritated her to hear his description of a typical woman. Froufrou flowers? But the man seemed sincere and genuinely interested in doing something sweet for the woman he loved. That had to count for something.

"Cinnamon Fields," she said confidently, spritzing some of the fragrance on her wrist and holding it up for him to smell.

The man leaned forward, casually resting his fingers against her wrist as he bowed his head to accept the unspoken invitation. The perfume scent was rich and tangy, and Noel felt her head spin slightly as he touched her. *Phooey. I must have sprayed on too much,* she thought as her stomach turned a small flip. She hoped her carelessness would not affect her sale.

"You said she's not into anything too flowery, in a manner of words." Noel withdrew her arm and pushed away the strange feeling that had arisen in her. "I assumed she was more spice than fruit. Am I right? Cinnamon Fields?"

He gave her a small smile that seemed to begin with his eyes instead of his lips. "Noel," he said, glancing at her name tag. "A Christmas baby, were you?"

She returned his easy smile. "No, nothing so romantic. My mom's French, and she had a friend once who was named Noelle."

"Well, it's beautiful. Just like you."

Not usually one to blush, Noel felt her cheeks grow warm at the compliment. The man grinned at her reaction. "Well," he said, stepping back, "you've convinced me. I'll take a small bottle of the Cinnamon Fields perfume and a jar of the body lotion."

Cinnamon Fields. Body lotion. His words reminded Noel of exactly why the man was there. Attractive or not, he was obviously taken. Time to get back to business.

Accepting the large bill he handed her, she rang up the purchase and turned back to him with the change and neatly bagged product.

"Thanks, Noel," he said warmly.

*Good-bye,* Noel thought regretfully, giving his strong jawline and stubbly five o'clock shadow one last appreciative glance. But, "You're welcome. Come again," was all she said. She watched as he turned on his expensive heel and strode out of Cosmetics.

"Well, he was the nicest customer we've had in here for days." Lia came to stand at Noel's side. "The job's not so bad now, huh?" she said knowingly, giving her friend a nudge.

"Well," Noel admitted with a rueful grin, "some days *are* more rewarding than others."

At six o'clock, Noel pulled off her white lab-style jacket and slipped into her red wool duster. "See you tomorrow, Lia."

"Okay," said Lia, who had pulled the closing shift. "Hey, is that coat new?"

"I got it last summer, but this is the first time I've worn it. I found it on sale at—" Noel dropped her voice to a whisper— "at Dillard's. They'd marked it down six times. I got it for twenty-four bucks! Can you believe it?"

"Incredible. And it looks gorgeous on you, too, with your dark hair and blue eyes."

"Thanks." Noel smiled and turned to go, then paused and spun back around. "Uh, Lia?"

"Yes?" Her coworker put down the brushes she'd been cleaning.

Noel cleared her throat nervously. "Look, I'm sorry about today. I didn't mean to say anything bad about your job. Our job, I mean. I just don't have the same vision for my career. I want to do something different. But I didn't mean to imply that what I want is better."

Lia stared at her for a moment. "Come stand over here," she ordered, as if she hadn't even heard the apology. Confused,

Noel did as she was told while Lia spun the stand of lipstick samplers and picked out a rich but subtle shade of burgundy called Merlot Mist. She pantomimed pursing her lips, and Noel again obeyed.

As Lia applied the lipstick, she smiled. "There. Very nice. Just your color." She paused and considered her friend thoughtfully. "It's okay, Noel," she said at last. "I know you didn't mean what you said as a slam. Not all of us can make the world beautiful in the same way." She handed Noel a small white mirror.

Noel glanced at her reflection and nodded appreciatively. "Thanks, Lia," she said, referring to more than just the lipstick.

"You're welcome."

Noel walked to the front door, nodding a good-night to the girls behind the other makeup counters as she made her way through the department-store aisles. Once outside, she took a long, deep breath of clean Seattle air. The pavement was wet from rain, but the skies were clearing now. When she looked up, the fast-moving clouds above her made her feel as though Sundstrom's were falling backward. She shook her head to clear away the dizzying optical illusion, then headed toward the Seattle Center.

On the nights she got off work at six, she routinely rushed down one block to the Seattle Center square to watch the giant fountain, music, and light show. The fountain had just been switched to a Christmas "gig," as Lia called it, which coordinated bursts of water with a number of accompanying carols. Great compressor pumps had been embedded beneath the huge basin, enabling "composers" to create magnificent displays of water sprays and spurts of liquid color and light that danced to the music. Noel found the show transfixing, a relaxing break before walking the three blocks to her cold apartment and her cat, Oscar the Grouch.

She was so intent upon watching the water that she hardly paid any attention to the people around her and was startled when the man next to her spoke.

"You like to come and relax here, too?"

Noel turned and, to her surprise, found herself face-to-face once again with her attractive Cinnamon Fields customer. "Oh…yes," she said, then looked back to the fountain. She hesitated, unsure whether or not to pursue a conversation. They had to speak loudly to be heard over the noise of the water and music.

The two of them watched as three teenage boys stripped off their shirts and ran down into the concrete basin, yelping and dodging streams of water. Nearby, a group of adult onlookers shook their heads.

"Someone's going to have to answer to his mother when he's sick tomorrow," Noel said, pointing toward the kids. It couldn't have been more than forty degrees outside.

Cinnamon Fields man smiled and nodded, then turned his gaze back to the water display.

*That's it,* Noel thought a bit grumpily. *I'm not saying anything else to this guy. I don't have to talk to him. He's a customer, that's all. End of story.*

But despite her resolve, she found herself wondering about the man's personal life. And before she had stopped to think about her words, she heard herself say, "I forgot to mention it, but we have free gift wrapping at the store. I mean, you know, if your perfume was a Christmas gift. For someone special." She cringed even before she had finished speaking. Based on idle curiosity or not, her words sounded like a blatant fishing trip for information about his marital status.

The man shook his head graciously. "Oh, no. Thank you, though. I guess you could call it an 'assignment' more than a gift."

"Oh," Noel said with a slight nod, though she had no idea what he meant by that. An assignment? Given by whom? His girlfriend? His wife? She automatically glanced down at his hands, but leather gloves prevented her from seeing whether or not he wore a wedding ring.

Suddenly, the seven-minute water-and-light show ended and, just as abruptly, the man rose to leave. "Well, have a good evening," he said, then looked around, appearing slightly worried. "Do you live near here? I'm not sure this is the safest place to be for one person alone."

Noel stood as well. "Don't worry, I'll get home okay. Good night."

She smiled politely and turned away. *Whew. That was embarrassing,* she thought. But at least it was over. The guy was gone, and she'd never have to see him again.

Behind her, she heard the man utter a soft good-night. As she walked confidently away, the next rotation of the water dance began.

# TWO

"You know, Mamie," Noel said, keeping her voice cool and even, "I've thought about what you said, and I agree. I do need to get to know the customer. Thank you for pointing that out. It was an important lesson to learn. And now that I *have*—"

"Now that you have what?" Mamie eyed her with what appeared to be a mixture of irritation and amusement.

Noel swallowed hard as she faced the Sundstrom matriarch. "Um, now that I have learned my lesson..."

Mamie pursed her lips, giving Noel that all-too-familiar disapproving stare. Noel tried to keep a brave face, but her shoulders slumped slightly and she felt herself shrink under that steely gaze.

The older woman rose with a sigh, stepped around her desk, then reseated herself in the chair next to Noel's.

"My dear," she began patiently, "I realize this is hard for you. You're very ambitious, and I think that's admirable. But I'm afraid you don't understand that you simply cannot rush the process.

"I assure you, I'm not trying to punish you or beat you down. There is simply something about being out there, on the front lines, so to speak, that proves invaluable to one's marketing career. I promise, the experience you are gaining will come in handy someday." She reached out and patted Noel's hand. "Cheer up. It could be worse. You could be working in Shoes."

Noel stared at her, feeling stunned. Was that a twinkle in Mamie's eyes? "All right," she said, and with her chin high, she rose to leave with what dignity she had left. "Thanks for your time."

"Oh, and, Noel?" Mamie called after her. "Speaking of the front lines, I need you to do me a special favor. As you know, Santa Claus will be in our store for the holiday season, starting tomorrow. We want to hire only minimum staffing. Therefore, I'd like you to fill in as an elf for two hours every day while the full-time elves take alternating lunch breaks. We'll have a temporary Santa during that time period as well. I hope you'll do everything you can to help." Mamie opened her mouth to say something else, then apparently changed her mind and closed her lips tightly.

Noel felt mildly relieved to have escaped whatever lecture Mamie had been about to deliver, but she could barely contain her disbelief at what could only be considered an insulting demotion. "An elf? Are you serious?"

Mamie sat up a little straighter. "Quite. Is there a problem, Noel?"

Noel bit her lip. "No. Of course not," she said carefully. "Whatever you say will be fine."

"Good." Mamie smiled benignly as she stood and made her way back around the enormous desk. "Think of it as more research. All those tired mothers in line will give you a perfect opportunity to ask focus-group questions pertaining to holiday sales."

"Yes, research," Noel said, pasting a smile on her face. *I'll be a focus group of one. The topic: what it feels like to be a green-clad freak.*

~ ~ ~ ~ ~

That night, Noel once again got off work at six o'clock. And again, she made her way to the fountain to watch the dance of water, music, and light. To her surprise, as she entered the square she caught a glimpse of her Cinnamon Fields customer exiting Key Bank, located on a street bordering the Seattle Center. That must be where he worked. She watched as he cast a look in her direction, apparently recognized her, then smiled and waved.

Noel raised her hand to return the greeting, then quickly turned away. Her face burned as she flushed with pleasure. *Stop it, Noel,* she told herself. *He's taken.* She took a seat and forced herself not to turn and watch to see if he was coming her way.

She felt rather than saw him take a seat beside her.

"Whew!" he said, breaking the silence. "It feels good to take a break."

Noel tried to look cool as she glanced over at him. "Tough day in the financial market?"

The man looked startled. "Financial market? How did you—?"

"I saw you coming out of the bank," she explained. "I assume you work with money in some way."

He stared at her for a moment, then grinned. "Well, actually...yes. I've always loved numbers. Some days, though, work is just that—work."

Noel sighed. "I know what you mean."

"Tough day at the makeup counter, huh?" he asked, looking toward the fountain as the music-and-water production began.

"You could say that. Although I did get a promotion."

"Great!" He looked impressed. "What will you be doing?"

"Oh, it's a terrific opportunity," Noel said brightly. "I'll be working with many different people and a younger clientele."

"Doing what?"

"Ah," she said, giving him a rueful smile. "I don't know if I can adequately communicate the weight of this move."

"Must be a big promotion."

"That's right. You see, I—and don't think just *anyone* gets to do this—I get to be Santa's elf for two hours a day."

To his credit, the man did not laugh openly. He just chuckled softly and smiled a gentle smile. "At least you're taking it with grace."

"Oh, you bet," Noel said dryly. "What could be more graceful than an elf? There's nothing like pulling on a green felt tunic and pointy boots to remind you that everybody has to start at the bottom. Maybe that's what God's trying to teach me. Humility. I figure I might as well learn fast and get it over with."

He tilted his head. "Oh, I don't know. It may not be so bad. Maybe it'll even be fun. You'll meet people who are in a good mood—"

"Or stressed shoppers."

"Kids who can't wait to see Santa—"

"And will stomp on any elf who gets in their way."

They laughed together, then turned their eyes back to the water show. After a few minutes, she ventured timidly: "You know, it just occurred to me that I never got your name."

The man turned and faced her once again. "Really? How rude of me. Please, call me Nick," he said and reached out to offer his hand.

"Hi, Nick. Nice to meet you. I'm Noel."

"I know." He grinned. "How could I forget a beautiful name like that? Or such a beautiful lady."

"Hey, watch it." Noel tried to make the words sound like a warning, but she knew she looked and sounded pleased. "I don't think the recipient of your Cinnamon Fields gift would appreciate your giving compliments to strange women."

Nick smiled into her eyes. "Trust me," he said, "this recipient would be pleased to hear that I shared a love of water fountains with such a delightful woman."

Noel tried not to grin too broadly and closed her eyes to concentrate on the lyrical melodies and the sounds of pulsating water.

"Do you like music?" Nick asked.

"Oh, yes," she said, squeezing her eyelids tightly. "Sometimes when I close my eyes here, I can visualize my own water-and-light show."

After a moment, Noel opened her eyes to look at him. She smiled when she saw that he had his eyes closed. "Very nice," he said simply.

They watched and listened to the rest of the show in silence. *Best to be the first to leave,* Noel thought as the fountain ran through its grand finale.

She rose. "Well, Nick, it was good to officially meet you." He remained seated but took the hand she offered, holding it a moment longer than necessary.

"It has been a delight, Noel. Again. You know, your name really is fitting."

"Oh?" She raised one eyebrow. "How so?"

"Because getting to know you is like a Christmas gift," he said. "I hope I'll see you here again soon. I'm looking forward to becoming friends."

*Friends?* Noel wasn't sure how to take that. One minute, Nick seemed to be flirting with her. The next, he seemed perfectly content to step back and take his time. He was unlike any man she had ever known.

"Oh," she repeated and pulled her hand from his, unnerved by his mysterious comment. "Well, uh, thanks. Good night."

"Good night, Noel."

# THREE

**N**oel gazed at her reflection in the full-length mirror, feeling sick to her stomach. She forced herself to take stock again. Maybe it wasn't as bad as she thought. Green tunic with deep *V* cuts in the bottom and neckline; bright red tights; long, pointy, green elf boots with tiny silver bells at the tips that jingled each time she took a step.

Her heart sank. Yes, it was bad. Really bad. Unfortunately, there was nothing she could do but get through this. She took a deep breath.

"Of course Lia wasn't hit up for the job because she's tall," she mumbled to herself. Once again, Noel lamented her petite stature. Oh, to be tall and statuesque like Lia or Mamie. Their very height seemed to command respect. And here she was, Santa's elf. *Am I on the bottom rung of this career ladder or what?*

One last glance at the clock in the employee dressing room sent her scuttling back out into the store. Being late would only make things worse. At least she was small. Perhaps that would work to her advantage for once. Noel hunched her shoulders and stared at her pointed toes. Maybe nobody would recognize her.

"Hey, Stevens," called Ned from Shoes. "Dig those boots!"

"Nice tunic," said Sara from across the aisle in Women's

Sportswear. "I think I have a customer who's looking for something just like that."

"Cute," Noel said with a sardonic smile. "Don't worry. You guys will get yours. Sundstrom's is an equal-opportunity employer, you know."

Resolutely, she strode through Children's Clothing, Women's Dresses, and Juniors, making her way to the front of the store. There, bordering cosmetics and facing outward into the mall, she found the huge Santa's Workshop display. A miniature building housed the hand-carved chair where Santa sat, with an elf at his side and a child on one knee. A second elf stood behind a tripod, taking Polaroids. All around them, extravagant decorations had gone up overnight: huge bows and fragrant evergreen garlands; ornate gold and white ornaments; wreaths on every column. It was beautiful and festive, Noel had to admit. The display staff had certainly gone to town this year.

Noel made her way through the crowd of parents and children clustered in a mass before Santa and climbed the stairs, which were covered in white indoor-outdoor carpeting—an attempt to simulate snow, she assumed. As she rounded the corner of the workshop, she nearly collided with a second Santa.

"Whoa, sorry," he said. Noel glanced up as he graciously nodded for her to go ahead of him. He must be the replacement Mamie had mentioned. Poor guy. She wondered which department he'd been pulled from.

"So, you have to do your time too, huh?" she asked as the two Santas switched places.

The replacement Santa shrugged while the other made his escape. "Actually, I volunteered for this position. I do it every year."

"Every year?" Noel asked, wondering why anyone would want to do such a thing. She motioned for the first child in line to approach them. "I'm Noel, by the way. What's your name?"

"Why, Kris Kringle, of course!" He spoke in a rich, booming voice, clearly trying to sound jolly. "Santa Claus. St. Nicholas. But you, my dear, can call me Kris."

Noel shot him another quick glance. There was something familiar about him. Had they met before? "It looks like you're really enjoying this."

"Of course I am. It's a lot of fun," he said, lifting the child onto his lap. "It gets me into the spirit of the season." He turned his attention to the five-year-old who was staring solemnly at him. "Hello, son. What's your name?"

"Benjamin. And I know you're Santa," the boy said solemnly, "'cause my mommy told me so."

Noel smiled in spite of herself. Maybe everyone was right. This might not be so bad after all: adorable kids trusting another with their wishes. It was sweet in a way.

"Well, that's right," Santa said with a booming laugh. "Ho, ho, ho! Have you been a good boy this year, Benjamin?"

"Mmm-hmm." The child looked quite serious. "I've been very, very, very good."

"Three verys, eh?" Santa nodded and somehow managed to remain straight-faced. "I see. That's good to hear, my boy. Very, very, very good. So tell me, what is on your wish list this year?"

"I want a Star Wars Death Star model," Benjamin said, "and a Han Solo action figure and the Millennium Falcon."

"Well, we'll see what we can do," Santa said cheerfully. "In the meantime, you be a good boy, Benjamin. My elf here will give you a candy cane on your way out."

Candy canes! Noel scanned the area around her and finally spotted a tin bucket loaded with the red-and-white-striped candy. She suddenly remembered last year's Christmas and the children's sermon her pastor had given. He told the story of a Christian candy maker who wanted to make something appropriate to remind children of what Christmas was all about.

Candy canes were the result. The shape was a symbol of Jesus' shepherd's crook; the color red symbolized the stripes of blood on Christ's back. What did the white stand for? Purity? She couldn't quite remember.

Her attention was jerked back to the present when Benjamin tugged on her tunic, impatiently awaiting his candy. "Oh! Sorry, honey. Merry Christmas!"

"That's the spirit," Santa said. Another boy climbed the steps in trepidation. Nearing them, his eyes grew big, and he turned and ran back to his mother, who quietly reassured him. While she and Kris waited, Noel turned to him.

"So, what department are you in?"

"The Gift Department," her companion boomed in his best Santa Claus voice.

Noel rolled her eyes. "I'm serious."

The man's light blue eyes flickered to hers. "Back office," he said quietly.

Great, Noel thought. She was working with someone who reported directly back to Mamie. No wonder Mamie had seemed appalled when Noel responded to her new assignment with less than enthusiasm. Apparently this guy seemed to consider it some kind of treat. She looked at him more carefully. For some reason, she still thought he looked familiar. After mentally running through all the executives she knew, she dismissed the thought. He was definitely not one of the ones she knew. Just a case of déjà vu, she supposed.

Her attention was caught once more by the child who had run back to his mother. Summoning up his courage, he approached Santa one more time. The man slowly stretched out his strong hands, beckoning the child with a warm, reassuring gesture. "Come here, son," he said soothingly. "Don't you want to chat with me for a moment?" The boy looked down at his feet, and Santa leaned forward. "Don't you want to sit on my lap?"

"Nuh-uh." The child shook his head, looking forlorn.

"I see. Well, that's all right. You can talk to me from there. Is there something you especially want for Christmas?"

The boy, an angelic-looking child with big blue eyes and blond hair, looked up at Santa. Tears filled his eyes. "I want my dad to come home."

Kris rested one arm on his knee and sighed. "I see. I can imagine how much you want that. You know, son," he said in a low voice, so Noel had to lean closer to hear over the noise of the crowd, "sometimes things on our wish lists are too big for even Santa to give. But I'll tell you what. I'll say a special prayer that God will bring your dad home, okay?"

"Okay," the boy said doubtfully.

"You see, God is so big, he made me and you, too. You can talk to him any day of the year. He hears whatever you say. He's with you, even though you can't see him with your eyes. And he loves you. He loves your mom and dad, too. Always. I think that's the best gift ever. How about you?"

That seemed to satisfy the child. "I guess so. Can I have a candy cane?"

"Of course," Noel jumped in. She handed him his treat, then watched as the boy ran down the stairs to rejoin his mother. She wiped away a sudden tear, hoping no one else had noticed her reaction. "That was amazing. But aren't you worried about your job? I mean, can't you get in trouble for saying things like that?"

"No," he said, waving forward the next child. "I know the boss, and he thinks it's okay." He gave her a quick glance, his blue eyes bright over red-rouged cheeks. "Does it bother you?"

"No. I admire what you just did. And I agree. You're hitting them with the truth. I just hadn't seen how my faith could fit into Santa's workshop."

"Well, today's your lucky day," said Santa with a smile. "You won't believe how many kids come who need an encouraging word. I don't have an agenda here, but when children need someone to turn to, I point them in the right direction."

Noel nodded, then looked out at the sprawling crowd, which was clearly in need of some line management. She decided to take charge. "Okay," she said, clapping her hands together and stepping out of the workshop. "Who's next? You wanna talk to the big guy? You think he's going to bring you something for Christmas? Well, you better have been good!"

Loud peals from the Episcopalian bell tower sounded at 8:00 A.M. the next morning, announcing the church's early-morning service. Noel groaned and pulled a second pillow over her head as the clanging continued. The sound made her think of a streetside Santa ringing his bell, a thought that reminded her of Sundstrom's enigmatic lunchtime Santa.

At first she'd thought he was a terrible brown-noser, trying to impress Mamie with his volunteer efforts. But it quickly became clear that his behavior was driven by a love for children and for God. Impressive. She liked the way he lived out his faith so courageously. Maybe she could learn to do the same thing.

She pushed the pillow off her head with a sigh. Now that her mind was in gear, she might as well get her body moving as well.

The comforter fell from her shoulders, and she shivered. Her studio apartment had high ceilings and old, highly polished wood floors, a combination that made her living quarters all the colder. Since the size of Noel's paycheck did not allow her the luxury of turning the furnace up high, she had loaded her bed with big, fluffy comforters and had to talk herself into braving the cold each day. Still, she loved the quirky characteristics of her home, especially the old, leaded glass windows that let the light pour in from two sides of her corner unit.

It was true that the church bells interfered with her sleep. Yet they, too, added to the apartment's ambience. From her windows, Noel could look out upon the huge, quarried stone bricks of the old cathedral across the street.

Her apartment walls were covered in countless layers of white paint. The building had once been a high-class ware-house but had recently been converted to living space. She had been lucky to get a lease. A friend of a friend had tipped her off even before it became available. Before she knew it, her sofa, bed, NordicTrack, trifold screen, card table, and chair were all moved in.

The home was perfect for her. A little artsy, and only a few blocks from Sundstrom's, where she had landed a job just prior to renting the space. It was a godsend, since she did not own a car and could not afford one. Her student loans took nearly every dollar she had left after paying for food and rent.

Noel sighed as she thought of her mountainous debt. Confident that she would find a high-paying job as soon as she completed grad school, she had borrowed left and right in order to pay her way through. And where did she find herself after graduation? In a cosmetics technician/elf entry-level position that paid little more than minimum wage. She simply had to get into marketing, and soon. If she could just get through the Christmas season, maybe Mamie would consider her dues paid in full. A regular salary and benefits would be a blessed relief.

Taking a deep breath, she shot out of bed and pattered across the cold floor to the tiny bathroom at the far corner of the apartment. She ignored the yowls of protest that rose from Oscar the Grouch, her blue-gray mutt of a cat. If Oscar had his way, she would stay perfectly still in bed, a permanent human heating pad for his berth.

Noel cranked the knob marked Hot, knowing it would take a few minutes for the warm water to reach the third floor. While she waited, she brushed her teeth and thought of her fountain friend. She wasn't sure what to think of him yet. But she had to admit she liked him.

She flashed a foamy grin at her reflection in the mirror. Yes, despite being at the bottom of the career ladder, she was in a great place. At least she had a job. She had her faith, her family. And she had a new friend, whatever that meant.

All in all, life was good.

"Guess who's coming to town?" Lia asked that Tuesday, as soon as Noel came around the corner after her elf shift.

"Uh, Santa Claus, I guess. I suppose that means we'd 'better watch out...'"

"Ha, ha. Very funny." Lia gave her a withering gaze. "I'm talking about Geoffrey Sundstrom," she said, raising her nose into the air and speaking in a pseudo-British accent. "Heir apparent to the Sundstrom fortune." She dropped her nose and returned to her normal voice. "People say he's a doll, inside and out. Wouldn't you just love to go out with someone like that?"

Noel shook her head. "Nope. Not me. I'm not going to waste my time dreaming of Cinderella stories," she said, searching under the counter for some Windex. "I didn't allow myself to go through six years of college—and countless hours of playing Santa's elf—just to marry into money. I'm going to make it on my own...no matter what." She didn't know if Lia would take her seriously, but Noel meant what she said. After years of living without a father, she had long ago stopped believing in the reliability of the opposite sex. She grabbed the bottle of cleanser she sought and stood, finding herself face-to-face with Nick.

If he had heard her last comment, he was being gracious enough to ignore it. "Hi," he said, suddenly looking and sounding like a sweet, awkward schoolboy. "I felt an urge to come by, though I'm not sure why. I'm not in need of any more Cinnamon Fields."

"Hmm." Noel thought for a moment. "Perhaps what you're feeling is an urge for a good cleansing regimen."

"Cleansing regimen?" He looked at her warily. "Oh, I don't know about that. That is, guys don't—"

"Don't be a chauvinist," Noel chided gently. "This skin-care system is designed especially for men." Nick still looked a bit nervous. "Come on," she said, smiling, "surely the idea doesn't threaten your masculinity."

He raised an eyebrow. "After that remark, I can hardly say no, can I?"

Noel patted his arm and smiled again. "Now, why don't you have a seat?"

Nick sat as he was directed, looking a bit ridiculous with his big body perched on the tall, narrow stool. He was about five-foot-ten, a good seven inches taller than Noel, with broad shoulders. He reminded her of her high school boyfriend, who had played quarterback on the school team.

She took a step nearer and softly cupped his chin in her hand, turning it to one side, then the other. She ignored his steady gaze and laughing eyes as she lent a critical eye to his epidermis.

"My goodness. What have you been using to clean your skin, sandpaper?"

"Isn't that what macho men do?"

Noel shook her head, knowing full well she wasn't about to get a straight answer. "From the look of things, I'd have to guess you're using some generic brand soft soap. But by the way you dress," she said, nodding toward his well-tailored suit,

"I'd guess you can spend a few dollars on quality skin care."

Nick shrugged noncommittally.

"Your skin isn't something to gamble with. Understand?" she said in a mock lecturing tone.

"All right, all right. That's why I'm here. Right?" He sent her a teasing glance again that sent a delightful little shiver down her spine.

"Right," she said, rubbing astringent on his face with a cotton ball. "Unless you're really here to buy more perfume for your girlfriends."

"I told you before," he said, turning farther to the side as she cleaned around his dimple, "I don't have a girlfriend."

"Not in so many words," she said lightly.

"Enough words that a college graduate should know."

"Smart aleck. I'll have you know that I have an advanced degree." She cleaned with an industrious tenacity, trying not to dwell on his nice cheekbones or strong jawline or that darn, darling dimple. She finished the first phase of the cleaning process, stepped back, and studied him. "Feels good, huh?"

Nick rubbed a broad hand over his face. "Actually, it does." He sounded surprised. "It's all tingly."

"Well, you ain't seen nothin' yet." She squirted a moisturizing lotion for combination skin into one palm and rubbed her hands together, then lightly spread the product over his nose, cheeks, forehead, chin, and neck. Suddenly, her skin felt all tingly, too.

"What's your advanced degree in?" he asked as she worked.

"Marketing."

Nick closed his eyes as if enjoying the sensation of her hands on his face. Noel finished quickly. "Mmm. I'll definitely need some of that," he mused. "Do your hands come with it?"

"I'm afraid not; I need them most days. Now close your eyes again." When he did, she spritzed a mint-laced spray over his face. Nick jumped slightly, startled.

"What's that?" he asked with a laugh.

"The Revitalizer," Noel said in all seriousness. "Anytime you're tired through the day, you can just pull that out of a desk drawer and give yourself a little shot."

"Right," he said with a laugh. "I'd be mocked by the entire office."

"Well, you at least need it after your cleansing and moisturizing regimen."

"I do?"

"You do."

"Well, okay. If you say so. You're the expert with the advanced degree. I'll take all three."

Noel nodded and moved away from him to grab the products from the shelves. Nick paid for them, and she met his glance once in the mirror as she rang up the sale. As much as he'd been flirting with her, she was surprised that he still had not asked her out, and was giving no indication that he would anytime soon.

"Thanks, Noel. I'm sure my skin will feel like a million bucks. Or should I say, it had *better* feel like a million bucks after what I just paid."

Noel grinned. "Thanks for coming. I hope it helps."

"Tonight at the fountain?"

Her heart skipped a beat. "See you then."

He smiled back at her, flashing her a row of straight white teeth, then turned and walked out.

Lia joined her at the counter, leaning down to rest her chin in her hands. "Mmm. He's dreamy."

"He is, isn't he?" Noel realized with a sense of surprise that Nick seemed even dreamier each time she saw him.

"Where'd you say he worked?"

"Key Bank, down by the Seattle Center. We're meeting at the

fountain again tonight. Maybe he'll finally ask me out." She sighed. "If he doesn't, I may have to ask Santa about it tomorrow. I have connections, you know." Her eyes twinkled merrily. "And a date with Nick is definitely on my wish list."

Noel walked the square, waiting for Nick to come out of the bank. Every once in a while, she allowed her attention to wander as she watched the people or the beautiful fountain. After several minutes, she spied him sitting down at their usual spot. She walked the curving sidewalk to him and plopped down at his side. "Hello, there."

"Well, hello. Where did you come from?"

"Took a little walk. It feels good to stretch my legs after being cooped up in the corridor all afternoon."

"The corridor?"

"You know, my two-by-six-foot cell."

"I take it you don't like working the cosmetics counter?" Nick leaned back, watching her.

"All in all, it could be worse. You're talking to an elf, remember. But we just talk about makeup and clothes all day. There's more to life, you know? Oh, and now that Geoffrey Sundstrom is back from grad school, he's another topic of conversation. Geoffrey this and Geoffrey that. No one's even seen him yet, but they're all talking as if he's the end-all.

"I bet he thinks the whole world bows down at his feet. Can you imagine? Finishing grad school and coming out to find the whole world on a plate before you. An only child and parents who own fifteen stores, with plans to open fifteen more in the next three years." Noel leaned back against the park bench. "I have to work to get where I'm going. And I have to pay for student loans en route. Mind you, I don't resent it. I just don't appreciate having to be an elf on the way."

Suddenly, Noel was aware that Nick was watching her with a slightly amused expression on his face. "Speaking of which, how is elfdom? Surely it can't be all bad."

Noel laughed softly and stared at the fountain. "No, it isn't. As a matter of fact, there are some really poignant moments with the kids. But I'm just dreading the day one of my old college friends comes in with her new baby and says, 'Noel? Is that you?' That's not something I look forward to."

"Maybe God really does want you to learn something from all of this, as you said earlier."

"Yeah. And as I said then, I want to learn it fast."

They laughed easily together. It had been a long time since Noel had felt so comfortable with a man. Surely she was not alone in her enjoyment of their easy camaraderie? She was wondering again if Nick would ask her out soon, when he stood abruptly and gave her an awkward smile.

"As always, it's been nice, Noel. But I have to be going. I have dinner plans."

Noel's heart fell. She hoped her face betrayed none of the sadness his statement had caused her. "Oh. Yes. Have a nice one."

"Thanks. Tomorrow?"

She nodded. "Maybe. I'll see how the day goes." Noel couldn't help herself. She was a little irked that he was going out with someone else. Maybe he really did have a girlfriend somewhere. Maybe this was just idle flirtation. Men did that sometimes; she'd seen it before.

He leaned closer, surprising her. She leaned back a little.

"I'll be here, Noel. I hope you will be too."

She watched as he walked away toward the parking garage. Puzzling. That's what her fountain friend was. Puzzling.

# FOUR

As the days went by, Noel found that she actually looked forward to her daily elf stint. It was, in fact, a nice break from her work behind the counter. When she commented on this one day before her shift at Santa's Workshop, Lia asked, "Is it being an elf, or is it being *Santa's* elf?"

Noel slid her white jacket into a drawer and scrutinized Lia. "What are you talking about? What other kind of elf would I be?"

"I'm talking about this particular Santa," Lia said. "I think he has nice eyes. What's his name?"

Noel smiled. "He says it's Kris. I can't tell if he's kidding. You'd think we were in *Miracle on 34th Street*. Apparently he works in management. Men's Wear, I suppose."

"How can you tell? His wardrobe? All that red and white—seems like he doesn't have much original flair."

"Ha, ha. Actually, this guy does have flair. You should see him with the kids. He can calm the most savage of beasts." She paused. "He has nice eyes, huh?"

"Yes." Lia rubbed lotion into her hands and studied Noel. "You haven't noticed? You've been working with him for two weeks."

"I guess I'm usually standing beside him, facing out toward

the mall. We've never really talked at length face-to-face. When did you have a chance to meet him?"

"I ran into him in the break room. I'm going to find out who he is. Maybe he's available. For me," she said, narrowing her eyes at Noel. "You already have Nick."

"If you can call it that. I guess I'm going to have to ask him out if we're ever going to get anywhere. It's cold out at that fountain. And speaking of cold, I'd better get going. I'm off to the North Pole."

"On, Dancer! On, Prancer!" Lia called after her.

After she'd changed into her costume, Noel hurried down the terrazzo hallway, in a rush because she'd chatted a little too long with Lia. She arrived slightly out of breath, and her heart sank as she spotted Seth Sundstrom, CEO and president, chatting with her partner, Kris.

"Well, hello there," Seth said, shaking her hand vigorously. "Santa here's just been telling me about you." Noel glanced at Kris, wondering just how high up he was in management. All she got was a twinkling smile in return.

"Well, I'd better let you two work. You have quite a lineup waiting for you," Mr. Sundstrom said. He turned to Noel. "It was nice to meet you, young lady. We do appreciate your filling in. Mamie told me all about it."

"Oh, it's fine," she said, feeling herself blush. "Better than I expected. It was nice to meet you, Mr. Sundstrom."

"Please, call me Seth." He looked at Santa. "I'll see you later, Mr. Kringle." Then he disappeared.

Noel turned back to Kris, ready to ask him about his position in the company. Lia would certainly want to know. But he was already in character, reaching out to the kids. She knew from experience what that meant: For the next two hours he would be Santa, for all intents and purposes. Her question would just have to wait.

Two hours later, the regular Santa was back, but by the time she remembered she had something to ask, her Santa was gone.


That night as she walked toward the fountain, Santa Claus was the last man on her mind. Her thoughts were focused solely on Nick. She refused to ask him what his dinner plans had been. It was none of her business. But his intentions toward her were her business. And she meant to find out what those were, once and for all.

Nick was waiting for her, and he watched her closely as she approached and took her place beside him.

"Good evening, Noel," he said. "I've been thinking about you all day."

"You have?" she asked, glancing at him. Nick studied the fountain, avoiding her gaze, and nodded. Patiently, she waited. When he finally dared to meet her gaze, she opened her mouth to ask the question she'd been wanting to ask for so long. "Nick?"

"Yes?"

"Um…have you been using a moisturizer on your lips?"

"No. I can't say I have."

"I can tell. You'd better come by tomorrow morning, and I'll rustle up a sample tube of our Ultra Aloe lip balm for you." Noel took a deep breath and gave it one last try. "And by the way, Nick, are you ever going to ask me out, or are we just fountain buddies?"

# FIVE

The next day, Noel's Santa partner was "in a management meeting." In his place was a temporary replacement: Theo, a black morning clerk who got a kick out of the kids' reaction to an African-American Santa. She was surprised herself by the contrast of his dark skin against the snow white of his beard, but his hearty "Ho, ho, ho!" had Kris's beat any day. They introduced themselves, then got right down to business.

"Hey, Santa's not black," said the first child in line, a sassy little blonde.

"He is in Africa," Theo retorted. "Now get on up here and tell me what you want, or my assistant just might mark you off as being naughty." His approach was one hundred percent effective.

Noel's shift went quickly; she was lost in thought, considering her nice, sweet banker. Tonight, at long last, Nick was taking her out, though she didn't know where.

"It's a surprise," he had said. "Wear something warm."

But she was already warm through and through.


Nick was waiting for her at the main entrance as she left Sundstrom's that night. Cheerfully, he led her down the street to the monorail. Noel was intensely aware of his proximity as they sat leg to leg in snug seats, soaring downtown. Her knee barely came three-quarters of the length of his thigh.

"Here?" she asked when they stopped.

"Here," he confirmed. "I figured a woman who could pick out Cinnamon Fields and a top-notch skin-care system could help me shop for Christmas presents. If you do well," he whispered, as if sharing a secret, "I'll reward you with something special."

"Oh? That sounds intriguing. Okay." Noel pretended to roll up her sleeves. He chuckled. "Who are we shopping for?"

Nick just grinned. "Friends, family, coworkers… Better to ask, who aren't we shopping for?"

For the next few hours, they poked in and out of dozens of downtown shops, enjoying the lights and the painted windows, the hustle and bustle of patrons on the street, the jingle of the occasional Salvation Army Santa. Being with Nick, talking to him as they picked out a gorgeous scarf for his mother and a blue cardigan for his father, made her heart sing.

At one point she found herself humming the fountain carols under her breath, and her heart filled with joy as Nick joined in. Walking down the street, he suddenly burst into song. "Shall I play for you? Pa-rum-pa-pum-pum. A tiny gift for you, pa-rum-pa-pum-pum." He grinned and nodded at passersby who gave him guarded smiles, then pulled Noel close when she pretended not to know him. She dissolved into giggles.

"Okay, drummer boy," she said. "I think we've accomplished your Christmas shopping mission of getting gifts for everyone you know, including your mysterious parents."

"Mysterious?"

"Yes. I don't even know their names. Come to think of it, I don't even know *your* whole name."

He gave her a quick, playful smile and said, "What's yours?"

44

She stuck out her hand. "Noel Stevens. Pleased to meet you."

His grin grew as he took her hand in his and shook it solemnly. "Delighted, Noel. I'm—" His eyes suddenly darted behind her as a vehicle sped by. "Whoa! Cabbie!" He put two fingers into his mouth and let go with a shrill whistle. Immediately, the cab pulled over and stopped. He hustled her toward the black-and-white checked car.

Noel looked at him in surprise. "Where to now? Are you suddenly anxious to get me home?"

"Not at all," he said as he settled in beside her. "The Four Seasons," he instructed the driver.

"I didn't realize it was so late," she said as she glanced at her watch. "I should be getting home. It's a 'school night,' you know."

"I know. But first, the best hot chocolate in Seattle. It won't take long."

They arrived at the elegant old hotel and hurried inside as the rain started to fall. Settling into plush armchairs around a cozy table for two, they stared out a window streaked with rain. "Looks like we made it just in time," Noel said.

"Yes." But Nick's mind was clearly not on the weather. He studied her in such an intense fashion that Noel struggled not to squirm under his gaze. She searched her mind for something to talk about.

"You were just about to tell me more about your parents."

Just then, the waitress came up, and Nick ordered two hot chocolates. He sat back and studied Noel some more, as if measuring his words. "They're both professionals," he said slowly. "But approachable. They've taught me a lot. I can only hope to be as good a person, in business and in life.

"Some of my favorite memories are from high school. My parents really cared about who I was becoming. They treated me like I was their greatest investment. Not as if I were a material possession, but like a gift they'd been given."

"No siblings?" Noel asked.

"No. Mom miscarried when I was two. As far as I know, they never tried again. You?"

"One younger brother. Ryan. He's coming to visit soon. I can't wait. I haven't seen him in so long—I feel like I need to get to know him all over again."

"I'm sure it won't be that tough. Family is family."

The waitress presented them with delicate bone china teacups, filled to the brim with swirling, dark chocolate and topped with a dollop of whipped cream and chocolate shavings. Before they knew it, they had finished their second cups and were in a deep conversation about politics. Just when Noel was commenting on their senator's recent vote, a man approached them from the bar, his eyes on Nick.

"Well, I'll be! If it isn't my old buddy—"

Nick practically leaped out of his chair to shake the man's hand. The way he placed himself between them, it seemed as though he was actually trying not to introduce Noel. But the man would not be dissuaded.

"And who's this?" he asked, taking Noel's hand and winking at Nick. "Your latest conquest?"

Noel shrank inside and pulled her hand away, trying not to show the distaste she felt for his comment. How many girlfriends did Nick have?

"Hardly," Nick said, passing it off as nothing. "Hal, this is Noel Stevens. Noel, this is Hal Camden. We're old college acquaintances."

"You sure know how to pick them," Hal said, still sizing Noel up as if she were a side of meat. "You work at Sundstrom's?"

"Yes," Noel said, her eyelids narrowing to mere slits. "How did you know?" Had Nick mentioned her to this man? Did the two actually hang out together on a regular basis? The thought alarmed her.

"Hey, Hal," Nick said quickly, before the man could answer, "last time I saw you, you were heading toward the altar. What are you doing in here by yourself?"

Noel was confused. Nick spoke as if he hadn't seen the man recently. But if they weren't close, how had the man heard about her?

Hal made a broad swipe in the air, and for the first time she realized that he was drunk. "Got myself out of that one. A gold digger, that's what she was." He cast a lazy eye over Noel and opened his mouth to say something else, but Nick gently led him back toward the bar.

"Bye. Nice to meet ya," Hal threw over his shoulder. "She looks like a model," she heard him say to Nick.

"Yes. She's beautiful, all right."

Noel smiled when she heard his response.

When Nick came back to the table, she asked casually, "Why did he assume I worked at Sundstrom's?"

Nick shrugged. "Who knows?" Then he picked up their political conversation where they'd left off, and Noel forgot about Hal.

IX

**N**oel awoke with a groan to the familiar sound of early-morning church bells. It had been two days since her date with Nick, and she hadn't been sleeping well. Every night, he showed up in her dreams. If only she could catch another twenty minutes of sleep...

Before closing her eyes again, she glanced out the window, and what she saw made her eyes fly open wide. Snowflakes—huge ones—were falling, a rare occurrence at Christmastime in Seattle. She smiled lazily and started to get out of bed to make coffee, but when her bare toes met the brisk air, she quickly pulled them back into her warm cocoon. Maybe she'd just lie there for a minute and watch the snow. She grabbed the remote control and started the Christmas music on her CD player.

It was the perfect morning off. A warm bed. A beautiful snowfall. Christmas music. Even grouchy Oscar stretched luxuriously, contentedly, before settling back into his comfortable nest.

Ten minutes later, she still didn't want to brave the cold, but her desire for caffeine was strong. Clad in a flannel nightshirt and cotton tights, Noel jumped out of bed and reached for anything she could find to layer over them. Old blue sweatpants she had worn while painting the studio white. A dark green turtleneck sweater that left her nightshirt fanned out at the bottom like a tiny skirt. Rummaging through her makeshift closet, she found a paisley wool scarf that kept her neck reasonably warm. Her final addition was a pair of bunny slippers Ryan had bought her as a joke. This was the pleasure of living alone, she thought with satisfaction. She could dress any way she wanted, and nobody could make an issue out of it.

Once she had her ancient Mr. Coffee gurgling and steaming, Noel padded over to the bathroom to wash her face. Grimacing at her grungy sink and toilet, she dug out a container of Comet cleanser, a brush, and a sponge, then set to work. She had just begun to scour a rusty-looking ring in her toilet bowl when she thought she heard a knock over Bing Crosby's "White Christmas." At first she ignored the sound, thinking she'd imagined it. But the knock, or what was now a steady pounding, persisted.

Noel hurried to her door. Someone must be in trouble to be making such a racket at that time of the morning. She opened the door without thinking.

"Nick!" she managed, her heart sinking as she realized what a sight she must be. Smiling broadly, he leaned against the doorjamb and crossed his arms. "Doing a little cleaning, I see?"

The toilet brush! Noel swung it behind her, as if by hiding it, she could make him forget what he'd seen. "Uh, yes. What are you doing here?"

"I came to surprise you."

"Mission accomplished," she said with a sorrowful glance at her getup. She wanted to cry. How could she have opened the door looking like she did? "I must look awful."

"No, no," he said, shaking his head emphatically. "You look more adorable than anyone I've ever seen."

"In an elfish sort of way, right?" She backed away from the doorway. "You might as well come in."

Nick took a step in and paused beside her. "Adorable in an unassuming, relaxed, fun sort of way," he insisted.

"All right, all right. Thank you very much, but the humiliation is over now. Come in. Have a cup of coffee, and I'll go change into something presentable."

"You don't have to," he said, planting himself in her director's chair, which sat next to the card table in the kitchen area. He watched as Noel poured him a cup of the rich, dark brew. "Is it colder in here than it is outside?"

"As a matter of fact, yes. Witness my clothing choices," she said, gesturing toward her outfit. Good grief! She was actually wearing the stupid scarf. And bunny slippers! *Oh, Father in heaven, I hope this is all part of some plan.* "My promotion to elf didn't bring a huge raise, and the high ceilings in here keep things pretty cold. I'm afraid that thermostat," she said, nodding toward the corner, "doesn't go above sixty."

Nick nodded gravely.

"I'll be right back." Noel walked back to her closet and selected a handful of clothing, which she carried behind a trifold screen. Moments later she emerged, wearing jeans and a blue wool fisherman's sweater. She wondered briefly why she hadn't bothered to begin with the ensemble from the start. It had just felt so lazy and wonderful to— Ah, well. There was no point in dwelling on it. Onward and upward.

Noel glanced at her reflection in a tiny oval mirror and ran her fingers through her hair in an attempt to tidy the wayward strands. She ignored her makeupless face. Lia would have had a fit.

She walked to the kitchen and poured herself a cup of coffee, then leaned against her countertop and studied her guest. Nick smiled back at her. "Nice outfit. But I liked the last one better."

"Yeah, right."

"I'm serious."

"Did you come here for a reason?" she asked, cocking her head.

"Other than to see you?"

"Other than to laugh at me."

Nick grinned. "I wanted to see if you wanted to venture outside. It's snowing."

"I know."

"Have you ever been on a ferry in the snow?"

Noel thought back and then shook her head.

"Well, it's time you were. Come on, I'll buy you breakfast on Bainbridge."

The offer was too good to resist. "Sounds great!" She paused and narrowed her eyes. "Wait a minute. This isn't some elaborate plan to get me to clean your toilet, is it?"

Nick laughed, his chuckle warming her heart. It sounded right as it echoed off the hard floors and walls. As if it belonged.


Half an hour later, the two donned their winter coats and emerged from the enclosed passenger area of the ferry, braving the open deck and delighting in the chill as they sped along the water. The weather was icy, but magical. The snowflakes were becoming more dense and fat as the temperature warmed; they obscured the view of the city. Only the eerie outlines of buildings could be seen through the whiteness. The engines of the ferry churned, and Noel went to the railing and watched the water as they cut through it, speeding their way to Bainbridge Island. The image of snow meeting water and disappearing was entrancing but could not compete with the feeling of Nick's arms casually wrapped around her shoulders.

"Do you mind?" he asked loudly enough to be heard over the engines.

"No," she said softly. Knowing he couldn't hear her, she reached up with gloved hands to hold his arms, hoping to encourage him to stay put. They stood that way, staring out at the sea, until she trembled with the cold. Instantly, Nick pulled away and offered her his hand. Glove in glove, they walked inside, the blasting heat of the cabin almost as welcome as the feeling of physical connection had been.

They sat together, and Noel brought her hands to her face. "Am I blue?"

"No," Nick said, tenderly stroking her cheek with a finger as he studied her. "Quite rosy cheeked, I'd say. Santa would be proud."

Then his expression changed, and his face turned slightly pale.

"What?" Noel squeezed his hand in alarm. "Are you okay? You look sick. Is it the water? We should be there any minute."

"No, Noel, there's something—"

"I used to get really seasick," she interrupted, not wanting him to be embarrassed over his nausea. She'd had a high school boyfriend who got sick after an amusement-park ride, then broke up with her because he was so humiliated. "It happens to a lot of people."

"Noel, listen to me," he said seriously, taking her hand in his. "I've been wanting to tell you something for a long time."

The intense worry on his face scared her. What was it? Was there somebody else, after all? Just then, the captain's voice came over the loudspeaker. "Bainbridge Island in five minutes. Please proceed back to your cars and wait for instruction."

Nick sighed and stood, pulling her up with him.

"What, Nick? What is it?"

"Nothing. Forget it. Maybe later."

Sensing that the moment was gone, Noel elected not to push. And, not wanting to ruin the rest of their date, she chose to lighten the mood with a story about the kid who had tried to look up her tunic the day before. "He said he wanted to see if I had green skin," she said with a laugh. "He was quite earnest. Never mind that my face and hands were normal skin color." They laughed together, and Noel sighed as their easy camaraderie was restored.

Noel couldn't remember ever having such a good time. Nick made her laugh constantly, and they talked all through their delicious meal. "Thought you'd like it," he said as they left the tiny café and climbed into his BMW. He groaned as he sat down. "Oh, but I always eat too much. Not that you'd notice," he teased, looking over at her.

"I could always eat more than my brother," she said with a smile. "What can I say? Small woman, big appetite. Lucky metabolism."

"I'll say." He turned the key. "I'll need to get a second job if we keep dating."

In protest, she slugged him playfully. But the words *keep dating* rang in her ears.

"Was that a butterfly on my arm?" he asked innocently, glancing around as if searching for the offender.

She punched him again, harder this time.

"Ow! Good one. I won't push it another round," he said, pulling out onto the main highway of the island and heading back to the ferry.

"My brother used to do that," Noel said, smiling. "He'd say, 'You call that a hit? It felt like a feather brushing my arm.'"

Nick smiled with her. "I missed having that. You know, sibling rivalry...and friendship."

"I'll bet," she said tenderly. She imagined Nick would have been a wonderful brother.

"Noel, would you go to church with me tomorrow? We could go to lunch at Elliott Bay afterward."

"Sounds great to me. Where do you go?"

"First Baptist, usually," he told her. "But we could go somewhere else. Where do you go to church?"

"The Episcopalian church right across the street from my apartment."

"Well, let's go there then."

Noel wondered what First Baptist was like, and if Nick lived near his congregation.

"Where do you live?" she said, just as Nick opened his mouth to say, "Noel, I—"

"Sorry, you first."

"No, that's okay." Nick sighed. He looked tired after their long day. Probably still suffering from seasickness, too, she suspected. "Queen Anne Hill," he answered.

"Nice neighborhood," Noel observed. "Are you near the Sundstroms?"

Nick turned pale. "Noel—"

She immediately felt guilty for probing when he was obviously ill, and shook her head. "Never mind. It's not important."

# $\mathscr{S}$EVEN

**N**oel pulled her short, navy merino wool dress on over her tights and studied her reflection in the mirror of her bathroom's antique medicine cabinet. She wondered how she appeared to Nick. Pursing her lips, she took stock of her features: dark brown hair, so dark it was almost black, styled in a chic shoulder-length cut; prominent cheekbones; large dark blue eyes. She sprayed the top of her hair again, lifting sections to add volume, then added mascara to her lashes.

For the most part, she was comfortable with her looks, despite the fact that she occasionally wished to be tall and blonde like Lia. Noel considered her only serious detraction to be her small lips; she longed to have a sensuous mouth like Audrey Hepburn. She added a subtle shade of lipstick inside her carefully drawn line, hoping to make the most of what she had. Sighing, she wondered if the time would ever come when Nick would want to kiss her.

There. Done. Noel glanced at the clock. She was ready a full fifty-four minutes early. When was the last time that happened? She smiled ruefully in the mirror. *Are you excited about being with this guy, or what?* she silently asked her reflection. The phone rang just as she was trying to think up a way to kill some time.

She breathed a sigh of relief when she heard her mother's voice. At least it wasn't Nick calling to cancel.

"Hi, honey. How are you? I know you're probably getting ready for church, but I was just thinking of you and wanted to tell you I love you." Noel's mother lived in Minneapolis, but the two had remained close and frequently visited over the phone.

"Thanks, Mom. I love you, too. Actually, I have some time to talk. I'm ready a bit early. I'm taking someone to church with me, but he won't be here for almost an hour. Wait 'til you hear about this guy. He's great!"

"Oh, sweetheart! Who is he? I want to hear everything."

Noel took a breath, realizing that even talking about him made her heart pound. "His name is Nick. He works at a bank near the store, and Mom, he's great. He's attractive and smart, but better yet, he's a Christian, and he treats me like gold. I'm almost afraid to breathe. I keep waiting for the other shoe to drop."

"Don't be silly. He sounds perfect. How long have you known each other?"

"A few weeks. We've gone out twice now. Yesterday he took me to Bainbridge Island. You won't believe how he surprised me; I looked like a wreck. But he didn't seem to mind. And today we're going to church together and then out for lunch."

"Oh, honey, I'm so excited for you. Nick," Mrs. Stevens said quietly, as if imagining what a "Nick" would look like. "What's his last name?"

Noel frowned. "You know, this is a little embarrassing. I don't know. If he told me, I don't remember it. I asked him about it once, but he just looked amused. I was so embarrassed; he must have suspected that I forgot. And now, after we've spent so much time together, it's even more awkward to say, 'Oh, by the way, what's your name?'"

Her mother laughed. "Well, how are you going to find out? You can't let it go forever."

58

"Oh, I'll figure it out. Super Sleuth Stevens will look at a piece of mail or a car registration. Or I could ask him how he spells it."

"What if it's Smith?"

"I'll say, 'I was wondering if it was with an *I* or a *Y*.'"

"Pretty clever, Noel. Let me know how it goes. Call me this week so I can hear all about church and your special lunch. By the way, has your brother shown up yet?"

Noel grinned. "I thought you called just to tell me you love me."

"Noel!" Her mother sounded slightly offended. "Of course I called to tell you—"

"Oh, Mom. I'm just teasing. I think he's due in this afternoon."

"Wasn't he supposed to get there last night?"

Noel glanced at her calendar. "No. I have him down for this afternoon."

"Oh," Mrs. Stevens said distractedly. Noel softened. She knew her mother worried about her kids. It was especially hard after her husband had walked out ten years ago, leaving her to be both mother and father to Noel and Ryan.

"Mom, Ry's twenty-two," she said gently. "He'll be fine. Stop worrying."

"I know." Her mother sighed. "You just wait until you're in my shoes. You'll see that you never stop worrying about your kids. I wish you two were going to be home for Christmas."

Noel smiled, feeling her mother's love and warmth from across the miles. "I know, Mom. We wish we were there, too. But with the store and all, it's tough for me to go, and neither one of us can afford it. Although I'll probably spend just as much on groceries for Ryan as I would on a trip to see you. You know how he eats everyone out of house and home."

"That's true."

"I promise, he *will* get here. And don't worry, I won't get so wrapped up in Nick that I forget to come home to let him in."

"You'd better not. Well, I'd better run. I'm catching a late service here. It was good to hear your voice, honey," her mother said. "Give me a ring tonight and let me know Ryan got there, okay?"

"Okay, Mom. Bye."


Nick and Noel ran across the street through the rain, Noel wearing her red coat with its wide hood. Nick teasingly called her "Little Red Riding Hood" as they left her apartment building.

Inside the old cathedral, Noel smiled as she looked up to the towering arches and giant stained-glass windows. "It's majestic, isn't it?" she whispered, conscious of the incredible acoustics of the sanctuary. She led him to a pew toward the back, where he could more fully appreciate the beauty of the place.

She struggled with her coat, and Nick quickly helped her with it. She leaned toward him and whispered, "I wonder how many thousands of people have sat on this pew. What they've prayed for, what they've cried over. Or celebrated." She leaned forward to see his face better. "Am I the only person who thinks like that?"

He smiled at her. "No," he said, shaking his head. He stared into her eyes intensely, and Noel finally had to look down at her hands. She leaned back, feeling suddenly overwhelmed by a rush of emotion for him.

As usual, Noel enjoyed the liturgical service, appreciating the hymns most of all. Neither she nor Nick had a terrific voice, but since it was Advent, half of the songs were Christmas carols, and they sang them with gusto. The singing of the congregation combined into one single voice that bounced off the terrazzo floors and high ceilings, gathering strength. It struck Noel as being a highly spiritual experience, the songs climbing toward God and growing in intensity as if backed by the shoulders of their praise.

*My God, you are magnificent.* She smiled upward, praying silently as they continued to sing. Tears welled in her eyes. *Thank you, Father. Thank you for all you have done. And today, thank you especially for Nick. Thank you that he cares for me. Thank you that he wanted to come here today, and that he loves you.*

She glanced over at Nick and was surprised to find him smiling tenderly at her. Gently he wiped the tears from her cheeks. For a brief moment, Noel felt slightly embarrassed to be caught in the midst of her intimate communion with God, and yet it was all right. She wanted Nick to know about her close relationship with Christ. She wanted to share that part of her life with him.

She quietly slipped her hand into his. Had such a simple show of affection ever felt so good, so right? *Please, Father, I pray that you go before us in this relationship. Please don't let me be imagining things. I pray that I don't feel something for Nick that he doesn't feel for me. Because, Father*—she glanced at Nick and then looked back up to the towering arches—*I think I'm falling in love.*

After the service, they paused in the foyer to greet the priest and compliment him on his sermon. He was elderly, with the marks of life showing plainly on his face and the light of Christ alive in his eyes. As they chatted, the post-service bells began to ring, and Noel's smile grew. Nothing could be heard over the loud peals, so they all simply waited. When the music concluded, the priest leaned toward his visitors. "I think that will be a sound we hear frequently in heaven. There is nothing more celebratory than bells, is there?"

"No," Nick said. "Especially bells that size."

"These came from Switzerland. A hundred years old, they are. If you'd like, one of these days I could take you two up the tower to see them."

Noel beamed. She'd always wanted to see them up close but had been embarrassed to ask. "That would be great!" she said and Nick agreed, smiling at her enthusiasm.

They said good-bye to the priest and made their way to the street, hailing a cab to take them down to Pioneer Square, Seattle's oldest neighborhood. Noel adored the old brick buildings that made up the heart of the historic district. She especially enjoyed browsing in the art galleries, the antique stores, and the Elliott Bay Book Company.

"I love this place," Nick said as the cab stopped in front of the bookstore. After he paid the driver, they hurried to the canopied sidewalk. "I've heard a lot of great authors read their work here."

Noel smiled up at him and took the hand he held out to her. "I wonder if we've ever been at the same readings. I've come here fairly often with friends. The only bad thing is I always come home with too many books."

"Well," he said, opening the door for her, "there's no such thing as too many books, right?"

They paused just inside the doorway and briefly perused the shelves of best-sellers in the front of the store. "Since it's Sunday," Nick said, "how about we each pick out our favorite Christian writer and compare favorite passages over lunch? We can eat downstairs in the café."

She grinned up at him. "That's a great idea. Let's go."

He followed her to the back of the store and up old, wooden stairs that looked as if they were part of the original building. Sandwiched between other religion books that encompassed the world's myriad faiths were many Christian gems. Nick quickly pulled a selection from one shelf but turned away when Noel tried to see what he'd chosen. "No peeking," he scolded. "Let's surprise one another."

"Okay, then you go downstairs and order us lunch," she said. "That way I can make my choice in secret, too."

"Right. What do you want?"

"Their soup and sandwich special of the day."

"It doesn't matter what it is?"

"I like surprises," she said.

After he had gone, Noel found her volume under the *Bs*. *A Sacred Journey* by Frederick Buechner had greatly impacted her life. She hoped Nick had not read it yet; she wanted to introduce him to a special author. Then again, who knew? Maybe he had picked the same volume off the shelf. He had chosen his author from nearby. What a marvelous idea this was. She headed downstairs to the café. Never before had she dated a man with such creativity and interest in life. She could hardly believe he was a banker. She smiled as she thought of the old cliché, *You can't judge a book...*

She spotted Nick at a table in the corner of the room. It was still early for lunch, so few people were downstairs. The atmosphere was perfect for sharing an intimate spiritual conversation and maybe other intimacies as well.... Noel blinked, startled at the thought. She reprimanded herself as she sat down across from him.

They ate quickly, chatting about church and what it was like to be lifelong believers. In between bites and sentences, they shared small smiles, as if both knew something special was transpiring between them. Noel finished moments after Nick and shoved her plate to the side. She leaned forward. "Okay, mister, show me what you've got."

He flipped his book over so she could see the cover. "C. S. Lewis. The master."

She raised her eyebrows in a skeptical manner. "Well, he's good. Very good. I'll grant you that. But can he beat the Beak?"

Nick looked at her dubiously. "The Beak?"

"Frederick Buechner. The *carpe diem*, salvation stud." She grinned, glad to have made him laugh, and enjoying his smile and deep, single dimple.

"Bet you don't know what 'C. S.' stands for," Nick said.

"Oh, you mean Clive Staples?"

"Ah, so you are a Lewis fan. Uh-oh. Now I'm worried. Your fellow might have mine beat if you chose him over Lewis."

"Well, I don't know. Lewis is really amazing. I'll read you some Beak, and you can decide for yourself." She was pleased at the chance to expose Nick to an author she loved. There was an aspect of the sharing that was delicious, intimate.

Nick read aloud from *Mere Christianity* for a bit, then looked at Noel. "You know, I was thinking. Your elfhood could be an analogy for Christianity."

Noel smiled in surprise. "How do you figure?"

"Listen to this passage: 'Hand over the whole natural self, all the desires which you think innocent as well as the ones you think wicked—the whole outfit. I will give you a new self instead. In fact, I will give you Myself....'

"Get it? We die to self to live in Christ. In the same way, you decided to let your own aspirations die, choosing to pursue not your will but the will of your master, in this case, your boss. Your new self, the elf, sees things you might not have if you'd stayed behind the cosmetics counter. The stories you've told me, the kids you've met—that's a special slice of life you might otherwise have missed."

Noel nodded, but couldn't help laughing at his odd comparison. "It's a stretch, but I'll buy it. Still, 'it's not easy being green.'"

Nick laughed with her. The moment was perfect, and Noel

found herself feeling extremely contented in his presence. Yet all of a sudden, his expression grew serious.

"Look, Noel," he said, looking uncomfortable. "There's something I've been meaning to share with you. You see, I—"

At just that moment, Noel's digital watch beeped. She glanced down, and her face clouded over.

"Oh, my gosh! Look what time it is! My brother, Ryan, is supposed to get here today," she said as she stood and slipped into her coat. "I'm afraid I need to get home. Can we keep talking on the way?"

"Of course." Nick stood and pulled on his own coat. But somehow, even on the drive back, the subject didn't come up again.

Hurriedly, they climbed the old warehouse steps to Noel's third-floor apartment.

"Glad I wasn't dating you when you moved in," Nick teased, pretending to huff and puff as they reached the landing.

"Yeah, you were lucky," she said, smiling back at him. When they opened the door to the hallway, Noel immediately spotted her brother sitting on the floor.

"Ryan! I'm so sorry; time got away from us. How long have you been here?" She embraced her brother, then pulled back to look at him. Despite their tremendous difference in size, the two could have been twins.

"Hey, Sis," Ryan said. "'Bout time you came and let me in." He looked over her shoulder at Nick and, leaving his left arm around Noel, reached out his right hand. "Hi. I'm Ryan Stevens."

Noel held her breath as she waited for her date's response.

"Glad to meet you. I'm Nick," he said, meeting Ryan's grip.

"Nick...?"

"Oh, no need for formalities," Nick said lightly.

Noel turned away and hunted for her keys. *Phooey. I thought I'd get his last name for sure that time.*

"Look, I'll get going now and give you two a chance to catch up," Nick said.

"Are you sure?" Ryan asked as Noel unlocked her two dead bolts. "I didn't mean to break up your date."

"You didn't." Noel looked at Nick. "Would you like to come in?"

"No, no." Nick shook his head. "You two spend some time together. I'll call you or catch you on the square tomorrow. You work then?"

"I'll be there."

Nick paused, as if he wanted to kiss her good-bye. From the corner of her eye, Noel saw Ryan duck his head awkwardly. Hurriedly, Nick brushed her cheek with a kiss, gave her a tender look, then left.

Ryan walked past her into the apartment while Noel stared after the man who had stolen her heart.

"I see you've gone all out in furnishing the place," Ryan teased, wrenching her thoughts back into the present. "And where are the Christmas decorations?"

"Hey, a girl's gotta eat," she retorted, and shutting the door behind her, she resolved to think of no man besides her brother for at least two hours. "And as to the decorations, I'm sorry—I just haven't had time."

"Well, let's go fix that," Ryan said, picking up his coat again. "Let's have a tacky Christmas. We'll buy the saddest Charlie Brown tree we can find and the most decorations we can purchase for whatever we have in our wallets."

Noel laughed. "I have about ten bucks."

"And I have about three. Come on, Sis, let's go to town."

# EIGHT

Ryan and Noel came out of the ancient five-and-dime store down the street from her apartment, giggling like children. In their hands were giant bags full of the cheapest ornaments and decorations they could find, and a scraggly two-foot tree Ryan had painstakingly picked out.

Noel stopped by a newspaper stand. "Ryan, do you have any money left? Let's buy a paper and find out what's happening in the world. I just need a little more change."

Her brother gave her a look of pity. "No TV, right?"

"Nope." She shrugged. "Too expensive. Besides, even if I had one I couldn't afford the monthly cable charges. Enjoy being at school while you can. You'll find it's easier to be at Stanford on scholarship than in your own place, paying the bills."

Ryan didn't respond to that. He simply gestured to the sad tree and the sack in his arms. "I don't think I have any money, anyway. Gave it all to the cause." He paused, then set his purchases on the ground and dug into a back pocket. Proudly, he held out two quarters. "Hey, look at this!"

Once the newspaper was purchased, they gathered their things and headed home. For the next few hours, they worked furiously at their task. When at last they stepped back to survey their handiwork, both dissolved into hysterical laughter. The apartment looked horrible and wonderful at the same time, with tinsel strewn across any available surface, Santa and elf ornaments valiantly trying to hang on to their assigned branches of the tree, and a huge, bent HO-HO-HO sign blinking on and off in one windowsill. The dusty, broken thing had been marked down to two dollars, and Ryan couldn't resist.

"It's festive; I'll give it that much," Noel said dubiously.

"All this decorating has me hungry," Ryan said once he'd quit laughing. "I hope you have some food in the house, since we spent our last dime on Christmas folderol."

"I'm afraid all I have is eggs and bread. I get paid tomorrow," she said, grinning at Ryan's worried expression. "And I bet Mom will send money any day now."

"Whew. That's a relief." He stretched out on her ratty couch to read the paper. As he opened its folds, he absentmindedly scratched Oscar's neck.

"No, Ry, don't get up. Don't worry, I've got dinner covered," she said in her best martyr voice.

"Okay," he said distractedly, reading on.

Ten minutes later she brought Ryan his plate, piled high with scrambled eggs and toast. "That's okay. You get cleanup," she said. "We don't want you to feel like a guest in what will be your home for the next ten days."

"Uh, thanks," he said, taking his plate from her. Noel curled up on the other end of the couch with her own meal. "So, anything interesting in the..." Her words trailed off as she stared at the paper. She swallowed hard and nudged some ads away from the People and Places section.

There, on the first page, was a picture of Nick.

Unable to believe her eyes, she pulled it closer. It was him all right. Nick. Or rather, *Geoffrey Sundstrom*. The caption read: "General Manager Geoffrey Sundstrom officiated at a quiet ceremony Thursday evening, honoring citizens for outstanding community service with the Sundstrom Sunshine Awards."

"What?" Ryan said midbite, staring worriedly at her. "What's wrong?"

Noel could not seem to find her voice.

Her brother pulled the newspaper from her. "What do you see?" He scanned the columns.

"The picture. *That* picture."

Ryan's eyes went to the photo, and his eyebrows shot up as he let out a long, low whistle. "'Geoffrey,' huh? And I take it you didn't know he was a Sundstrom?"

Noel shook her head, numb with disbelief. How could he? How could he have lied to her? After all they had shared? She groaned, wanting to cry at the utter humiliation of being played for a fool. It only got worse. She read the article beneath the picture and learned about Geoffrey Sundstrom's involvement in various charity events. The story closed with a paragraph about his current stint as a fill-in Santa during the lunch hour at Sundstrom's main store.

All at once, the bits and pieces began to come together: the relief Kris Kringle who would not reveal his name but spoke about God to little children and was on friendly terms with the company president, Seth Sundstrom, who was his *father;* Nick's interest in her work as an elf; his aversion to telling her his last name. What was it he had said when he first introduced himself at the fountain? *"Please, call me Nick."* And all the while knowing that she would be working as an assistant to his St. Nicholas.

Noel groaned. "How could I be so blind? He must think I'm a total idiot for not figuring it out. And why? Why wouldn't he tell me?" She put her plate down on the floor, no longer hungry. The eggs tasted like rubber, the toast like sand.

"Maybe he wanted to get to know you first, then tell you."

"The time has come and gone. He should've come clean a long time ago."

"Maybe it's one of those situations where the rich guy just wants to be loved for himself," Ryan offered helpfully. "He's gotta be one of the most sought-after bachelors in Seattle."

"Quit defending him!" she spat out. "As far as I'm concerned, he can go on being a bachelor. He's a lying, scheming rat!" Noel jumped off the couch and headed to the bathroom, knowing she was about to cry and wanting the only privacy the apartment afforded. Thankfully, Ryan honored her wish and left her alone.

When her tears finally abated, she considered calling and confronting Geoffrey Sundstrom, but she couldn't quite find the words. She felt completely disappointed, weak and debilitated by feelings of anger and betrayal.

She sat near the window in the dark, looking up at the night sky as their sign blinked HO-HO-HO and Ryan snored on the couch. Where was he now, this Geoff, and what was he doing? How long had he intended to keep his identity a secret? How long did he think it would take her to figure it out? Tomorrow she would get her answers. *Oh, dear God*, she prayed, *how could you let me get in this deep?*

The following afternoon she pulled on her elf outfit though she would have preferred to shred it. But today, at least, she would face him. Noel would tell Geoffrey Sundstrom that she knew the truth.

She reached the workshop five minutes early, wanting every chance to meet his eyes when he showed up in costume. *In costume.* Was he always playing a part with her? Did she really know him at all?

Geoffrey rounded the corner and raised his fake white eyebrows in surprise at the sight of her. "Ah, my loyal elf Noel," he said, smiling. "You're here early. Nothing like a job you love, hmm?" He climbed the steps to join her.

Noel hoped her gaze was as murderous as she felt inside.

He stopped short. "Noel," he said in a low voice, "are you all right?"

"I'm fine, *Kris*," she said coolly. "But maybe I should call you Geoffrey? Or is it Nick?"

He frowned and moved closer to her. "So you know. Yes, I'm Geoffrey Sundstrom. Geoff. And Noel—"

"No." She looked up at him, on the verge of tears once again. "You're not just Geoffrey Sundstrom. You're Nick…my Nick." She heard her voice rising and knew she was about to make a scene, but she could not seem to stop herself. "How could you?" she asked, shaking her head. "How could you not tell me?"

"Noel, I—" he reached out to grab her arm as she struggled to leave.

The tears crested and fell down her cheeks. "You lied to me!" she cried. "You had every opportunity to tell me, but you didn't. You made me feel like a fool." She wrenched her arm away.

"Wait. Noel, I—"

"Forget it," she said to him coldly. "I'm feeling a bit sick to my stomach. I'm afraid you'll have to hand out your own candy today, Saint Nick."

And with that, she turned and fled.


Noel paced her apartment, staring out the windows and debating about going to the fountain. Geoff owed her an explanation, but she really didn't feel like seeing him. Their confrontation earlier still stung. Yet a part of her wanted to see whether he was man enough to face her, and what he'd have to say.

"Go, already," Ryan called as he cut up vegetables for stir-fry.

"You know you want to."

"What? Go see him? No way."

"It's killing you. I can see it. And you're going to go and ruin my Christmas if you don't get this worked out." He gestured with the knife in his hand, glancing down at it and then at her. "I'll keep all the sharp objects here, though."

Noel laughed in spite of herself. "That's okay. All I need is one good blunt instrument to do the job." She sank onto the couch, chewing a fingernail and thinking. What would he have to say? Could he possibly begin to explain the motivation behind his actions?

Ryan sat down beside her, rubbing his hands on a towel. "Go see him," he repeated, then looked at her skeptically. "Uh, you do know where he lives, don't you?"

"Queen Anne Hill." She laughed hollowly, shaking her head at the memory of how she had learned that one lone fact about him. "At least that's what he said. I'll bet you anything he lives down the street from his parents in a tiny mansion. Who am I in comparison?" she asked, waving toward her sparse apartment. "The little match girl?"

Ryan stared at her. "Go."

"I don't know what house it is, Ryan," she protested. "Anyway, if he really did care about me at all, he wouldn't be home. He'd be at the fountain, where we used to meet."

"So go there. Go find out what he really feels. Find out if he's got a decent excuse."

Noel doubted that he did. But she knew she had to go anyway. "Okay, okay," she said, giving in at last, then marched to the bathroom to pull herself together.

Geoff paced back and forth, looking at his watch for the fifth time. What was he doing? She wasn't coming. It was fifteen minutes past her usual quitting time, and he'd already found out from Lia that Noel had gone home sick earlier in the day.

Still, he had hoped she would show up so he could explain in this place why he'd done what he had. He knew her brother was at her apartment, and he'd go there if he had to. But he had hoped to talk to Noel here, where they had good memories. This fountain had brought them together, in a way. Geoff believed God had been there with them in those precious moments. Maybe Noel thought so, too. Maybe that alone would give him a chance.

He scanned the square one last time and spotted Noel standing near a sculpture, her arms crossed, watching him. Geoff went to her without hesitation. Her cheeks were splotchy and her eyes swollen from hours of tears. "Noel, please," he began, wanting to sink down before her and beg. "I'm so sorry. Please let me explain." He reached out to take her hands, but at his touch, she pulled away.

He took a deep breath and gestured toward a nearby bench. After hesitating for a moment, Noel went to it and sat down. He paced in front of her.

"Look, I was an idiot. I suppose it won't help to tell you I tried to come clean several times. Obviously, I didn't try hard enough. I was just so afraid, Noel. Afraid of losing you."

"Losing your latest conquest, like your friend Hal said? Who was I, the poor little girl you made an elf? I suppose that was your idea too," she said bitterly.

"No, no. It just happened that way. Maybe it was a coincidence. I like to think it was God. I admit, the first time I met you was a setup. Mother sent me to your counter on assignment. It was a routine Sundstrom employee check. You know, sending someone in undercover to see how an employee treats customers. But I swear, every interaction between us since then has been by chance or because I wanted to see you."

He looked at her, desperately willing her to understand, to believe him. "At first I didn't know how to tell you who I was. I figured you'd be mad. But when I decided I had to find a way, I tried. Several times. But something always happened. And it was so complicated, because somewhere along the way I fell in love with you, Noel. I only wanted to be with you, and for one of the few times in my life, someone was with me because of me, not because of my name."

"Yet I really didn't know who you were, did I, Geoff? I still don't know who you are."

"Yes, you do. You know me better than any woman I've known. You know me for who I am inside." He sat down beside her, struggling not to reach out and take her hand.

Noel shook her head. "I know you deceived me. Is that who you are? A liar?" She stood and began to pace herself. "Did you enjoy your fun at my expense? Good grief, do you have any idea how humiliating this is?"

"I know, I know," he said, his head sinking into his hands. "All I can say is that I made a terrible error in judgment. But it wasn't all a lie." He looked up at her, hoping his eyes conveyed the pleading of his heart. "I really do work over at the Key Bank building in a special office for Sundstrom finances, in addition to the work I do from home. And I volunteer every year for Santa duty, just like I said, because I really do love it. It was Mother's idea to make you an elf. It had nothing to do with me. I didn't object, mind you. As a matter of fact, I was thrilled. But it wasn't some scheme. I wanted you to fall in love with me just as I fell in love with you, Noel. On our own, for who we are inside."

She stared at him, her deep blue eyes brimming with tears. "How do I know what's true?" she whispered, as much to herself as to him. "I don't even know which end is up anymore."

Geoff rose from the bench and stood beside her. "You know,

there were ethical concerns as well. If a Sundstrom had asked you out, wouldn't you have felt pressured to agree?"

Noel frowned at him. "Now you're reaching for excuses, Geoff. Sure, that makes it sound better. But you and I know that you just got deeper and deeper into your own lie."

Geoff swallowed hard and nodded. "Probably."

Noel turned away from him, watching as the fountain began its routine. "My father walked out when I was fourteen. He told me he would be home after work, and he never came back. Call them untruths or half-truths; make excuses if you want. But I can't handle lies. The truth is always better, no matter how painful it might be."

Her revelation stung him to his very core. *Dear God, this is terrible. I've done the one thing that could hurt her most. Please. Please help me make it up to her.* "I'm so sorry," he said, tenderly taking hold of her shoulders. Noel tensed beneath his touch. "All I can say is, I was wrong. I thought my reasons were sound in the beginning, but it soon became clear to me that they weren't—even before you found out the truth. Please, Noel," he said, turning her around to face him. "Can you forgive me? I promise, no more secrets."

She just stared up at him, her face mostly in shadows, her eyes holding the look of a betrayed little girl. She said nothing to him. Just dropped her head and walked away across the dewy grass without another word.

Her look would keep him awake and staring at the ceiling all night.


The following morning, unable to face any of the Sundstroms, Noel called in sick. She was moping about, still lying on the couch at ten-thirty when her doorbell rang. "Can you get it?" she asked Ryan.

Dutifully, he went to the door. Within moments, twelve glorious, fragrant bouquets filled her apartment. On the table, the kitchen counter, and the floor stood giant arrangements of irises and white Casablanca lilies. Ryan handed her the card.

"Irises because I can't get your eyes out of my mind," the note read, "white lilies to signify my pledge for nothing but honesty between us from now on. Please forgive me, Noel. Geoff."

"The guy's got it bad." Ryan picked up her feet, sat down, then lowered her feet back onto his lap. He took the note from her without asking and read it. "I think you should forgive him," he said at last.

"You say that even after knowing the whole story?" Noel said wearily. She was emotionally exhausted. Even talking seemed to take more effort than she could exert.

"He blew it," Ryan said with a shrug. "But the only thing he lied about was his identity. And now he's sorry. Everyone makes mistakes. Relationships are full of them. Nobody's perfect, Noel. If you don't learn how to forgive, you'll die a lonely, bitter old woman."

"I'm just afraid." She stared out the window, past the blinking HO-HO-HO sign.

"Of what?"

"Of ending up like Mom. Heartbroken. Alone."

Ryan frowned. "You can't let Dad's failure haunt every relationship you have."

"I know," Noel said quietly. She glanced at him as he rubbed her feet absentmindedly. "Just how did you get to be so smart?"

Ryan shrugged. "Most of it's common sense. The rest of it is the gospel."

"I'll just have to remind you of these little bits of wisdom the next time someone breaks your heart."

Ryan gestured to the flowers around them. "It seems like

Geoff is trying to mend what he's broken."

Tired of Ryan's preaching, she sat up and stared out the window at the bricks of the Episcopalian sanctuary. "I think I need some fresh air. I'm going to wash my face and then go over to the church to do some praying and thinking."

Ryan nodded.


Noel prayed for a while, then simply sat in the ancient cathedral, listening and waiting. For what, she didn't know. Did she expect God to speak to her? To tell her what to do? She wondered what Buechner would say about such a moment as this. That she was learning more about the importance of faith in tough times? That she should embrace the moment, tough as it was? More and more she felt the urge to go to Geoff, to tell him again how angry she was and how he had hurt her. And even to forgive him. Was that urge the voice of God?

She was staring up at a stained-glass window depicting Mary, Joseph, and the baby Jesus, when she heard someone sit down behind her. Noel glanced over her shoulder and opened her eyes wide.

"Mamie, what are you doing here?"

"I came to your apartment to give you this," the woman said, handing an envelope over Noel's shoulder. "Your brother told me you were here. I was going to give it to you the day you left early," she said carefully. "Note the date. Please don't think this was anything but well-earned."

Noel slowly tore open the envelope and read the contents of the letter, which told her that Mamie was giving her the spot she had coveted on the marketing team. Slowly, she let the paper sink to her lap and shook her head. "I don't know, Mamie," she said in a soft voice. "I don't know if it's appropriate for me to work at your store anymore."

Mamie stood and came to sit beside her, lowering herself as a model would, with perfect elegant ease. "Don't be ridiculous, my dear. Regardless of what happens between you and my son, I believe you are an excellent employee. Bright, ambitious. You are someone I want, sincerely want, on my marketing team. You've paid your dues."

Noel still felt doubtful, even in light of the praise from a woman she so admired.

"I need to apologize and explain my part in all of this," Mamie said, leaning forward to look into Noel's eyes. "I was up late talking with Geoffrey last night, and I saw how much he cares for you. I would hate to know that my actions are what stands in the way of your forgiving him. You see, when I sent him in to buy product from you, I was asking him to perform what truly is a routine Sundstrom test. I had to know how you treat the customer when I'm not around. I believed you have what it takes. But I needed to know my intuition was true."

Mamie gave her a look of approval. "You did beautifully, of course. Not only did you make the sale, you captured my son's heart. Geoff's subsequent visits were made completely of his own accord. I almost told you the swing-shift Santa was my son. But Geoff doesn't like to make a big deal out of being the boss's child. He likes to be his own man, to introduce himself to people when he's ready.

"Honestly, there was no great scheme behind my assigning you to your elf role. I simply saw it as a good way for you to see the customer in a different light. And, as I believe you found out, it was an opportunity to have some fun, too. I know that cosmetics can be drudgery at times."

Mamie took Noel's hand with her long fingers. "Noel, I've never seen my son so taken with a woman before. And for all his blundering mistakes, I believe he's a good, honest boy… man," she corrected herself. She smiled ruefully. "It takes a mother awhile to get used to that. He'll be at the Christmas party tonight. And I know he wants to see you. I hope you'll be there."

She stood and looked down at Noel. "Well, I won't meddle any longer. I am sorry for my part in hurting you, Noel. I truly had only the best of intentions. Please forgive me."

Noel nodded, feeling awkward forgiving her boss.

"I'll expect you in the marketing office on Monday. Your hours are eight to five, Monday through Friday, regardless of your decision about my son."

"Thank you," Noel managed. Mamie's words were softening her hardened heart. She could feel it.

Mamie made her way out of the pews and was walking down the aisle when Noel called after her.

"Uh, Mamie," she began hesitantly. "I'd like to come in the rest of this week. Work the counter. You know, say good-bye to the girls and all."

Mamie nodded once, giving her assent.

"And...I think I'd like to finish out my stint as elf. After all, Christmas is just around the corner, and I haven't even told Santa what's on my wish list."

Mamie nodded again, a slow smile spreading across her face.

"Of course, I'd appreciate it if you'd let me tell Santa myself."

"Of course." Mamie turned to walk away, then stopped. She turned back to Noel, then apparently decided to keep her mouth shut. She gave Noel an odd little wave and went out the door.

Noel sat back in the pew and smiled. She'd finally seen Mamie Sundstrom not entirely confident about something in her life. Somehow it made her feel less insecure about her own uncertainties. And, strangely enough, it made her even more convinced of what her next move had to be.

# NINE

Noel dressed for the holiday party in an elegant gown of luxurious purple velvet. Weeks before, she'd decided to splurge on it after hearing Lia talk endlessly about what a fabulous evening it would be. The event was held annually in the restaurant of the Space Needle, and long-term employees like Lia waited for it with anticipation. Yet in spite of her confidence in her appearance, Noel couldn't help feeling anxious as she thought about what lay ahead.

When she walked out from behind her trifold dressing screen, Ryan whistled. "Man, you'll have Geoff on his knees for sure." Noel laughed, feeling self-conscious, and came forward to look at him in his rental tux.

"You look great, Bro. Thanks for agreeing to go with me. I have to admit, I'm a little nervous." She ducked her head, not meeting his gaze. She still hadn't told her brother that she planned to forgive Geoff. She wanted Geoff to be the first to hear.

Ryan studied her and opened his mouth to give her his latest advice. "You know, Noel, I think you should—"

"Please." She held up a hand in protest. "No speeches."

"Okay," he said. "But this is the moment of truth. Can you forgive him, or is it *hasta la vista*, baby?"

"I said no speeches." She shot him a warning look.

"Okay, okay," he said, putting his hands out in mock surrender. "Just want my big sister to be prepared for one of those remarkable moments when a person is faced with a decision that will impact the rest of her life."

"Thanks for not adding pressure to the situation."

"You're welcome." He offered her his arm. "I am here only to serve. And to scope out any hot Sundstrom babes."

Noel slugged him on the shoulder.

"What was that? Did a feather land on my arm?"


The moment Noel arrived, it was as if Geoff could sense her presence. He turned and gasped, then wondered if his response had been audible. He glanced quickly about. It was a miracle no one had heard him; his mouth was hanging open like a cartoon character's, and his heart was pounding so loudly he half expected someone to complain that it was drowning out the music.

Noel looked lovely on her brother's arm, a vision in a long, purple velvet gown that hugged her body. Her hair was done up in a knot with soft tendrils falling down at her temples. Sparkly earrings hung from her earlobes. He stared openly at her, waiting for her to meet his gaze. He had to wait through Lia's greeting and her introduction to Noel's brother before Noel looked across the crowded room.

Their eyes locked, and suddenly it was as if no one else were there. The music seemed to fade. Dancers who drifted through their line of vision were ignored.

Someone came up to his side, but Geoff ignored the greeting, his attention riveted on Noel. He knew that if they were to have a future together, they would have to talk things out, and soon. Tonight would tell the tale. Perhaps she had chosen to walk away from him. Perhaps their relationship would survive.

Either way, he had to know. This state of limbo was driving him insane.

He was about to make his way across the dance floor when someone bumped into him from the side.

"Oops. Sorry! Oh, there you are!" Angie Frick said, fluttering her eyelashes at him. Angie was one of the full-time elves who worked before and after Noel's shifts. But tonight, her behavior was incredibly un-elflike. She had obviously had too much to drink. Her skimpy black suede dress was practically falling off, but she didn't seem to care. He glanced down at the floor to avoid seeing too much and realized that she was wearing her elf boots. He raised his eyebrows in surprise.

"I've been looking for you everywhere," Angie breathed. "I have a present for you." She held up a cheap drugstore Santa's hat with his name misspelled on the brim in silver glitter. "Lean down. I'll put it on for you."

"Angie, thanks, but I don't think—"

"Lean down!" She yelled, her brow furrowing in frustration.

Wanting only to avoid a scene, Geoff obediently bowed slightly, closing his eyes to avoid a view of her ample cleavage. Angie carefully placed the hat on his head, moving slowly as if to concentrate on her task; then before he could straighten, she grabbed his head in her hands and planted a sloppy kiss on his lips.

Geoff, horrified by her advances, wrenched himself away, barely controlling the urge to wipe his handkerchief across his mouth. Several employees had witnessed the scene, and he felt himself blush a hot, bright red. "There's more where that came from," Angie said, reaching up to straighten his bow tie. Then she turned toward the bar. Several men hooted their approval.

*Noel.* His eyes raced back across the room. She was nowhere to be seen.

～～～～～

"Okay, come clean," Lia said as Noel splashed cold water on her face. "How long have you known you were actually dating Geoffrey Sundstrom?"

Noel sighed and leaned against the counter in the ladies' lounge. "Two days." She glanced up at Lia. "How did you figure it out?"

"Well, your running out of the ballroom like that was a big clue. Everyone's whispering about how Angie is throwing herself at the boss's son. Apparently she met him while he was playing Santa Claus." She gave Noel a meaningful look. "Man, I feel like such a putz. There I was, talking about that adorable Kris Kringle, when he was already taken—by you! I can't believe it, Noel. You're actually dating the famous Geoffrey Sundstrom."

"Not anymore, I'm not. Lia, I've been out with him three times, met him at that fountain for weeks, and he never told me!"

"Ohhh. Wait a minute. I get the picture," Lia said, crossing her arms. "He was sent in on the customer check, right? Then he forgot to tell you who he really was? Is that how all this happened?"

"Right. And now he wants me to forgive him."

"So forgive him, already. He's the key to your future!"

"No," Noel said, turning around and facing her reflection. "*I'm* the key to my future. I'll never count on a man."

"What are you talking about?"

A group of women entered the ladies' room and Noel just shook her head. "Oh, never mind. Ghosts from the past. I'm just trying to figure out what God wants of me and to be obedient. Which is rather tough at times. Especially when I look across the dance floor and see the man I had planned to forgive kissing another woman!"

"Come on, girlfriend. You know Angie would go after any available man, especially the most eligible bachelor in Seattle. She grabbed him and kissed him. I saw it."

"Yeah? Well, he did pull away...." Noel admitted.

"Exactly. Now get your buns out there and claim your man."

Noel resolved to stick out the rest of the party not to "claim her man" as Lia put it but to maintain her dignity. Ten minutes later, her face fresh and makeup reapplied, she was dancing with her brother when a sleazy guy from accounting cut in. Graciously, Ryan left her to the man, ignoring her wide-eyed outrage. Couldn't he see that this character was a slug? Still, trying to be kind, Noel forced a smile and tried to keep her distance from her new dance partner.

"It's good to see you, Noel," he breathed. "How come we haven't gone out yet?"

"I don't think it would be a good idea, Leo."

"Oh, I do. Give me a chance. You'll see."

He was barely as tall as she, and seemed to grow an extra set of hands as they danced. Firmly, she moved the one that was drifting low at her back to its appropriate position. Leo laughed nervously. "Sorry, I get nervous around beautiful women. Nervous hands."

"Yeah, well, keep those nervous hands to yourself, Leo." *Please God, let this be a short song.* She shot a look to the big band director as if he could read her mind. He did not meet her gaze. Unconsciously, she scanned the room for Geoff.

"I hear you're moving to the back office," Leo was saying. "Maybe someday we can have lunch."

"Maybe," she hedged, not wanting to be unkind. But then her brow furrowed. His hand was moving south again. She backed out of his arms. "I think our dance is over."

But Leo was not to be put off. He quickly pulled her back into his embrace, so close she could smell the alcohol on his breath. "Come on, baby, let's just finish this song."

Noel was about to give voice to her outrage when Leo abruptly stopped swinging his hips. His hands left her and Noel stepped away, plowing right into the person behind her. Someone large. "Sorry, I—" she glanced over her shoulder and saw Geoff glaring at Leo. Noel crossed her arms confidently and stared along with him at her offender.

"As I was saying, Leo," she said with a smile, "I'm sorry you're not feeling well. You'd better go home and sleep it off before it gets worse."

Leo glanced from Noel to Geoff and nodded hurriedly. "Right. Home. On my way." He made his way off the dance floor like a rabbit dodging a dog's maw.

She turned to Geoff. "Thank you. I appreciate the assistance."

He looked at her earnestly. "You're welcome."

Noel opened her mouth to speak, but her carefully prepared speech would not come to her. Suddenly, forgiving him seemed too difficult. Too risky. "But don't think that gets you off the hook," she found herself saying. "I came here wanting to make up, but what do I see? You, making out with…with another elf!"

Geoff followed her off the dance floor. "You don't understand. *She* kissed *me*. Uninvited."

"Geoff, you haven't even kissed *me*."

"You want me to kiss you?" Noel looked up to see several onlookers staring at them. She had wanted so badly to see Geoff again. Now she wanted nothing more than to disappear.

"I did once. I don't know anymore."

Before he could say another word, she stepped into the

crowd and dragged her brother from the side of a pretty Shoe department intern who was laughing at his jokes.

"Come on, Ryan. It's time to go home."

There was nothing Geoff could do but let them go.

The evening after the party, Noel and Ryan sat on the couch, dressed in sweats, and sipped cocoa.

"You know, Geoff took me to the Four Seasons for hot chocolate," Noel said morosely.

"Yeah, well, I bet it wasn't as good as this instant I made," Ryan said. He was in reasonably good spirits, especially considering the fact that the night before she had made him dress in a tuxedo for what amounted to all of an hour.

"No," she lied, giving him a tiny smile. "It didn't compare."

Ryan threw her a quick glance. "So, what happened last night?" he asked. After the party, she had refused to discuss it, choosing instead to go straight home and directly to bed.

Although Noel had not worked the next day, she had remained busy cleaning house and running errands. Now, for the first time, Ryan had her full attention. "One moment I see you two lovebirds ready to make up and kiss," he said, "and the next thing I know, you're dragging me out by the ear."

"Hardly by the ear," she protested mildly.

"Practically."

Noel sighed. "Oh, Ryan, I don't know. He was standing there after he'd saved me from this sleazy guy, giving me an earnest look, and I just froze up. It was weird. I kept seeing Dad telling me that he'd be home after work, when he'd been planning all along to leave us. And the whole time I trusted him. I don't feel I'm a very good judge of character anymore. I'm afraid Geoff's just playing with me."

"Geoff is not Dad, Noel."

"So you've told me."

"Well, it's the truth. The Bible says we're supposed to forgive and go on. Maybe you need to forgive Dad for being a deadbeat. Holding a grudge is messing up your life. You and Geoff could have a great relationship. I'd hate to see you blow it."

She stared at him in wonder. His words had hit home. "You really are getting smart."

"College," Ryan said, looking smug.

"Really. Well, thanks, little brother. I'll think about what you said. I think I'll go for a little walk. You know, have a little conversation with God. Maybe even an imaginary one with Dad."

"Good luck." Ryan looked pleased. "And don't worry about me. I'll just be here reading this old magazine, wishing for a giant TV with a good cable sports channel." He waggled his eyebrows mischievously. "I don't suppose when you make up with Santa you could pass along my wish list, too? And meanwhile, ask for a television set for yourself? I mean, not only does the guy have connections at the North Pole, he's also stinking rich."

"I only have one thing on my wish list," she said quietly. "And it has nothing to do with money or connections."


Three hours later, Noel stumbled back through the door of her dark apartment. She'd walked past Sundstrom's, past the fountain, past the Episcopalian church. So many places, so many memories shared with Nick...with Geoff. And while she walked, she had searched her soul, acknowledging the ache in her heart, the unfulfilled longing for her father's arms, the feeling of betrayal upon seeing Geoff in Angie's embrace. Anger, loneliness, and fear flooded over her. And as each emotion surfaced, she turned it over and over, viewing it from all sides, weeping, and finally giving it over to God.

From the couch, soft snores rose from her brother as she tiptoed past him to the phone. It was late, but she was already late in doing what she knew had to be done. She dialed the number from memory.

"Hi, this is Geoff," he said, answering after the second ring.

"I forgive you," she said quietly, her heart pounding. Then, for some reason she could not identify, she slammed the phone down before he could answer. "Oh, no. What did I do that for?"

The snoring had ceased. "Probably afraid he wouldn't forgive *you*," Ryan whispered back from the couch.

 EN

F ive days after Noel's late-night call, she still hadn't heard from Geoff.

During lunch break with Lia, she shook her head in dismay. "I was right. He's played me for a fool. Just wanted my forgiveness to ease his conscience."

"No way. I heard he was on a business trip. He'll come back around."

"How'd you hear that?" Noel looked up in surprise. "I thought I was the one with back-office connections these days."

"Yeah. But you can't top the gossip queen," Lia said, biting into a carrot. "Believe me, honey. I saw the way he looked at you. He's practically married to you already. There isn't any chance for anyone else with you in the picture."

"Maybe that was true once," Noel said, picking at her salad, "but I think he's angry at me now. Angry because it took me so long to forgive. Angry because I did it in such a stupid way. Sometimes I think I should call him again and apologize for the way I apologized. But I don't want to beg, for goodness' sake. I mean, he knows where I am." She turned to face her friend, looking forlorn. "Why hasn't he called?"

Lia reached across the table and clasped her hand. "He'll come around. You'll see."

∽ ∽ ∽ ∽ ∽

With the frenzy of Christmas shoppers growing stronger by the day, and because she was learning the ropes of a new department, Noel was excused from elf duty for the rest of the season. With Geoff gone, she didn't miss it too much. Still, she managed to find an excuse to walk past the workshop each day. She watched with longing as Theo and a girl she did not know filled in during their shift. Geoff's. Hers. Hers and Geoff's. She longed to turn back time and do some things over again.

Ryan took her out to lunch on the twenty-third in an effort to lift her spirits. He asked what she wanted to do on Christmas Eve and the following day, but Noel couldn't muster enough emotion to care. It was making her crazy. Where was Geoff? What had she done? Had she driven him away forever?

After an exhausting, twelve-hour Christmas Eve shift that ended at eleven-thirty, Noel walked the block down to the square, hoping against hope that Geoff would be there. He was not. She slumped onto a bench, shivering in the cold, and watched as the fountain rose and fell in rhythm with the Christmas carols for the last time. Why hadn't she set aside her stupid pride and just asked Mamie where he was?

Shivering uncontrollably, she sat forward, resolving not to ruin Ryan's Christmas. She would put on a happy face for the next twenty-four hours for his sake, even if her heart was breaking. Even if Geoff was gone from her life forever. She still had reason to celebrate. She still had her family, her life, her God. Noel stood and put her hood on.

She turned and gasped, realizing she was not alone. Her heart skipped a beat when she saw the face of the man standing next to her. "Geoff!"

He smiled gently. "I got home this afternoon. And I have to say, I don't know what it did to make you angry, but it was nice of you to forgive my answering machine."

"Your—" Noel gaped at him. "Your answering machine?"

"I'm sorry. I realized when I listened to that message that you must be wondering why it's taken me so long to respond."

"Well, maybe a little."

"Believe me, if I'd been home when you called, I'd have been on your doorstep in minutes."

Noel's eyes widened. "Minutes?"

"Count on it." He grew serious. "Noel, after the party I almost decided to try to forget you. I thought I couldn't do anything else to convince you and I knew we'd never make it if you couldn't forgive me when I did something wrong. But every time I looked up into the night sky, just after dusk when the stars are beginning to sparkle, I thought of your eyes. And then I remembered your spirit," he said, kneeling before her. Noel met his steady gaze, wondering if she was dreaming.

"Your faith," he continued, "and your ambition. And your willingness to be an elf to get there. And then I realized that I'm very much in love with you. Let's start over, Noel. Will you have me back now, as Geoffrey Sundstrom?"

Her heart burst with gladness and relief. "No more secrets, Nick?"

"No more secrets."

She couldn't remember ever feeling such joy. *Thank you, Father! You've worked a miracle for us.* Reaching down, she pulled him up from his knees. Gently, he took her face in his hands and softly kissed her. It was late; the fountain had quit. But in the distance, the Episcopalian church's bells rang as if on cue.

"Do you hear heavenly bells, or is it just me?" Geoff asked with a smile.

"It's just you," she teased. Then she lifted her face for one more Christmas Eve kiss.

# MYSTERY AT CHRISTMAS

LAURA KRAUSE

# ONE

"H ello?" Bridget panted into the cellular phone she cradled on her shoulder. Her purse swung from one arm and a grocery bag balanced in the other while she wrestled with the front door.

"I didn't think I'd ever talk to you in person," came Aunt Victoria's voice. "Your Uncle George and I haven't heard from you in ages. I've left dozens of messages on your machine, but I thought I'd try your other phone number before putting out a missing-persons bulletin."

With all her strength, Bridget wrenched the doorknob and shoved with her foot. The door flew open, bounced off the wall, and slammed back in her face. "Oh, Aunt V., has it really been that long?" She narrowed her eyes, then seized the knob in a death grip. She was about to ram her shoulder against the wood, but the door eased open in oiled perfection.

"Two months, four days, sixteen hours." A pause. "And thirty-two minutes."

"Aunt V., you're such a character." Bridget smiled and stepped into the foyer, feeling her tension recede. She kicked the apartment door shut and hung her purse on an antique coat-stand, then walked to the kitchen and set the groceries on the counter.

"Anyway, I called to congratulate you on your new book.

Your mother would have been proud." Aunt V. paused. "I'm still disappointed you won't be home for Christmas. This makes two in a row. I haven't seen you for a year and a half!"

"That may change. I just talked to my editor this morning. She said my work's suffering and suggested I take Christmas off." Bridget said it calmly, but her stomach balled up again. The two-hour conversation had been an emotional walk over hot coals. So much so that she'd immediately reached for her bag of chocolates, and had to run to the grocery store when she realized she was out of them. But perhaps Christmas with the family wouldn't be so bad. She could relax, rest up, and come back brimming with inspiration.

"What about your deadline?"

"That may change, too. Gloria said my last chapters weren't up to my usual standard, whatever that means. I don't know how to please this woman. She wants me to finish this next book, then tells me to take a week off—with no writing!"

A soft cough interrupted her tirade. "Dear, I thought *you* set that deadline."

Bridget paused. "I did suggest it, didn't I?"

"Suggest it? I imagine you shoved it in her face and gave her the option of answering 'yes' or 'yes, ma'am.'"

Bridget winced. Aunt V. knew her too well. "Maybe I'll spend Christmas in Cancún."

"Oh, no! You've said you're coming, and come you shall. Cally and Robert will be here with the boys. You'll come for the whole week, won't you?" Giving Bridget no time to reply, she continued, "I'll expect you the Wednesday before Christmas. And Bridget, Mark will be here."

Bridget froze. Aunt V. couldn't mean Mark. She must have the wrong name, or maybe she meant a different Mark.

"Mark Fielder?"

"Who else?"

"Why?" Bridget sank, weak-kneed, into a Louis XV side chair.

"Aren't you glad, my dear? You two were such good friends," Aunt V. said.

"You know exactly what we were to each other, Aunt V. Why will he be there? Are you trying to get us back together?"

"Of course not, dear. I've only just found out you're coming. For the record, he and I have struck up a friendship, and he didn't have a better place to spend the holidays."

"And off the record?"

"I never say anything off the record." After a slight pause, Aunt V. said, "I'll see you on Wednesday, dear. Everyone will be here then. Good-bye."

The line went dead. Bridget placed the phone on the coffee table and slowly sat forward in her chair. Where had her idea of a nice, relaxing holiday gone? Right out that squeaky door.

She pounded the chair with her fist, then stood up. Thoughts crowded her brain as she paced the hardwood floor with nervous energy.

It looked as if Mark would be reappearing on the stage of her life. She had cut him out of it as thoroughly as if she'd taken scissors to a picture and snipped off a part. And that's what it felt like sometimes—part of her was missing. She closed her eyes and drew a deep breath.

She remembered the night he'd asked her to marry him. He had been so sweet, so earnest. He'd said they'd get married after college, and she'd trusted him. And then he'd betrayed that trust.

Hot tears rose to her eyes, but she choked them back. She would not give in to tears now. She hadn't cried for Mark since the night he'd betrayed her, and she wasn't about to start. Walls she'd built for just this purpose slammed into place. There was no reason this visit should bother her. After all, it had been eight years; both of them had changed.

She marched into the kitchen, microwaved a cup of water, then dunked an instant-coffee bag into the mug. She had her writing now—her ministry. She had this beautiful old apartment filled with the antiques she'd inherited from her parents. She was fulfilled. Bridget Deans did not need anything, or anyone, else. So why should she get upset? Mark was ancient history. A week with him would prove it.

Tuesday, eight days before Christmas, Mark Fielder slammed the door on his blue Plymouth Duster and looked up—way, way up. Rutledge Place still amazed him. It was enormous. He'd never forget how intimidated he'd been when he picked Bridget up for their first date. Driving this far out of Denton, Texas, he'd expected a farmhouse, not a mansion.

But a mansion was what it was. The huge Victorian had been built in the late 1800s by Jedediah Rutledge, Bridget's great-great-grandfather, and the family had added on and modernized it over the years. It now sprawled over thousands of square feet.

Mark raced up the stairs and across the gingerbread-trimmed veranda. Before he could reach for the bell, the door flew open and Aunt Victoria swept out to meet him, closing the door behind her.

"There's something you should know, Mark."

"A change in plans?"

"No, an extra hitch. Bridget will be here tomorrow."

His jaw dropped. Bridget? He hadn't bargained on that. His heart ached every time he thought of her. He wondered if she ever thought of him, and if so, what she felt. After what he'd done to her, she probably hated him.

"She's dropping by?" he asked, daring to hope she wasn't staying.

"No, she'll be here for the duration." Aunt Victoria patted his cheek and ushered him inside.

"I can't play spy and deal with Bridget," he whispered.

"Then why not let me deal with her? She won't know a thing about it."

Mark climbed the stairs behind Aunt V. and followed her to a back bedroom on the second floor. It was nearly as big as his entire apartment near the college campus in Denton. But he'd stake his last dollar that there wasn't a roach war in progress here. After Aunt V. left to let him unpack, he sank into a deep, upholstered chair.

He rested his eyes on the muted blue wallpaper, his nerves wound tight. He ran his fingers through his hair. Aunt V.'s scheme had sounded so easy before. Now Bridget was coming, and Aunt V. wouldn't allow him to tell her what he was doing here. That would go over well. He'd have to avoid Bridget. It was the only thing to do.

Bridget rolled down the window of her red Miata. North Texas wasn't any colder than Austin. The weather and the scenery brought back a lot of memories, though. She'd spent almost every Christmas at Rutledge Place, first as a guest with her parents and her sister, Cally. When she was eleven, her parents died in a car accident and she and Cally had come to live there with Victoria and George, her mother's sister and brother.

Bridget turned off on a rural route just north of Denton. After a few miles, the land rose slightly and, suddenly, the natural beauty of the roadside became a cultivated winter garden. To the right and back from the road, Rutledge Place appeared.

She followed the driveway, twisting between the tall pine trees that lined it on either side, and drew in her breath as she gazed at her favorite place in the world. The Victorian mansion was still painted in the same cream, wine, and forest green colors it had been when she was a child. Bridget sighed in contentment. She was home. The lane wound around the back of the house, and she pulled up on one side of the garage.

She hopped out, unlocked her trunk, and began to tug at her suitcase. It bulged with Christmas presents for the family and shifted only slightly with her efforts. How on earth had she managed to get it into the trunk in the first place?

The thought of all the presents she'd purchased dampened her holiday spirit. She hadn't gotten a gift for Mark. Oh, why did he have to be here at all? It would be so much easier if they didn't have to see one another. God must have a reason for this, but what possible good could come of it? It was a mystery to her. Then again, if she'd been on closer terms with God, perhaps she would have found out. Well, it wouldn't matter in the long run. She'd be here one week, and after she left on Christmas evening, Mark would be out of her life for good.

She pushed up her sleeves and was getting into a position to give her suitcase one last tug when she heard the purr of an engine coming up the drive behind her.

It was the family Cadillac. The huge car pulled up in front of the garage, and a familiar figure jumped out of the passenger seat. Uncle George! His bushy white hair and round potbelly set him apart in any crowd.

She almost ran to give him a hug but held back, puzzled by his actions. Apparently he hadn't seen her. She watched as he looked around furtively, then pulled a huge shopping bag from the trunk. Bundles bulged from inside it. Mr. Stout, the chauffeur, stood ready to help, but after nearly thirty years of service, knew better than to offer assistance to the feisty older man. Bag in hand, Uncle George trotted over to the side of the house and down the steps that led to the wine cellar. Why on earth was he going down there? It was just a musty old storeroom now.

Bridget was about to go follow Uncle George, but again she stopped as another movement caught her eye. The back passenger door of the car was opening, but no one was inside.

Suddenly a pair of hands descended from the car's interior, then a pair of knees. Next, a head of light brown hair appeared around the end of the door. It was Mark.

Bridget gaped. What in the world? Mark crawled around the door and gingerly shut it with one hand. Then he lay flat on the rough pavement and looked under the car in the direction Mr. Stout and Uncle George had headed.

This insanity smacked of Aunt V. As quietly as possible, Bridget edged across the drive and tiptoed up behind Mark. She squatted down, inches from his face. He jerked his head around, and she found herself staring into his eyes. Back in high school, she'd called them tiger eyes. Gold flecks of light danced in a light brown background that matched his hair.

Her pulse raced just as it had all those years ago. But things had changed. Mark had grown up, his shoulders broadened, his muscles developed. The lines of his jaw were stronger and more angular, and a quiet maturity was written on his face. He was even more attractive than he'd been before. The thought snapped her to attention. She fixed a look of disdain on her face and plunged in.

"Enjoying yourself down here?"

Mark didn't look as though he was enjoying himself. A stunning array of emotions passed through his eyes before he carefully hid them. The effect took her breath away.

"Actually, no. And you?" His smile was forced.

"Let me be frank, Mark. I'm stuck with you this week. I'd rather you weren't here. Aunt Victoria has some little secret going with you, but I'm sure I'll figure it out soon enough. In the meantime, we'll be distantly cordial."

"How sweet of you."

"Oh, it's not on your account. I don't want to ruin my family's Christmas." She stood to leave.

"Wait, Bridget." She looked back at him, and he pushed himself up from the ground. "I didn't want you to accidentally step on me."

She cringed at his sarcastic tone and watched him stride to her car. He reached into the trunk and hefted her suitcase with one easy motion.

Even after she'd been rude to him, he was being nice. Or was it distantly cordial? Bridget wasn't sure. Nodding her thanks, she turned on her heel and strode to the back door of the house.

She encountered no one as she passed through the kitchen to the long back hall, then through the library and into the front hall. Turning to bound up the stairs, she almost ran into Aunt Victoria. Her white hair, unlike Uncle George's, sat neatly atop her head. She patted it after regaining her composure.

"Bridget, my dear! I'm so glad you've arrived." Aunt V. studied Bridget with her clear blue eyes. "You look as if someone is after you."

"Good to see you, Aunt V. Maybe we could go to the sitting room and have a good talk." Bridget told herself she was not trying to escape Mark; she just hadn't seen her aunt for a while and wanted to visit with her.

"Of course not. Everyone's got to greet you." She turned and hollered up the stairs, "Cally! Robert!" She said to Bridget, "They're in their room on the third floor. Perhaps I should get the maid to go up."

She had hardly spoken before a clatter of footsteps sounded on the stairs. A moment later, Cally's auburn hair flashed into view.

"Bridget! It's been forever," Cally said. "Oh, my word—look at you. You're so tiny! You're twenty-six, right? No kids, though—that's got to be it. Look at these thighs...ack!"

Bridget looked at her sister, amused. "Cally, you look great. You actually have a figure to talk about." She gave Cally a hug, then stepped back to look at her. How she missed talking with her older sister.

"Hello, Robert." Cally's husband, a tall, handsome, black man, came down the stairs, and Bridget stepped forward to give him a hug. "Where are the kids?"

"Robby and Luke are at the tank, fishing," he explained. "You won't recognize them. They're full-fledged adolescents now."

Mark arrived and set Bridget's suitcase on the floor.

"Hello, Mark." Aunt V. gave him a knowing glance. "I assume you've greeted Bridget already."

"Yes." He inclined his head toward her. "Bridget."

"Hello, Mark." The words shot out like the crack of a whip and lasted just as long.

"Ah, reunions," Aunt V. said with a smile. "You two need a good long talk. Mark, you wait in the living room while I show Bridget to her room. She'll be down in five minutes."

Aunt Victoria's word was law. Mark headed in the direction of the living room while Bridget, lugging her suitcase, followed her aunt upstairs. As soon as they reached the second floor, Bridget turned to Aunt V.

"I don't want to talk with Mark. You are being an obvious matchmaker. I've told you time and again that I'm not going to marry anyone, ever. I'm married to my ministry." She set down her suitcase with a weary sigh. "This is so embarrassing."

Aunt Victoria planted her hands on her hips and spoke quietly. "I don't want to go through the holidays in a deep freeze. You two had better hammer out your differences and make the best of it." Her tone softened slightly. "Even if I do matchmake, you shouldn't be embarrassed. Everyone expects an old woman to do it."

She took Bridget's face in her hands, kissed her forehead, then smiled through unshed tears.

"Although I've never married, the Lord has taught me a great deal over the years. Let me pass it on to you. Love is a beautiful thing. It may inconvenience you, but…" She paused. "Are the heroines in your stories willing to die for the men they love?"

"Yes."

"A thing isn't worth living for unless it's worth dying for. Like your faith in God. Go freshen up. I'll tell Mark you're coming." She started back down the stairs, then stopped and turned around. "Five minutes!"

Bridget went to the room that had been hers since childhood and flopped across the bed. This was ridiculous. Aunt Victoria chose to forget, at the worst of times, Bridget's decision to stay single. She didn't mean "not Mark"; she meant "not anybody."

Five minutes later, Bridget stopped short in the entrance to the living room. There he was, lounging shamelessly on the medallion-backed sofa, facing the far windows. She forced herself to move forward. How could Aunt V. do this? She knew how painful this was for Bridget.

She edged a little farther into the room, reminded of Daniel being shoved into the lions' den. Mark turned around and met her eyes. The lion had seen her; there was no escaping now.

"Hi, Bridget. Want to sit down?"

Bridget crossed the rug. She was trapped. Now she was going to get eaten.

# Two

**M**ark watched as Bridget perched on the far end of the couch.

"Still being distantly cordial?" He gave her a pleasant smile.

"I'm being distant, but the cordial part is coming hard."

"It's only a hunch, but I'd bet money you've never forgiven me." The words came out smoothly, but he felt a half-second of raw pain before burying it again.

"Mark Fielder, that's none of your business."

"None of my business? You don't know how my mistakes have affected me." He paused, then said softly, "Come on, Bridget. Let's call a truce. Can we be friends…distant friends?" he qualified when he saw the stubborn look on her face.

She closed her eyes and sighed. Mark waited silently.

"All right," she said finally.

Mark let out the breath he hadn't realized he'd been holding. He searched for a nonoffensive topic of conversation. "So, I hear your writing is really taking off." He extended the statement like jumper cables to a sluggish engine.

"Yes." She didn't take the nudge.

"Your first two books were pretty big. High hopes for the new one?"

"I've heard it's selling well."

He looked at the woman sitting so stiffly at the end of the couch. The sight of her reminded him of high school days, but that teenage girl had been a shadow of what she'd become. Her thin, pretty figure had developed beautiful, slender curves. Her rich brown hair, now cut in a chin-length bob, beckoned his fingers to touch it; and her delicate face, dominated by chocolate eyes and soft, full lips, raised his blood pressure. He swallowed, pulled his thoughts into line, and asked the first thing that came to mind.

"What did it feel like, getting your first book published?"

"You really want to know?" Interest sparked in her eyes.

"Yes."

She bit her lower lip and paused as if to search for adequate words. "You really want to know what it felt like?"

"I said I did."

"Okay, then, imagine this: A hot day in Texas. It's ninety-eight degrees, 80 percent humidity, and you're working in the sun. Suddenly, a big front moves through, it's eighty degrees, and the work day's over. You drive home down a rural route with the windows open and the radio on full blast." She grinned. "It was great."

Mark laughed. "You have a way with words."

"I hope so." Bridget's expression was half-proud, half-embarrassed. "What about you? What are you doing with your business degree?"

"I teach ballroom and modern dance at the university, and I do some spots on TV and radio commercials."

"No way. Really?" Bridget's eyes were wide, but she was smiling.

"The university wants me to get my master's in physical education and stay on with them. I'll get better pay, tenure, all that. Business didn't suit me well."

"I could have told you that when you started."

"Why didn't you?" Mark almost reached out physically to pull the words back. But it was too late. Bridget stiffened, and the light camaraderie vanished into the air. *Argh! You idiot!*

"I could tell you why, but you already know."

"Yes, I do. I'm sorry I brought it up. I'd rather remember the good days, though. My junior and senior years of high school were some of the best years I've had. We had a lot of fun together, and I miss that."

There was nothing more he could say to her now; he knew that. After a long moment of tense silence, he walked out of the room, through the hall, and up the stairs. Distant cordiality was best, as Bridget had said. Anything else dredged up too much pain.


Dinner at Rutledge Place retained the old-fashioned, formal flavor of the past century. Bridget, wearing a blue silk dress, pulled out a chair across from Robert, the room's only other occupant.

"You look nice." He stood politely, waiting while Bridget tucked her short skirt around her legs and sat down.

"Thank you. You look dashing yourself. Where is everyone?"

A thunder of running feet echoed across the polished wood floor of the hallway before she finished speaking.

"Sounds like the kids now."

He was right. The door was flung open, and in rushed the two boys. Bridget's jaw dropped. They looked much older than she remembered; in the year and a half since she'd seen them, they had become smaller versions of their papa.

"Aunt Bridget!"

Luke rushed to her side and gave her a hug.

"Wow, Luke. I can't believe this is you. You're so much

older—twelve now? Come here, Robby."

She gave the older boy a brief hug so as not to offend his thirteen-year-old manliness.

"It's good to see you guys. I hardly recognize you."

Aunt Victoria strolled in on Uncle George's arm, followed by Cally. They all took their seats at the long, ornately carved table. A minute later, Mark arrived, out of breath. Bridget followed his gaze to the only remaining chair, which was right next to hers. He compressed his lips and sat down.

This could be a long, uncomfortable Christmas. She closed her eyes and willed the looming image of disaster away. Surely something good would happen during the holiday.

The maid, Elaine, clad in a neat black-and-white uniform, wheeled in a serving cart full of food. Bridget inhaled the spicy aroma of another of the chef's masterpieces. Armand had been the chef here for years, and Bridget had eaten hundreds of his meals, but he was certainly in top form tonight. Slices of veal topped with marinara and smothered in mozzarella filled a platter next to a large bowl of fettucine Alfredo, and a basket overflowed with freshly baked Italian bread. Mark may have stolen her peace, but he couldn't steal her appetite.

During dessert, Aunt V. rose and clinked her water goblet with a fork.

"Ladies and gentlemen, attention. I would like to remind you of my annual Christmas party this Saturday evening. I trust you brought formal wear. Caroling is on Friday night, and the church's annual charity supper is still on Christmas Eve. I've drafted you all to help serve."

Mark tapped Bridget on the shoulder and whispered in her ear. "Do you remember when she used to draft us in high school?"

Bridget smiled and nodded, for an instant transported back to their old companionship. His voice next to her ear awakened a tingle that shot through her body like lightning. Then she stiffened. She couldn't let her guard down now. *If* she did—and that was a big if—she had to work through a gaggle of unruly emotions first.

After dinner, Aunt V. declared they needed a moonlight walk, and just a short while later, they were all strolling two by two down the drive. Mark couldn't figure how she arranged it, but Aunt Victoria managed to place Bridget and him together.

The moon shone, unhampered by clouds, and the stars dimmed in its brilliance. It was what Bridget used to call a "blue night." Everything was a cool, peaceful blue, and their footsteps echoed as if they were inside a room. Eerie. Beautiful.

Mark sighed as he thought about what happened at dinner. He hadn't meant to whisper in her ear like that, but it hurt more than he would have thought to see her warm response turn cold. Still, that instant of warmth had lit a fire in his heart. He'd known it would happen. He also knew that he would dodge her that much more, since neither of them wanted to renew their relationship.

Walking beside her in the dark, he realized how easy it was to fall back into step with each other. Easy but not comfortable, like stepping into a hot bath. If that was what he'd done, someone had electrified it. Mark snorted at the thought, and everyone turned to look at him.

"What's so funny, Mark?" Aunt Victoria called.

"I, well, I was thinking about, uh, electrified baths...." He trailed off lamely.

Aunt V. raised her eyebrows; then Luke launched into an exposition on a detective show he'd seen on TV. All of them were startled by a loud "ha!" from Uncle George.

"Ha, ha! You're right, my boy. I've had some thoughts about

those myself. Too dangerous for practical jokes, though. Remember that."

Mark looked at Bridget, and they shared a grin.


On Thursday morning, Mark was crouched on the back floorboards of the large Cadillac when he heard footsteps approach the car. He pulled a thick, rough blanket over his head. Uncle George opened the front door on the passenger side.

"Take me to the mall, Mr. Stout."

Oh, not again. This made the third day in a row Mark had followed George from one shopping mall to the next, then through several neighborhoods. How did the man do it? He had to be over seventy—a very strong seventy.

Mark hunkered down under his covering. If this didn't have to be so cryptically secret, he could sit in the seat like a real human being and help George with his work openly. But he couldn't break his promise to Aunt V.


At noon, lunch was served on the veranda. Bridget walked outside to a white, wrought-iron table and dropped into a chair. Aunt Victoria smiled at her and inhaled deeply.

"Hello, dear. What a beautiful day for lunch outdoors."

Before Bridget could respond, Robert, Cally, and the boys trooped through the door from the library. In a whirlwind, they found seats at the round table.

"I hear we're having quiche." Cally beamed. "Armand makes the best crusts in the world. Flaky, buttery…they almost melt in your mouth. I have his recipe."

Elaine brought out the food, and a wedge of spinach quiche was placed in front of Bridget. Despite the enticing smell of cheese and eggs, she frowned as she counted the gathered family members. Where were Mark and Uncle George? Out in the Cadillac again? This mystery grated on her nerves. But there was no need to be subtle; this was her family, after all. She could ask a direct question and expect a direct answer.

"Aunt V.?" Bridget took the plunge.

"Yes, dear?"

"Where are Uncle George and Mark? I haven't seen them all morning."

"Oh, probably out shopping," her aunt answered vaguely.

Aunt V. was never vague. And she always knew everything about every person in the house. Her brother, George, was no exception. Something smelled fishy—and it wasn't lunch.

"Now don't forget the charity supper at church on Christmas Eve," Aunt V. was saying. "We'll have to do the cooking ourselves because I gave Armand two days off. Pastor Burkett says to bring two stuffed turkeys and a dessert. Cally, could you roll out a couple of those pie crusts you do so well?"

Aunt V. continued to delegate, but Bridget listened with one ear. She wondered what Uncle George and Mark were up to, and why Aunt V. was hiding it. She'd just have to find out on her own.

When lunch was over, Bridget strode to the garden near the front of the house. She hopped the loosely hung chain that bordered it and walked down the main path.

Aunt V. was covering for Mark and Uncle George, which meant she must know where they'd gone and what they were doing. Aunt V. said they might be shopping. Aunt V. never lied. So it had to be possible, at least, that that's what they were doing.

Denton boasted one mall and a few shopping centers. Where would men shop? Bridget guessed the mall. Her mind made up, she turned and ran for the garage. As she reached her car, she realized what a silly idea this was. Why should she care what Uncle George and Mark were up to? But, she rationalized, she didn't have anything else slated for that afternoon. And a trip to the mall hardly qualified her as a fanatic. It wasn't as if she were going to follow them to Dallas.

She pulled out of the driveway and sped down the two-lane road. A large, white Cadillac with gold trim should stick out like a sore thumb. If they were in the mall, she'd know it within a matter of minutes. Hopefully.

The Cadillac pulled up to the front entrance of the mall. Uncle George opened the passenger door and stepped out. He smiled his thanks at the chauffeur, then turned and walked toward the wide glass doors.

Mr. Stout drove through the parking lot and found a place to stop. The back door opened and Mark climbed out, breathing gulps of fresh air.

"Why don't you go in and have a soda or find a book to read?" Mr. Stout said.

"I'd do better to find an oxygen tank. Do you think I could fit one under the blanket with me?"

"Hardly. Might I suggest a snorkel? You could stick it out when you feel faint."

Mark grinned at him as he shut the door. He dusted off his khaki pants and polo shirt, ran a hand through his hair, hoping to dislodge any fuzz from the blanket, then turned and walked toward the mall.

The Miata sped down I-35 in the fast lane until Bridget saw the sign for Loop 288. She squeezed into the line of cars at the exit. Christmas was next Wednesday, and she supposed everyone was doing last-minute shopping.

She made it to the traffic light. For some reason, she was feeling nervous about this. What would she tell Mark if she found him? She commanded her nerves to calm down. She was nearly there; the mall was just on the other side of the intersection.

The light changed to green, and Bridget turned under the highway. There it was—the long, sprawling building loomed ahead and to the left. She pulled into the turn lane in front of the mall's main entrance. The light was red, so she would have to wait. Again. She closed her eyes and rested her forehead on the steering wheel. Inhaling slowly, she willed her breathing to steady. There really was no hurry.

At that moment, a long, white Cadillac with gold trim pulled out of the mall parking lot and turned right onto the street, passing within a few feet of the Miata. It drove a short distance down the street and pulled into a gas station.

Bridget looked up. The light changed to green, and she turned into the crowded parking lot. Now, where to start?

Two hours and one tank of gas later, Bridget returned home. There had been no sign of Mark or Uncle George. She didn't want to think right now about how foolish she'd acted; her brain was too tired. She pulled up the drive toward the garage and planned on taking a long nap.


That night, Robby and Luke convinced their dad and Uncle George to drive them into town to pick out a Christmas tree. Bridget sat on the hearth, watching the exchange and remembering the same scene from her childhood.

"Sure you don't want to wait till tomorrow? Tomorrow sounds nice. Or how 'bout Saturday?" Uncle George teased them as he would small children.

"No, Uncle G.!" they cried.

"Let's go tonight," Robby pleaded. "We always put up our tree at home right after Thanksgiving."

"That's because your tree comes out of a box." Uncle George wrinkled his nose in disgust. "There's a *real* tree out there waiting for us. I guess we should go tonight, before someone else gets it."

"All right!" The boys high-fived and clapped each other on the back all the way out the door.

When at last they returned, they dragged in an enormous blue spruce that seemed to fill half the living room with its fragrant branches.

Bridget shook her head and laughed. "How are we going to dance around that at the party this Saturday?"

The foursome looked from the tree to Bridget. *Oops* was written across their faces. Bridget laughed again.

Mark strode in through the sitting-room doors, toting an array of gloves, handsaws, and other tools. "Here I come to save the day!" he sang in a booming voice.

Cally hooted, and Aunt V. covered her mouth with the back of her hand. Bridget fought a laugh all the way back down to the pit of her stomach.

While the men cut the tree so that it would fit in its stand, the women climbed up to the attic to retrieve the decorations.

The strains of Christmas carols drifted from ceiling speakers as the family trimmed the tree. Mark and Robert had stood it in the corner by one of the front windows, displacing a Louis XV commode. When they were finished, they all stood back and admired their work.

"I think this room is loveliest at Christmas." Aunt Victoria's voice had a dreamy, nostalgic quality. "The green and gold and red, and all of the lights. It is a vision."

Bridget sat on the arm of the couch and watched her aunt make a few final adjustments to the ornaments. The flaming log in the fireplace set each ornament ablaze. The effect dazzled her senses.

Uncle George stepped forward, a small box held gently in his hands.

"Gather 'round! George is placing the nativity!" Aunt Victoria clapped her hands and gestured the family to press in.

Robert turned off the music and joined the group around the tree for the family tradition. When Uncle George had finished arranging the nativity at the base of the tree, they all held hands to sing carols.

Of course Mark would end up beside Bridget. She reached out her hand to him, though her racing heart called it folly. Her fingers brushed his palm hesitantly. Bursts of heat raced up her arm, and she almost jumped back. Perhaps if she grabbed his hand more firmly this time. She took hold of it as if it were the knob on her stubborn apartment door. That didn't help.

The singing began. Bridget stumbled through familiar tunes whose lyrics had suddenly escaped her. She stared at the flashing lights on the tree.

"Star of wonder, star of night…" The singing sounded distant as a little voice in her head taunted her. She wasn't over Mark at all. His hand around hers felt warm and vibrantly alive. Inside her head, thoughts tumbled over and around each other as if her mind couldn't figure out which one to settle on. As soon as the singing ended, she dropped the hands on either side of her and hurried out onto the veranda.

# THREE

B ridget?" Mark couldn't think what asinine idea had made him rush out after her, but she did look upset. She was staring distractedly into the yard, chewing on her bottom lip.

"Are you okay?"

She didn't respond. Mark walked to where she stood by the rail and touched her elbow. Her gaze met his, and her eyes cleared for a moment.

"Sure, I'm fine." She turned back to the yard.

He followed her stare into the deep shadows that stretched forward from the far corners of the lawn. His uneasiness grew as the silence lengthened, but he didn't know what to say. She seemed troubled, but since he knew it was his fault, he didn't know if pressing the issue would make things better or worse. They'd been snipping at each other from the moment she'd arrived and found him on the ground beside the Cadillac.

"Bridget, I'm sorry I upset you yesterday. I shouldn't have brought up our past. Your aunt wanted us to make up, and I ruined it."

"No." She looked back at him. "I had my feelings on my sleeve. I still do."

"You're still angry?"

"That's not what I meant." She paused. "No offense, Mark,

but I can't talk to you about this. It's personal."

"It's about me, then." He grinned as he looked down at her serious face.

She returned a faint smile. "Yes and no. I have some unresolved emotions to deal with. Let's change the subject, shall we? I want to talk about why you're here at Rutledge Place."

Mark carefully schooled his features before he responded. "You know I can't talk about that."

"No, I don't. I don't know anything at all except what I saw on the driveway and what I heard from Aunt V."

That stopped him for a second. "Aunt V. told you something? I don't believe it."

She laughed. "You're right. It's more what she didn't say. I know she's got you up to something, though. You didn't invite yourself here."

"Now you're assuming things. Oh, I might as well tell you the whole thing." He darted a glance around the veranda, then spoke in a conspiratorial whisper. "I'm an agent for Household Spies Anonymous. Is your butler dipping into the peppermint supply, your maid cleaning up on your wardrobe? Call HSA, and we'll nail 'em to the wall. You see, Mr. Stout has been siphoning off gas...."

Bridget choked on a giggle and pressed her hands to her ears. "Enough! You're incorrigible." She set one hand on her hip and pointed inside. "Get—before I tell Mr. Stout what you've been saying."


The next night, the weather turned cold. In preparation for Aunt Victoria's caroling trip, Bridget pulled a thick cable-knit sweater over her turtleneck. Maybe several heavy layers would keep her from feeling such an attraction to Mark. Each touch they shared shot lightning through her veins. Each conversation broke down another bit of her defenses. She knew she needed time away from him or she'd be in danger of falling in love with him again. Unfortunately, Aunt V. was doing her best to throw them at each other.

Her black wool coat strained over the bulky clothes while she fastened the buttons. She shoved her gloves into her pockets and opened her bedroom door. If things got out of hand tonight, all she had to do was pull out her memory of Mark's unfaithfulness. There. It was working already.

Bridget dashed out the front door and climbed into the minivan, where the rest of the family was waiting. She took one look at the backseat and saw that the boys were back there with Mark so that there was no room for her. Relieved, she slid onto the middle seat next to Aunt V.

Robert started the engine and rolled out of the driveway. "Which area will we victimize tonight?"

"Oh, I hope we're not that bad." Aunt Victoria waved a blue folder she held on her lap. "I have the typed sheets our church used two years ago. We visited a neighborhood near the university then. How about that nice little area off McCormick this year?"

Robert pulled onto the highway and exited on McCormick. After he stopped the van next to a park, they all piled out and Aunt V. passed the song sheets around.

"I'm g-glad you made me bring my coat, Mom." Robby shivered visibly, his breath coming out in white puffs.

Cally gave him a quick hug. "That's what moms are for."

As Bridget watched them, she felt a stab of pain. It had been so many years, but she still missed her mother. All the things she'd done and been through since then, both triumphs and sorrows—and she hadn't been able to share any of them with Mom.

Aunt V. hollered to get everyone's attention. "Okay, family, let's warm up with a few songs. Watch me for stop and start signals or we'll have a cacophony rather than a choir."

All the talking settled down to a few whispers; then Aunt Victoria raised her hand and signaled the start of "Hark, the Herald Angels Sing." Uncle George led off with a bass rumble, and everyone else attempted to match his key and tempo.

Mark leaned next to Bridget's ear. "Is something wrong? You looked really sad for a minute."

Bridget's eyes met his, and the tenderness there melted her resolve to keep her distance. She nodded and tilted her head to speak in his ear.

"I'll tell you later, when we're not singing."

Mark agreed politely, then backed away. First one song, then another, drifted on the night air. Traditional carols and the classics about snowmen and reindeer mixed together in raucous holiday abandon.

Just when Bridget was beginning to think they were going to warm up with every song in the book, Aunt V. pronounced them ready to go. Robert took the lead, booming "Forward, march!" His silver watch was the only thing that distinguished his dark, upheld hand from the night.

Again, Bridget ended up next to Mark, and he slowed their pace until the two of them brought up the rear. Feeling his hand at her elbow, Bridget glanced up at him.

"It just hit me how much I miss my mom." She paused, then added, "Of course, I miss both my parents, but right now it's Mom. I was watching Cally and Robby back there, and I…" Tears welled up in her eyes, and she dropped her gaze to her shoes. After a brief hesitation, Mark wrapped his arm around her shoulder.

"I can't even imagine how you feel, but I know it's got to hurt."

Robert stopped the group at the first house and knocked on

the door. When a man answered with a little girl peeking out behind him, Aunt V. gave the signal to start singing.

Nestled under Mark's arm, Bridget felt her misgivings slip away. She fit here. She felt safe and warm.

After several carols, they all waved good-bye to the collection of people now gathered inside the front door. Bridget and Mark stepped back and let the other carolers pass in front of them. Again, they brought up the rear.

"Feeling better?" His deep voice was close, his breath warm on her ear.

"Y-yes."

Mark slipped his arm from her shoulders. A tangible loss crept over her in its place. She tried to tell herself that her reaction proved only her physical attraction and that when the holidays were over, she'd forget about him. But deep down, a small voice whispered that it wasn't true.

The others were singing again, but Bridget stood still, her coat sleeve brushing against Mark's. No sound came from him, either. They had to look silly. Perversely, the corners of her mouth turned up into a grin. She wondered if their audience was thinking what a nice family of singers, except for the two stiffs in the back.

A laugh vibrated in her diaphragm. She bit her lip to hold it back, but the more she resisted it, the more funny the whole situation seemed. Tears spilled down her cheeks as she muffled her hysterics behind her hand. Then her efforts to keep quiet gave her the hiccups, and she would have fallen over if Mark hadn't caught her. His look of alarm sent another deluge of laughter over her. She clamped her fingers tighter around her mouth. Tears streamed down her face and hiccups jolted her until her sides ached.

"Quiet. They'll hear you when the song ends," Mark whispered.

She tried, but just as the singing stopped, she hiccuped loudly. Every face turned in her direction, and she collapsed in a gale of laughter again.

"Bridget, collect yourself," Aunt Victoria reprimanded.

"I'm sorry." She hiccuped. "I've got the hiccups. Mark…could you…take me back to the car?"

"Drink a cup of water upside down. It works every time," Cally called as Mark steered Bridget back in the direction they'd come.

"What on earth were you doing?" he asked when they were out of earshot of the group.

"It was so funny. You and me…standing there like a couple of wooden puppets." Out loud, it didn't sound as hilarious as it had in her mind. Her laughter died away, and she said nothing the rest of the way to the vehicle.

Mark sat her down on the first bench seat of the van and knelt next to her. She hiccuped. He took her face in his hands.

"Hiccup."

"What?" Bridget stared at him.

"I said hiccup. If you've got the hiccups, prove it." His eyes were inches away.

"I can't."

"I know—it works every time." Instead of letting her go, he moved closer. His hands cupped her face gently, and his lips came down toward hers. Bridget's heart pounded as she waited for his kiss.

"Hello, in there. Victoria sent me to…" George's voice trailed off when he peered into the van.

Mark dropped his hands from Bridget's face and scooted back a few inches. Bridget cleared her throat and broke the embarrassed hush.

"Did you need something, Uncle G.?"

"Oh, no. Your aunt wanted me to see if you needed any

help, but you seem to be doing fine without me. Ah, carry on."
He waved his hands in an indication to continue, turned, and
walked back down the street.

Bridget sunk her head in her hands, but Mark laughed out
loud. He took her hand to help her from the van.

"Come on. We'd better join the others."


Saturday dawned clear but cold. Bridget tugged a red cashmere
sweater over her head and felt her hair prickle with static. She
spritzed hair spray on a comb and pulled it through her hair
while her pulse did the two-step. The thought of Mark's hands
on her face, his lips a fraction of an inch from her own, made
her feel more alive than she had in years. One touch from the
tip of his finger and her defensiveness turned to Jell-O.

She pursed her lips and crossed her arms over her chest.
What had happened to her strong walls, her stony indifference?
Mark was still what he was. Why did she have to change?

She didn't. Bridget lifted her chin and stared back at her
reflection in the mirror. One couldn't *fall* into love. It was a
choice. She chose not to. Mark had proved eight years ago that
he had no sense of right and wrong when it came to women.
She had every right to refuse to love him. Gradually, her fluttering pulse slowed to normal.

As she opened her door, the salty smell of fried bacon and
the rich aroma of coffee reached her nose. Her stomach rumbled.
Real breakfast? Armand never came to work before eleven. Her
tingling taste buds pushed her down the back stairs and into
the kitchen. There, she saw Mark and Robert standing over the
stove.

"Hey, Bridget. Ready for the Christmas party tonight? Pass
me that platter." Robert motioned to a stoneware dish on the
counter. He smiled his thanks as he took it from her hands.

Thick slabs of bacon, smoked sausages, and scrambled eggs tumbled from skillets into serving dishes. A basket full of hot biscuits sat on the island work space. Mark passed her a plate, then turned back to a pan of gravy on the stove.

Bridget filled her plate with the hot food, then perched on a stool at the counter.

Robby and Luke burst into the kitchen, followed by Cally and Aunt V. When they had all found seats, they barely fit around the large island.

Cally bumped Bridget's elbow with her own. "For such a tiny person, you sure do take up a lot of space."

"Don't look at me. It's that husband of yours. Every time he flexes, he knocks me over five inches." Bridget nudged Robert, who was sitting on her other side. He smiled widely. "Where's Uncle George?" she asked Aunt V. "Isn't he hungry?"

"Oh, he's down in the wine cellar," her aunt answered. "It's a kind of office for him."

"What could he possibly do down there?" What did he do, ever? His life seemed so simple.

"He takes on projects once in a while. Last year, he whittled whistles and dolls for kids at the orphanage."

Bridget thought about Uncle George while she spooned gravy over her biscuits. He grew more complex all the time, between this new revelation and his penchant for shopping with Mark. For years she'd assumed his life consisted of checkers and card games, but she realized now that she didn't know him as well as she'd thought.

Mark leaned over Uncle George that evening, watching him program the CD player. The man had placed five different CDs on the turntable and was now choosing which ballroom classics would play and when.

Excellent equipment. He didn't have anything like it at home, and he used a record player at the university.

"House is too small for a live band," Uncle George explained as he worked. "I don't know what the old man did when he whooped it up."

Mark's forehead wrinkled. "Who?"

"The old man, Jedediah Rutledge. He built this house."

Mark nodded and gazed around the open area. The folding doors between the living room and sitting room were opened wide. The two rooms looked bare now that most of the furniture had been shoved against the walls or moved to the dining room.

Bridget stood on a ladder in the middle of the front entrance to the living room. He watched as she tied a ribbon with a sprig of something green to a cup hook affixed to the top of the doorframe. Mistletoe.

She climbed down and repeated the procedure in the doorway between the two connected dance areas.

Mark stood in his corner with Uncle George, smiling. It would be fun to see who got caught under that mistletoe. Then his smile drooped. What if he found himself under it with Bridget? He touched his fingers to his lips. He'd have to plan a strategy to keep himself out of trouble.

Boy, did he. Each touch they shared drew him in deeper, even though he knew it was wrong. She hadn't forgiven him, not really. He hadn't even forgiven himself.

"Oh, look at the time!" Aunt V. stood up from her crouched position in front of the hors d'oeuvres table. "We'd better dress."

"Drat. I planned to quit half an hour ago. Now I'll have to hurry." Cally followed her aunt across the room, and Bridget brought up the rear.

The women left the finishing touches to the hired servers and climbed the stairs to the bedrooms. Mark watched them

127

leave and scratched his head. He'd never understand how women could take an hour and a half to dress.

Bridget stood on the landing, surveying the party below her. Most of the guests had arrived. Cally and Robert stood together, holding hands and talking with Mr. and Mrs. Thompson from church. Aunt Victoria was leading Pastor Burkett to the hors d'oeuvres table. And where was Mark? She finally spotted him, standing with his back to her and staring into the roaring fire.

Her fingernails strummed the banister as she waited a moment longer. Aunt V. had told her to make a grand entrance, but she wasn't going to stand on the stairs and clap for attention. Cautiously stepping to the ground level, she slipped unnoticed into the living room.

Christmas carols on harpsichord floated down from the speakers. At least forty people besides the family were gathered in chattering bunches around the two rooms. Bridget edged through the crowd. At last she reached the hearth. From just behind Mark's shoulder, she spoke.

"When I was a girl, I used to imagine the flames were orange satin flowing up from a draft below."

Mark started at her voice. He turned, and his tiger eyes met hers. His gaze swept over the midnight blue silk dress she'd splurged on, lingering on one bare shoulder, before his eyes traveled back to her face.

"You are beautiful." His voice held depths as rich as velvet. His eyes captivated hers.

"Thank you." Bridget forced her gaze away. She examined his tux instead of the unnamed emotion on his face.

"The dancing will start any minute now. Do you want something to eat first?"

At her nod of assent, Mark took her elbow and led her toward the refreshment table. When Bridget glanced up, she realized their path would lead them directly under the mistletoe hanging in the doorway.

# FOUR

A larms went off in Bridget's head while her heart pounded in anticipation. But, as if on cue, just then the doorbell rang. Aunt V. hurried past them to open the front door.

"Dear Jolene! Mrs. Rogers! Come in. I'm so glad you could make it."

A moment later, a pretty young blonde entered the living room, sequins from her sleek dress shimmering in the soft lighting.

"Oh, Mark, honey! I'm so glad to see you," she gushed as she walked toward them. She gave him a warm hug and fluttered her long eyelashes. Bridget ignored a bout of senseless jealousy.

"Hello, Jolene." Mark returned her hug, then introduced Bridget, his arm still around Jolene's waist. "Bridget, this is Jolene Rogers. She and I work with the same ad agency, and her mother is a friend of Aunt V."

Bridget forced a polite greeting from her lips.

"How about some punch?" Mark took a woman on each arm and guided them toward the buffet table.

"Oh, mistletoe!" Jolene said brightly, to Bridget's horror. Now he would have to kiss them both. She squeezed her eyes shut on a picture of Mark swooping Jolene back in a dramatic kiss.

131

Before Mark could do anything, Jolene took his face between her manicured hands and planted a quick kiss on his mouth.

Bridget turned abruptly away. "I think I'll have that punch now."

Her heels clicked as she crossed the floor and grabbed a cup of punch from the table. As she lifted it to her lips, someone came up behind her and stood very close. She didn't have to look to know it was Mark. She turned slowly.

"Are you going to get some punch for me, too?" His breath stirred the strands of hair around her ear.

"I thought you were busy with Jolene. I didn't want to feel like part of the harem."

Mark's smile froze. "Of course. Well, the first dance is starting. I'd better gather Jolene and the rest of the girls so they can belly dance around me and feed me grapes." He pivoted on one heel and stormed away.

Bridget set her cup on the table and trotted after him. "Please, won't you let me feed you the grapes? Or I could at least grab that big wicker fan off the back porch and cool your—"

Mark turned and grabbed her wrist, leaning close to her face. "Look around you!" he hissed.

She looked. They were surrounded by waltzing couples who watched them with delighted curiosity. Blood rushed to her face, and she started to back away, but Mark took her in his arms. One hand just above the small of her back, the other holding her hand, he led her around the dance floor. Exhilaration replaced her embarrassment as they glided across the polished floor.

Mark had always been a good dancer, but now he was an expert. He moved smoothly, adding art and passion to simple dance steps. Bridget surrendered to his lead. He twirled her out and pulled her back to him effortlessly. Her eyes met his and saw the intensity there. She closed her eyes and stepped lightly through the moves, guided by his hand.

The music stopped. They stood in each other's arms for an instant, unwilling to let go. Another piece began, and Mark released her.

"I never did get you something to eat," he said lightly.

Bridget let him lead her to the bay window in the sitting room. There were side chairs there, carved in a grapevine motif. He motioned for her to sit.

Her clouded mind quickly began to clear. She couldn't sit next to him, share this cozy little alcove with him. She was too vulnerable. She needed space to gather herself together.

"Oh, no, you don't have to do that. I should be mingling, and you dare not let Jolene become a wallflower." Bridget tried to sidle away, but Mark stepped in front of her.

"Jolene can hold her own. You sit there, and I'll play the gentleman. Still like the same foods?" Bridget nodded mutely and sat down. One of these days she was going to stand up to this man, and he'd see he couldn't cow her. One of these days.

Mark strode to the hors d'oeuvres table, a frown deepening the crease between his eyebrows. He needed this time away from her. How could he make it all evening without kissing those smooth shoulders? They'd been tempting him since she'd appeared on the stairs, and he'd had to quickly turn away.

He shook his head and sighed. This was going to be a long party.

After he'd filled Bridget's plate, he balanced it in one hand while he held her cup in the other. He wove through the dancing couples and carefully made his way to the alcove. It was empty. He glanced around the room. The chair sat forlornly where he'd left it, and Bridget was nowhere around. He plopped the food down on the chair, sending a piece of shrimp to the floor. He set her cup on a rococo tea table nearby.

The room bulged with people. He stood on tiptoe and still couldn't spot her. Finally, he caught a flash of midnight blue in the entrance to the living room. He straightened his bow tie and dove into the churning mass of dancers.

He might as well have been dancing, too. He dodged and twisted past a few couples and dove in front of others. At last he reached the place where he'd spotted Bridget. A rhythmic, tropical drumbeat undulated through the rooms. The rumba—the dance of love! Bridget swayed in the arms of Grant Galloway, one of Cally's old boyfriends, and recently divorced. Mark clenched his fists by his side as they swept near the fireplace and then away.

Bridget's eyes met his as the couple twirled close to him. She raised her eyebrows before moving away again. That did it. Mark left a wake of disoriented dancers in his path as he plowed through to the front of the room.

This song wouldn't last forever, and when it ended, he'd be waiting for her. He planted himself in front of the French doors that led to the veranda and stood, legs apart, arms folded over his chest.

The music paused, and most of the couples left the floor. When the next song started, he swept the room in a glance. There she was, still dancing with that pawing, fawning Grant Galloway. Enough was enough.

He butted his way across the dance floor until he reached the other side. In front of the fireplace, he caught up with them. His finger tapped Grant's shoulder, a little too hard.

"May I?"

"Sure, buddy." Grant backed off, surprise on his face.

Mark grabbed Bridget's waist and guided her back into the flow. She glared at him.

"What's my line here? Oh, yes. Please, Rhett, don't leave me!" She feigned a Southern accent, thick with sarcasm.

He ignored her remark. "Why did you leave?"

"I was offered a dance. Am I your date? I don't think so."

"You were avoiding me on purpose."

"I'm allowed to do that." Her large brown eyes hardened, but her beautiful, full lips trembled slightly when she spoke.

"We need to talk." His voice softened, and, without warning, he maneuvered her to the French doors and out onto the veranda.

The night air was a still, brittle cold. He'd forgotten the weather. Bridget shivered in his arms, and he left the door open a crack to allow some warm air out from the living room.

"This won't take long. Just tell me what's going on. I'm confused. One minute we're friends, the next minute I'm on your blacklist." Mark rubbed her upper arms to keep her from getting too chilled.

"You're so arrogant, Mark. I don't like being told to sit and stay, as if I'm some sort of…poodle. In fact, I don't like being brought outside for a talking to, either." Bridget's eyes bored into him.

Something in her, perhaps her defiance, or maybe it was her determination, drew him. He stopped rubbing her arms and traced the stubborn line of her chin with one finger. It took all his willpower to keep from pulling her into his arms.

"I'll not force you to stay. You can go if you want to." He withdrew his hand from her face.

Bridget stared at him. She started to leave, then stopped. Anger arched her brow and tightened her lips into a thin line. He'd stolen her thunder.

"You're—you're shoving this ball back into my court!"

Mark narrowed his eyes and grinned a crooked grin. "So you *want* to stay here with me, even in the cold?"

"Oh!" The single syllable rang through the night air. With every muscle in her body, she stiffened, pulled herself to her full height, and lifted her chin. "I'll not waste more of this dance on you, Mr. Fielder."

She stepped back through the doors and into the warm room. He stared at her back until she'd disappeared into the crowd. Why had he said such a stupid thing?

The dance broke up at midnight. Careful to stay out of Mark's way, Bridget dragged her tired body up the stairs and onto her bed. She was still fuming. His suggestion that she wanted to stay out in the cold with him pushed all her buttons. And he'd known it would. She pummeled her pillow with her fist.

A quiet knock sounded on the door. "Who is it?" No answer, just another soft knock. "Cally, it's twelve-thirty!" Bridget pushed herself off the bed and opened the door.

Instead of seeing her sister's face, a strong hand grasped hers and pulled her gently from the room. It was Mark.

He stood to the side of her door, still in his tux, and held her hand. Her jaw dropped at seeing him there. She unconsciously lifted her free hand to straighten her hair.

"I apologize for my brutish behavior tonight." His voice was slow and deep, spreading over her senses like warm honey. He lifted her hand to his mouth and pressed his warm lips against it, his gold-brown eyes never releasing hers.

Then he bowed slightly and replaced her hand by her side. She stared after him, unable to utter a word, as he walked to his room.

His door clicked shut, and still she stood like a statue in the hall. Warmth flowed from her hand to the rest of her body. His single sentence filled her mind with a slow-moving excitement.

As if in a trance, she floated into her room and shut the

door. She didn't know what to do with this sensitive side of Mark. It gathered her in and carried her away, body and soul.

She quickly undressed, climbed into bed, and fell asleep immediately.

She woke early in the morning and snuggled deeper under the blankets. The air whispering around her face felt cool. She hadn't slept so well since she'd come to Rutledge Place. All that dancing must have worn her out.

A burst of warmth spread from her heart to her toes. Mark. An image shimmered in her mind's eye—Mark holding her hand to his lips, his thumb rubbing her shaking fingers.

She sat upright in bed. Frigid air coursed down the back of her nightgown, prickling the hairs at the base of her spine. Realization spread down the same path, raising more goose bumps than the chill. She stood on the brink of a cliff called love. She saw it better than she could on a big-screen TV. No one could decide the next move for her. She had to choose— either step off the cliff or back away.

"I'm not ready for this!" Her voice rang clear in the crisp, cold air. She looked up, directing her thoughts and words to God. How could she give her heart over to be bruised again? But how could she step away, knowing that she'd never again stand in the circle of Mark's arms, never watch a laugh light up his eyes? "Oh, Father, I can't decide now!"

Bridget raced for her closet and some warm clothes. She must escape her thoughts before she did something foolish. After she'd dressed, she made a beeline for the kitchen. There, Aunt V. and Uncle George sat on stools, cradling cups of steaming coffee.

"Bridget," George said as she filled a mug, "will you play dominoes with us after church this afternoon?"

Bridget sniffed the rich, roasted aroma rising from the carafe. "All right, I'll play with you, so long as I get to win."

"Youth seldom wins over wisdom, dear," Aunt Victoria said.

"But nothing beats genius!" Uncle George laughed and rubbed his wild white hair.

That afternoon, Bridget sauntered from the library and headed toward the stairs. She pulled her hair away from her face and breathed deeply. Dominoes had diverted her mind from Mark for a while. Every thought of last night she'd squelched with a one-liner to George or a gulp of French Roast. Now what?

Thumping steps sounded on the stairs, and Cally came into view. "Bridget, we need to talk. Care to visit in my room awhile?" She gestured up the staircase.

"Sure." Bridget followed her to the third floor. "Did you find string to hang the cinnamon pine cones?"

"Yes, but that's not what I want to talk about." She nodded toward the chairs clustered around a Victorian tea table.

Bridget edged into the plump, flowered seat and braced herself for the inevitable. "You want to talk about Mark, right? There's nothing to talk about."

Cally sat down across the table and sighed. "You say that, but I find it hard to believe. First, you can't stand the sight of him. Then, you two are kissing on the sly—"

"What?" She bolted upright in her chair.

"I've got my sources.… Okay, Uncle George told me."

"Uncle George is wrong. Besides, I've told you and everyone else for years—I'm staying single."

"Oh, come on, Bridget. That's just backlash from Mark's rejection, and it's about time you let it go."

The breath rushed from her as if Cally had kicked her in the stomach. Is that what everyone thought? She stared open-mouthed at her sister.

"Listen, I don't want to hurt you, but you've got to get over this sometime."

"I am over it." The words lacked the conviction she was striving for. "As soon as Christmas is over, I'll go back home and forget all about Mark." She crossed her legs and strummed the cherry finish of the table with her fingertips.

"Bridget, I can't believe this! You know he's hook, line, and sinker, off-the-deep-end crazy about you. How can you be so cold?"

"Cold? I'm being cold? You know what he did to me. You know I was still a girl when he promised to marry me. No one had ever kissed me before or held me...." A knot rose in her throat.

She looked down at the table, then closed her eyes as tears slid slowly down her cheeks. Cally reached out and stroked her hair in a steady rhythm.

"Honey, I know. I was mad at him, too. Remember? I offered to hire a hit man. But even I can see he's not the boy he was. You should give him a chance."

Bridget lifted her gaze and looked into Cally's hazel eyes. More than anything, she wanted to give in and stop fighting her heart. She saw again the gentle way Mark had held her hand last night. The sweetness of his apology begged her not to give up on him.

"Maybe you're right."

# FIVE

**M**ark rummaged through the woodpile on the back porch, searching for the perfect log for a Sunday-evening fire. When he heard Aunt V. clear her throat, he looked up and saw her poking her head out the back door.

"Follow me, young man. I have a job for you."

"Can't I choose a log first?"

"No. This is urgent."

He dusted his jeans and stood up straight. Little particles of dust and wood made his nose twitch. He followed Aunt V. through the kitchen and up the hall toward the front of the house.

"Right here." She stopped in front of two Hepplewhite chairs. They stood under the mistletoe between the living room and the front hall. "That cup hook keeps coming loose. Could you climb up and fix it?"

He tilted his head and stared at the woman. Had he heard her right?

"This is what's urgent?"

"Absolutely. But take your shoes off before you climb on my chairs."

Mark said nothing. He removed his shoes and climbed onto one of the chairs. The hook wiggled loosely when he grabbed it.

"Looks like the hook's too small for the hole, Aunt V." He stared down into her eyes suspiciously.

"Just as I thought. I have a bigger one. Stay where you are and don't move."

The mischief maker walked primly from the hall, through the library, and into the kitchen.

Within a minute, footsteps approached from the kitchen. He leaned down to see under the door frame to the library. Shapely legs clad in green leggings strode into view. Yes sirree, Aunt V. had something up her sleeve.

He should have seen it coming. She'd planted him under the mistletoe and created a good reason for Bridget to "happen" along. He stood up straight, rubbed a hand over his five o'clock shadow, then grinned. He supposed it wouldn't hurt to go along with Aunt V.'s scheme.

"Aunt V. said you needed this cup hook?" Bridget looked up at him, then her eyes widened in sudden understanding. A shy smile spread across her face and she backed up a couple of steps.

"Well, are you going to give it to me or not?" He held out his hand but didn't stretch too far. She could come a little closer.

"You come down and get it."

"Oh, no. We couldn't disappoint your aunt like that." His mouth twitched at the sides.

"I'm not coming closer. You'll have to reach." She stretched her arm toward him, the hook held precariously between two fingers.

He leaned out. In a quick move, he grasped Bridget's wrist and pulled her toward him.

"No fair!"

"Maybe, maybe not."

Mark reached down and lifted her to the other chair. Bridget's laughing smile melted and warm color rushed to her

142

cheeks to replace it. She drew him like a magnet. He bent down and gently touched his lips to hers. The feel of their softness overwhelmed him. He entwined his fingers in her hair, massaging the nape of her neck with his thumb.

Bridget reached her arms around him, and her lips trembled under his kiss. He pulled her closer, his mind crying out for a way to keep her with him forever. But it seemed just the briefest second later that she broke away.

"Oh, Mark. What are we doing?"

"I don't know." He cradled her head in his hands. "I've tried, but I can't stay away from you." He sprinkled kisses along one cheekbone.

"I thought I could get rid of all the feelings you've aroused in me." Bridget stared into his eyes and his stomach flip-flopped. "Now I'm not sure," she whispered.

Mark stiffened and pulled back a few inches. Alarms were going off in his head.

"What's wrong?" Bridget looked at him with wide eyes.

"Oh, darling," he said, stroking her hair one last time, "there's no one in this world who wants you more than I do. But I can't risk hurting you." He hopped off the chair, then helped her down, holding her at arm's length.

She bent down and retrieved his shoes. As she handed them over, he saw confusion in her expression.

"Bridget, a relationship between us would be a disaster. I don't want to, but I have to back off."

"I tell you I have feelings for you, and you drop me like a hot potato?" She stepped away, disbelief on her pale face.

"No, Bridget. That's not it at all." He struggled for words. "I haven't been able to forgive myself for what I did to you, and if you're honest with yourself, you'll see you haven't forgiven me, either. A relationship between us now would only cause more pain."

"What I see is that you can't make a commitment. Don't worry, I wouldn't want one from you anyway." She turned on her heel and stormed away.

After the evening meal, Bridget went upstairs to her room and flopped onto her bed. The confident expression she'd been wearing all evening melted into pain. She couldn't hide her hurting heart any longer.

Tears rose up and tingled behind her nose and eyes. A knot of misery rose from her stomach to her throat and begged to be released. She punched her pillow. She wouldn't cry for him. She would not let him control her, especially when he wasn't even here. But if she didn't do something to divert her mind, her brittle resolve would crumble.

She pushed herself off the bed and strode out the glass door to the balcony. The sun had set, and darkness surrounded her. She buttoned her sweater and warmed her hands under her arms.

Vigorously she paced, even counting her steps, but one thought consumed her. Mark had rejected her. For whatever reason, he didn't want her enough to keep her. And that hurt far worse than she'd ever imagined it would.

Her breath came shallow and ragged. She couldn't run anymore. Bridget sank to her knees, her hands clinging to the railing. Bitter sobs tore from her soul and shook her body.

"Why, God?" she cried out. "Why did you let me get my heart involved, only to have it broken again?"

Hot tears fell from her eyes. Her empty heart convulsed, and she had nothing to ease the pain.

In time, the cool wind whipped her cheeks dry. Her eyelids stung, and her head bowed, too heavy to hold upright. Nothing could lift this heaviness from her, not ever.

The thought jerked her head up. This was pathetic. She was

an adult, a writer, a professional with a God-given ministry. No man could take that away from her. She wouldn't let him.

She stood up and brushed dirt from her knees. She had a life outside of Mark. It was time to get on with it. Wiping her eyes, she walked inside.

On her desk lay a pad of paper and a couple of pens. She wouldn't break her promise to Gloria by writing on her vacation, but surely she could jot down a few ideas for a future book.

She sat at her table, pad in hand, and uncapped her pen. Unlike other writers she knew, the prospect of a fresh page or a blank computer screen excited her, filled her with creative ideas. But now the pad of paper in front of her seemed barren, depressing.

An hour later, she was staring at the same blank sheet of paper. She didn't have a single idea. And what was worse, she didn't care.


The next afternoon, Mark returned from another trip with George and marched to his room. Every muscle in his body was tight; he felt ready to pounce.

He stood in the middle of the room and realized he couldn't stay here. He needed to work off his frustration. And he knew just the place to go. He ran down the back stairs to the garage, then jumped behind the wheel of his car. Although he forced himself to drive the speed limit, it still took less than fifteen minutes to get to campus. He parked in faculty parking and sprinted to the gym.

He changed into his workout clothes in the locker room, then unlocked the cabinet containing his music and record player. He selected albums of contemporary numbers with fast tempos and challenging beats. Right now, he needed a sweat-drenched workout.

The music started. Mark stretched his muscles in a warm-up routine. He stood, knees straight, palms on the floor, nose touching his legs. Next he jogged in place. No, that wasn't good enough. He started a more demanding piece and sprang into a sprint around the polished floor.

A few laps of rubber squeaking on wax, in rhythm with his heartbeat and even breathing, and he was ready. The record player automatically started the song again. He kicked off his shoes and stood still in the middle of the room.

The first notes started rhythmically, and he raised his hands over his head. The music stopped for a fraction of a second. He clasped his hands and dropped to his knees. An explosion of rhythm and sound blasted him to life. He sprang to his feet and leaped up, twirling in midair. The moves were haphazard, unplanned, but they satisfied his need for action and speed, running, sliding, twisting in the air. Finally, the music stopped.

He stopped, breathing hard. The record player began the tune again, and on impulse, he dove into a series of back hand-springs. He came upright a few feet from the machine.

Before he could get to it, a dark hand reached out and lifted the arm from the record. The music stopped. Mark looked up into Robert's face.

"I'm impressed," Robert said.

Mark stood still, sweating and gasping for air. "Robert, why are you here?"

"I followed you. Walk with me, and we'll talk." Robert tilted his head toward the back door.

Mark nodded. "Let me just put this stuff away first." As he gathered the albums, Robert leaned down and picked up the record player.

"You looked fit to be tied when you left the house. I thought I'd better follow."

"Why?"

"For one thing, I could help if your crazy driving got you into a wreck."

"I drove just fine."

"Yeah, sure." Robert's mouth turned up in a grin. "Anyway, I also wanted to talk to you, preferably somewhere more private than the house."

Mark changed quickly; then they walked out of the building. The sun was setting, and the air was rapidly cooling off.

"Let's get inside somewhere before it gets cold," Mark said. "How about the pizza place off Fry? Do you think Aunt V. will be offended if we skip supper?"

"I don't think so."

It took only a few minutes to walk across campus to the pizzeria. Mark was amazed by how different the place was during vacation. Not only were there a number of vacant booths, but someone had turned the sound system down from ear-blasting to dull roar.

The two men found a table on the empty second level. Robert waited until the server had taken their order, then launched in.

"I've seen that you're going through something lately. Maybe talking about it would help."

"I don't know." Mark closed his eyes and rested his forehead in his hands.

"Hey. I'm a friend, remember? That's unconditional. I've decided to be here for you, and that's that."

The waiter arrived with their soft drinks. Mark tossed the straw from his soda and guzzled half of his drink in one gulp. He plunked the cup down on the table.

"I told Bridget we couldn't have a relationship."

"Oh."

"Look, Robert, I don't know how much you know about our past, but Bridget hasn't forgiven me for what I did to her, and I can't even forgive myself. You can't build a future on a foundation like that."

"Did you explain this to her?"

"I tried. She's too hurt to care."

"I see. What are you going to do now?"

"Bury myself in work. Try to forget about her. I thought I'd take up drinking," he said with a weak attempt at a grin, "but I decided to start a ministry instead."

Robert snorted. "Good choice. What kind of ministry?"

"I only have a few half-baked ideas so far."

"Half-baked ideas are okay. Tell me about them. If they're really bad, I'll laugh at you. On the other hand, they might not be as bad as you think."

Mark chugged the other half of his drink, then set it down with a thud.

"I'll tell you, then. You've laughed at me before." He grinned. "You know, those charity suppers the church has are good, but they're only once a year. We need more contact with the people if we're going to help them financially or win them to the Lord. That's where I draw a blank. I have a few ideas, but—"

"But this is where they get half-baked?" Robert finished for him. "Pick out your best one and tell me about it."

The waiter arrived with a steaming pan of sausage-and-pepperoni pizza. After sorting through the flurry of plates, napkins, and forks, Mark continued.

"I guess the café idea is my favorite. You know about charity kitchens? This would be like that, but not fully charity—say, twenty-five cents per meal. I think it would attract a lot of the millworkers. And there could be a bulletin board listing available jobs in the area." He glanced up from his food, searching Robert's expression for a response.

Robert was silent for a minute. Mark waited a little nervously.

Finally, Robert said, "That's good, but have you thought of holding classes there, too? I mean reading classes, Bible studies—that sort of thing." He rubbed a hand across his clean-shaven jaw. "Just remember, following your ministry's great, but it won't fulfill you. You were made for a relationship with God."

After they finished eating and had headed to their separate cars, Mark continued to think about what Robert had said. It was true. And he knew that before he could resolve his problems with Bridget, he'd have to talk things over with God.

# $\mathscr{S}$IX

**R**obert's words tumbled over and over in Mark's head as he paced through the garden in the dark.

"You were made for a relationship with God," he repeated aloud.

He stopped under a lone pear tree alongside the path and sat on a bench. He remembered that day when he was ten years old when he'd responded to the invitation at church and accepted Christ. He'd been trembling with fear and embarrassment, but he had come. And he'd done it with a sincere heart.

What was that Scripture? "If we confess our sins, he is faithful and just and will forgive us our sins and purify us from all unrighteousness." He had done that. He'd confessed his sin to God and knew God had forgiven him, but for some reason he didn't feel forgiven.

He stopped as a new thought gripped him. He may not feel forgiven, but God never lied. He remained true to his Word. Mark absently tore apart a dry leaf while his thoughts churned. "It's me, isn't it, God? I haven't forgiven myself, and Bridget hasn't forgiven me. Lord, I know I can't make Bridget forgive me, but I'm sinning against you if I don't forgive myself. After all, if you can forgive me, I certainly don't have any right to hold onto this sin and allow it to keep me from a relationship with you."

He paused for a moment, then closed his eyes. "Lord, I know you've forgiven me and cleansed me from all unrighteousness, and I believe you can take this unforgiveness from my heart. I've tried on my own, and it's impossible. I ask now that you would help me, Lord, and also that you would put it upon Bridget's heart to forgive me, because I don't want that bitterness to keep her from you, either."

Mark raised his head and opened his eyes, smiling. He felt better than he had in a long time.

That night, Bridget crept to the third floor and into Great-great-grandfather Rutledge's retreat. It was used for furniture storage now, so no one would find her. Besides, Great-great-grandfather had spent a lot of his time here. Maybe his wisdom would somehow soak into her. She almost smiled at the thought.

Dusty antiques and haphazard piles of clutter filled the room. Weaving around old settees, card tables, and the huge circular sofa, she found her way to the Beidermeier couch. She drew her knees to her chest and hugged them close, her hot face nestled against the nubby fabric.

Half of her ached for Mark and what they'd lost. The other half chafed with bitter memories until her anger and pain made her physically sore. She didn't know whether to cry or scream.

It was too late to decide. Scorching tears spilled in streams down her cheeks, pent-up hurt fueling them until she thought they'd never stop.

A quick rap sounded on the door. She froze.

"Bridget?" Mark called softly through the door.

She didn't answer.

"I know you're there. I heard you shuffling around. Can I come in?"

"Not now, Mark. Not ever. Go away."

"Listen." His words came through loud and clear this time. "I've got something I have to tell you. Unless you want me to holler it through the door for the whole house to hear, you'd better let me in."

Great. What horrible sentiment awaited public revelation now? Maybe he'd discovered he didn't love her after all, and Jolene Rogers was waiting in a car outside to take him away. Her heart wrenched painfully.

"Okay," he called, "I just wanted to tell you—"

"Wait! Give me a minute, okay?" Bridget sprang into action. She dabbed her eyes with the sleeve of her sweater and blew her nose on a wadded-up piece of tissue paper. Leave it to Mark to catch her in the middle of a private cry. He had no decency.

Desperately, she waved an old sheet of newspaper in front of her face to dry her eyes. If he saw them all red and puffy, he would think she was crying for him. Which she wasn't. She was mourning a lost ideal, not a lost man.

"What'd you do? Jump out the window?"

No, the man certainly wasn't lost. He was standing in the hall, making a nuisance of himself.

"Okay, Mark. You can come in."

The door swung open, and in he came, as handsome and cocky as ever. "Bridget—" He stopped short. "Have you been crying?"

Bridget scowled at him. "Just say what you have to say; then get out!"

An impish grin quirked at the side of his mouth, but he quickly grew serious again. "I'll try. Why don't you sit down? This will take a little while."

She perched on the edge of an end table and waited. She had meant to remain aloof, but something about Mark's demeanor drew her attention. What was it? She watched through narrowed eyes as he found a chair, hauled it to the small clear space in front of her, and sat down.

His movements were strong and sure, as always, and he looked straight at her. She saw that something had changed. He was excited to tell her something, but in back of that, there was something stable, a peace about him.

"Bridget?" He frowned. "Are you listening to me?"

"Mark, just tell me why you're here; then leave." Her whole body shook with emotion. Anger and…something else.

"Okay." His voice remained calm. "God is, and always will be, first in my life. He's shown me that. Nothing else will work. What I need to talk about now takes second place, but it still outweighs anything else in this world." His eyes caught hers, the heat of their intensity burning into her mind. He walked over to her and stood, a breath away.

"If you ever decide you can forgive me, I'll be here for you. There will never be anyone else, and, if you give me the chance, I want to cherish you and protect you forever." He rubbed his thumb over the line on her cheek where tears had flowed moments before. "I'll love you for the rest of our lives."

Bridget was stunned. She couldn't move away from Mark's touch. His words pounded against the walls around her heart, threatening to crack her defenses. Her heart had craved those promises for eight years. She wanted to hug them to her, feed them to her starving soul. But as soon as she thought it, her skin crawled with humiliation. She was almost naive enough to fall for the same lie a second time.

"How dare you?" The words were quiet, almost whispered, but they carried the weight of years of grief. "You betrayed me. You hurt me like no one else ever has."

Mark backed up a step, and Bridget leaned toward him. "Remember? You told me you wanted to marry me. You said to wait for you until we finished college. I believed you. I would have waited until the end of time. But you—you didn't." Her voice broke. Bridget clenched her fists and tightened her jaw. She wouldn't cry. She had to finish this. Her voice low and husky, she ground out, "You made a fool out of me. I agreed, like a brainless little girl, to wait, while you turned around and stabbed me in the back!"

"That's not true, Bridget. Yes, I went out with Becky—"

"Oh, you did a lot more than that."

"What do you think I did, Bridget—sleep with her?" He was in her face again, his arms spread wide for her scrutiny. "You saw the whole thing. I kissed her—once. That was it. I was sick to think I'd lost you. I never even talked to her after that."

The years fell away, and she lived it again—spotting his car in the empty football-field parking lot, walking over without a clue in the world. What she saw made her sick to her stomach.

It had been no innocent kiss her future husband was sharing with the pretty blonde. If Bridget hadn't shown up when she did... She ground her teeth now in an effort to shake the image.

"How could you have betrayed me like that?"

Mark sank back onto the couch, a heavy sigh escaping his lips. He shut his eyes, and Bridget watched the visible pain cross his features. Good. He deserved to hurt after what he'd done to her.

"I'd grown away from God, and..." He swallowed and tried again. "It started with one little thought. Here I was, eighteen years old, and I'd only dated one girl. At first, I ignored the idea, horrified that I could even think it. But it came back. And it kept coming back.

"Finally, I decided to date Becky. Just once. I knew she liked me, and, Bridget, when you saw us in that car, it was our one and only kiss."

"You sure moved a lot faster with her than you did with

me!" Bridget watched his face turn pale. Even if it had been only a kiss, his wanting someone else, touching someone else, hurt just as much. "Can't you see how you killed me inside?"

"I know." Mark looked her in the eyes. "I died, too. From the moment I saw you standing outside the car, I knew I'd lost you. I've never felt as devastated as I did right then. For eight years, I couldn't forgive myself for what I did to you. Just today, I've finally realized that if God has forgiven me, I'm clean in his eyes, as if I never did it. I've finally forgiven myself, and I need your forgiveness, too."

Forgive him? Bridget stared into the pleading eyes in front of her, and the twinge of compassion she felt was overpowered by the ache in her heart. Her conscience couldn't pull together enough strength to do as he asked.

"I can't, Mark." The words were wrenched from her soul. She had thought she'd forgiven him years ago, but she realized now that the hurt and pain had simply been buried. "I just can't."


On Christmas Eve morning, Mark went downstairs using the front staircase, hoping to see Bridget as he went past her room. He needed every possible chance to show her his love and devotion before she went home tomorrow. Unfortunately, she was nowhere to be seen.

As he walked down the front hall, Mr. Stout emerged from the kitchen. The chauffeur saw him and nodded almost imperceptibly. Mark groaned. Didn't Uncle George ever rest?

He grabbed his jacket from the coat rack, then jogged to the garage. George always gave Mr. Stout fifteen minutes' notice, but how much of that time had Stout spent looking for him? He'd have to hurry. He quietly opened the back door of the Cadillac and settled into his cramped hiding place.

"Watch your head back there; we're in a rush." Mr. Stout revved the engine and pulled out into the drive.

No sooner had he squealed to a stop in front of the veranda than Uncle George hallooed from the direction of the house. Talk about close calls. Mark hunched down closer to the floorboard.

A short drive through town ended in bumpy railroad crossings and pitted streets. They waited for five full minutes while coal cars clacked along tracks that crossed the broken asphalt.

"You know, Stout," Uncle George said, "I think I've shopped every store in town, and I still can't find a tomahawk. I suppose they're simply not in style anymore." He rustled the long list on his lap.

"You may be right, sir," said Mr. Stout. "Perhaps you could make one." Uncle George grunted a response. "And, since you have knowledge of so many stores, maybe you could help out a friend of mine. He's looking for a snorkel."

Mark jammed the blanket against his mouth to muffle a laugh.

"What's that noise? Do we have a cat in the car?" The seat cushion squeaked as Uncle George shifted to look in back.

"No, sir. Definitely not. It's flatulence, sir."

"Oh."

Mark shook with the effort not to laugh when he heard the electric window roll down on Uncle George's side.

On the other side of the tracks, the Cadillac pulled to the edge of the road and stopped.

"I'll go to the park today, Stout. Don't bring the car around. You know how it intimidates the folks. How about an hour from now? We'll meet back here. Go have yourself a doughnut."

It happened the same way every day. He gave his speech and walked off. Five minutes later, Mark crawled out from under the blanket and followed. The park was easy. No one gave him funny looks for hanging out there. The neighborhoods posed a more difficult problem. He had to keep George in sight without being seen—but people worried about a strange man prowling around their street. He was sure someone had called the police on him the first day.

The park consisted of a collection of rusty playground equipment surrounded by a few rickety benches. Uncle George sat on one of them, waiting for some of his new friends to happen along. Moving soundlessly among the dead leaves and fallen twigs while at the same time trying not to look like James Bond on the prowl, Mark crept forward until he was near enough to come to Uncle George's assistance should it be necessary. He found a tree and sat against it, his back to his charge.

# SEVEN

ey, George."

Mark glanced around the tree and saw a shriveled old man. He wore an oil-stained, ancient jacket, not thick enough for the chill in the air. His gray pants were too long, and they frayed at the hem. Gray hair hung in wisps around his ears.

"Winston, fine to see you. How's that cough?"

"That's not me; that's Charlie. He'll be all right, though. Too many cigarettes. Doctor wants him to quit. That'll be the day!" Winston laughed a paper-thin laugh until tears rolled down his cheeks and he had to blow his nose. "Stubborn cuss," he added, tucking the tattered hanky back into his pocket.

"Did you talk to your granddaughter?" asked Uncle George. "What does she want for Christmas?"

"Had to talk to her mother. Says Becca's been wantin' that ballerina doll, the one that turns 'round on her toe. You know how little girls are, they see a thing on TV and they've gotta have it."

"Are they coming for the supper, then?"

"Far as I know."

"And you?"

"Oh, I don't know. Never have believed in Santa myself." He laughed again.

"Please come. I don't want to be there alone."

"That'd be the day, George. You've got some sort of plan up your sleeve, gettin' me an' the boys to the rec center. Just might come, though. You got me curious."

The old man meandered off, and Uncle George sat alone for a while. Fifteen minutes passed before a young mother strolled up with her baby. A similar conversation passed between George and the woman before she too moved on.

Noting the time, Mark stood to his feet, careful to make no noise. He started back to the meeting spot, keeping a tree or bush between him and Uncle George whenever possible.

Aunt V. had made this job sound easy when she'd asked him to do it. Well, it wasn't. His heart pumped two-fifty a minute when he made these getaways. Almost as fast as when he thought about Bridget.


The recreation center was decked out in holiday finery. Bridget looked at the huge Christmas tree and long, food-laden tables without really seeing them. She hadn't been able to focus on much of anything since her conversation with Mark last night.

Her mind was a record skipping on a scratched spot. *"I'll love you for the rest of our lives. I'll love you..."* kept echoing in her head until she thought she'd go insane.

Glittering lights hung from the high ceiling, catching Bridget's attention as they played off the foil-covered platters on the tables. Any minute the double doors would open and hundreds of hungry guests would pour in. She took her place behind a table, serving spoon in hand.

Six o'clock struck. A couple of teens opened the doors to the expectant faces outside. In an instant, the river of people flowed from the door at the back to the tree at the front, where the food lines would start.

Pastor Burkett stepped onto a makeshift stage and spoke into the microphone.

"Merry Christmas, everyone, and thanks for coming. We know you're all ready to eat, so we're going to start this ball rolling with prayer." He paused while more people edged into the room. A hush fell. "Father, we come to you in Jesus' name. Thank you for the privilege of blessing the folks you've brought here, whom you love so much. Nourish this food to their bodies and touch their hearts. Amen." The pastor looked up and signaled for dinner to begin.

For the next hour, Bridget served up mashed potatoes and gravy to an endless line of guests. There wasn't even time to sip from the cup of water another church member had brought her. Finally, the torrent slowed to a trickle. Everyone must have had their first helping.

At that instant, a tingle of excitement raced audibly through the children in the crowd. Bridget followed their stares and pointing fingers to the front of the room. There stood Uncle George, a Santa hat on his head and a monstrous bag bulging at his side. Mothers shushed their children as he took the microphone from its stand.

"These gifts are for you, children." A high-pitched cheer rose from the kids. Uncle George waited until it had died down, then said, "I hope you like them. You see, I found out some of your names and what you wanted, but I don't know everyone, so I brought a lot of extras." He shifted his feet and held up a hand for their attention.

"You see, dear children, there's no way I can know you all, but there is one who knows everything about you. Do you know who that is?"

"Mommy!" a little girl called out. He chuckled.

"She knows you pretty well, doesn't she? But there's someone who knows you better. He knows all the dreams you hold in your heart. It's the Lord Jesus. So while I couldn't get all of you presents with your names on them, he knows you through and through and wants to make those dreams in your heart come true.

"I'll put the presents with names in one pile and the presents labeled 'boy' and 'girl' in another. Then come and line up."

Bridget stood behind the table, ladle in hand, while tears blurred her view. Dawning respect choked her throat. What love Uncle George had for these children! She watched as he tenderly leaned over them with a kind word for each one. Her own selfishness amazed her. She'd been so caught up with her confusion over Mark that she'd had no concern for others.

She suddenly became aware that a man stood in front of her, waiting for mashed potatoes. Bridget looked up at the tall African-American and smiled.

"Isn't that the sweetest thing?" She pointed at the scene up front, where George hugged a toddler.

"It's good for the kids. Some of them don't get much out of life."

Bridget studied the man who eyed his plate hungrily. He wore torn jeans and a faded T-shirt, and his eyes drooped with fatigue. "How about you?"

"Can't complain. I got a job at the mill. Pays the rent."

The man moved down the line. Bridget thumped her spoon down onto the steaming mass of potatoes. If this man couldn't complain, what right did she have to be wallowing in self-pity over her own relatively small troubles?

Late that night, Bridget sat on the floor in her room wrapping gifts. The clock in the hall chimed twelve, and she rubbed her eyes. She wished she'd been able to finish her gifts earlier, but it couldn't be helped. They hadn't returned from the recreation center until after nine-thirty.

Winding ribbon around her fingers to make a bow, Bridget's mind drifted from her task to the thrilled faces of the children at church. She was sure most of them had never had such wonderful gifts. How did Uncle George know what those kids wanted? She chewed a fingernail. Aunt Victoria's excuse for his absences lately had always been that he'd been shopping. That made sense, but how did he know what to buy?

But George hadn't been the only one shopping. Somehow Mark was involved in this thing. But when she tried to decipher how, her brain knotted up like a ball of twine.

He'd done whatever he did secretly. Uncle George hadn't known of Mark's presence in the back of the Cadillac that day she'd spied on them. Yet Aunt Victoria knew; Bridget had no doubt about that.

Aunt V. must have hired Mark. But for what? Bridget pushed aside a wrapped present and started on another. This whole mess revolved around the charity supper and those gifts. Somehow. And she had until tomorrow to figure it out.


Robby and Luke were sitting by the tree when Bridget arrived in the living room on Christmas morning. She struggled across the room with her pile of gifts and nudged Luke's side with her toe.

"If you want your presents from me, you'll have to move. I can't reach the tree."

"Yes, ma'am!" Luke sprang from the floor and found a seat by the fireplace.

Bridget got on her hands and knees and crammed presents under the already-crowded tree. Pine needles scraped her hands, and the swaying branches released a wave of spicy perfume. She pulled out of the branches and sniffed the air appreciatively.

Mark, Cally, and Robert shuffled in with more packages, and then Aunt V., followed by George, who was carrying a huge log. With tender care, he placed it on the fire just so. Then he dusted his hands and looked at the faces around the room.

"Let's start, shall we?" He turned to the boys. "To work! There is no holiday for Santa's helpers. Pass out those gifts."

Soon, piles of presents sat in front of each person. Now the ritual of opening the presents began: Each person opened one until everyone had undone a gift. Then they went around again until the last package lay dismembered on the floor. Bridget's heart warmed to the age-old procedure. The Rutledge family had done it this way since before she was born. She opened a large, shiny package when her turn came.

"Oh! Thank you, Cally and Robert, guys." She held up an intricate pink-and-cream quilt. "It's lovely."

And it went on. Gift after gift lay in open boxes, and finally, they reached the last round. Robby and Luke crashed into theirs simultaneously and came out with small, remote-controlled airplanes from their parents.

"Cool!" they said in unison.

Aunt Victoria opened a pair of tapestry-and-beadwork house slippers, and Cally found a pair of earrings from the boys. Then it was Bridget's turn to open her tiny package from Mark. She'd saved it until last.

As the paper fell away, an old jewelry gift box appeared. Something clicked in her memory. She'd seen this box before. Her fingers hesitated, afraid to discover its secret. The lid creaked back on rusty hinges. The box had never been quality, but what lay inside jerked her back nine years. A fragile, gold-plated chain with a nameplate lay curled up on the shabby blue velvet liner.

Bridget touched the bracelet, then lifted it from its case. There, carved on the nameplate, was her name with tiny hearts on either end. Tears pooled in her eyes. The room around her fell silent.

"I found it in the floor of my car after we…argued that last time." Mark's gentle tone sent the tears spilling down her cheeks. He reached over and touched her knee. "I've always wanted to give it back to you, but I didn't know if you'd accept it."

Bridget sniffed and wiped her face with a tissue Cally handed her. "I'd almost forgotten it. You gave it to me on the anniversary of our first date."

Mark nodded. "You're not upset to see it again?"

"No," Bridget whispered.

# EIGHT

Bridget was still struggling to recover when George walked to the middle of the room holding a small, wrapped present. She dabbed her eyes and watched.

"I have a gift for you all, but since it's one package, I'll ask Victoria to open it."

"Thank you, George." Aunt V. took the package and carefully pulled back the paper. "What is this?"

She held up the crumbling leather volume and opened the front cover. "It's the diary of Jedediah Rutledge. Oh, my!" Tears filled her eyes. "Did you know, George, that I've known about this journal and looked for it most of my life? Where did you find it?"

"I was down in the wine cellar last week doing some...er, that is...taking care of business, when I needed some tape." Uncle George leaned back on his heels, obviously enjoying his audience. "I knew I had an extra roll somewhere, so I searched all around my desk, looking in all the cubbyholes. It used to be Old Man Rutledge's desk about a century ago," he added, for the benefit of the younger generation.

"Anyhow, I looked into one of the slots I thought was empty and stumbled onto this. Quite a surprise, eh?" He chuckled.

The family gathered around to look, anxious to learn more

about the man who had built the family fortune—and Rutledge Place.

"We can all hear it together, if you approve, Aunt V. You could read and we'll listen," Robert suggested.

The family matriarch smiled at him, then beamed over her whole, collected family.

"That sounds wonderful. Thank you, Robert. And George." She placed a kiss on her brother's weathered cheek.

The faded blue eyes twinkled merrily, and Bridget smiled to see the rose-colored hue on her aunt's cheeks.

Ten minutes later, they gathered in the sitting room. Bridget backed into a cold corner of the couch with a china cup of delicately scented tea. With great care, Aunt Victoria lifted the brittle leather cover of the journal and read the inscription on the first page.

"'To Jedediah Moses Rutledge. From Mother. June 1, 1850. Ten years old.'" She looked up at the family, mist lighting her eyes. "Interesting already!"

Bridget watched Cally snuggle closer to Robert as they sat on the floor by the fire. She sighed. It was good to see them so openly affectionate, but it hurt at the same time. She'd been so close to a relationship like that, yet so far.

She glanced at Mark across the room. He leaned against the wall, listening, his gaze directed toward the ceiling. Her heart began hammering, the way it did whenever she looked at him, but the pain was still there as well.

Aunt V. turned another fragile page and continued reading. It seemed Great-great-grandfather Rutledge didn't write much as a boy. But he remedied that during young adulthood. At age twenty, he began working full-time in his father's antique store. He loved the work, and the business flourished when his father placed more and more of it in his hands.

The summer Jedediah turned twenty-three, an evangelist

held meetings at the family's church, and Jedediah gave his life to the Lord. His writing changed from that time on. He still worked frantically, but he had new purpose. "Doesn't sound so durned puffed up," as Uncle George put it.

Two months later, Jedediah met Emma St. James. Robby's interest perked up, along with his ears, and Aunt V. chuckled softly. "He writes, 'I never saw a creature so lovely in all my life—chestnut hair, eyes like cinnamon, and I dare not dwell on form!'" She laughed again. "What a gentleman!"

Bridget found herself listening more closely as their romance progressed with all its ups and downs. Jedediah had to woo the beautiful Emma away from another man who vied for her attention. Bridget bristled with frustration when Emma allowed the other man to walk her home from church and call on her at her parents' home.

How could she flip-flop from one man to another? Bridget bit her lip to keep the words back. Jedediah worked his fingers to the bone just for money to buy her flowers. What had this other fellow done? Nothing. His family "owned the cattle on a thousand hills, as the Lord's book says," Jedediah wrote.

For two years, the occasional journal entries chronicled Jedediah's struggle to gain Emma's love. Then, suddenly, he stopped. He wrote instead of his rededication to the Lord.

"'I must consider Emma a thing of the past. She loves another. My hope for happiness is in God.'" Aunt V. brushed a tear from her thin cheek. "What a tragic story! Bridget, you should write a book about this." She blew her nose and read on.

Only three weeks after the sorrowful entry, Emma broke down crying on Jedediah's mother's shoulder in the middle of a ladies' tea. Now that he'd left her alone, it seemed, she couldn't live without him. They were married three months later.

Bridget shook her head, half in wonder, half in anger. She didn't like Emma, her own great-great-grandmother. The woman couldn't make up her mind—didn't know her mind until someone pointed it out to her! It brought up Mark's speech about calling off their relationship with dazzling clarity.

But the journal continued. Emma and Grandfather eventually brought three children into the world. He worked long hours, but he was never happier than when he was with his beloved wife. Eventually, his fortune increased into a "princely sum," and he built his beautiful house and dubbed it Rutledge Place. Emma did him proud, he wrote. She was as gracious a society hostess as she was a hard worker and mother of three. In fact, Jedediah's journal brimmed full of stories about his "beautiful bride" and their offspring. Right down to his old age, his God and his family kept him alive. The antique business pulled in a fortune, but his relationships brought him joy.

A spasm twisted Bridget's heart like hunger pangs in an empty stomach. Grandfather had had it all. And it was Emma who gave it to him. She started at the realization. She'd misjudged her—she'd thought Emma was like Mark, shifting and unstable. Another pang racked her heart.

Finally, Aunt V. turned to the last page. Jedediah, now an old man, wrote that Emma had died. Aunt Victoria stopped reading and wiped tears from her face with trembling hands.

"'I don't know how to live without her.'" Aunt Victoria choked up again. Bridget put a finger to her own face and realized her cheek was wet. "'Maybe it's time to go on to be with the Lord. I've survived two of my own children and now my beloved wife. Our grandchildren are devoted to God, so my work here is done. Oh, Lord, I'm ninety years old. Take me home. Life has been good, but I want to go home.'"

Aunt Victoria closed the book. "That's all he wrote." She cleared her throat. "Great-grandfather Rutledge died in 1935, five years after his last entry. I was only two, and your mother hadn't been born yet." She nodded at Bridget and Cally.

"I remember him well," Uncle George broke in. "He was more like a grandfather to me than a great-grandfather. After all, the old man outlived Grandfather by almost ten years. I don't recall him being sad, though. Just looked forward to going home."

The room held an almost palpable silence. It should have been a sad moment, but Bridget felt the odd elation that leapt in each heart. Love conquered in the end—conquered heartache, conquered death. They were together again: Jedediah, Emma, and Jesus. Quietly, she eased out of her seat and slipped from the room.

She climbed the stairs to her room and closed the door behind her. After grabbing her hairbrush from the dresser, she sat down cross-legged on the bed. This evening she would leave, returning to her one-bedroom apartment to live alone. As she brushed her hair, she envied Jedediah Rutledge his beloved family and his joy. The way it looked now, she had a computer to snuggle up to. She sighed. Maybe she would get a pet.

Mark said he'd love her for the rest of her life. She considered the possibility that he meant it. After all, he'd searched the entire house to find a woman who hated him and put himself in a position to get his head bitten off. He must sincerely feel something.

Experience taught her otherwise, though. If she believed him now, she'd have her heart battered again. There was a precedent already set.

Then he'd asked her to forgive him. Or had he asked? Bridget stopped brushing. She set the brush in her lap and played with the plastic bristles while her thoughts took an uncomfortable turn. God wanted her to forgive Mark; she knew that. For one thing, that Scripture she'd memorized in high school kept tapping at her conscience.

"'Bear with each other and forgive whatever grievances you

171

may have against one another. Forgive as the Lord forgave you.' Colossians 3:13," Bridget whispered.

The other reason was the still, small voice in her heart. Without having to pray, she knew God's will. But she couldn't do it, not without his help. The revelation fell into her lap, startling her with its truth. Her own strength had very real, very big limits. Forgiving Mark was beyond those limits by half the globe or so.

Bridget picked up the brush and yanked it through her hair with a vengeance. Tears sprang to her eyes when the bristles caught a tangle and tore several hairs from her scalp. Her fingers rubbed the spot while her mind continued on. Okay, she needed help. There were things she couldn't do by herself.

"What *can* you do by yourself? What talent do you have that I haven't given you? Even your physical existence is a gift from me."

Bridget realized that the voice came from her heart. Immediately, she slid from the bed to her knees. "Lord, I'm sorry I've ignored you." Her ears strained to hear the inward words again. He'd given her every talent; he'd given her physical life. She could do nothing without him. "Lord, forgive my pride. Take it out of me—I can't even do *that* by myself."

She couldn't forgive Mark; anger built up inside her at the thought of him. She'd ignored it, pushed it aside, tried to forget about it, but it gnawed at her heart constantly.

"How can I forgive him, God? I've tried time and again. I thought I'd already done it, but it's obvious I haven't. Help me, Lord! I need your grace."

Memories flashed before her mind's eye—but not the betraying kiss or their arguments. Not this time. She saw instead a dozen roses propped against the front door after she'd broken up with him. She felt the bulk of each letter he'd sent her, which she'd returned unopened.

Finally, she tasted the sweetness of the last week. The tenderness of his kiss, certainly, but much more than that. His honesty rose before her. Risking his own heart, he'd told her he still loved her. And she admired him for the way he'd stepped back when he'd been tempted to start a doomed relationship. That wasn't the same Mark she'd known all those years ago. But his forgiveness and unconditional love were what broke her heart.

She'd tried deliberately to hurt him, and he hadn't shoved back. She'd thrown his guilt up in his face and smirked at his love, but he forgave her.

Bridget pulled her head up from the bedspread. That still, small voice inside spoke again.

"And how much greater is my love, my forgiveness, my power. Child, I love you. I'm not finished with you. Remember that I'll never leave you nor forsake you."

Bridget smiled through the tears. At that instant, another realization filled her with peace and salved her wounds. She'd forgiven Mark. The years of anger and pride were past. They were gone, and there was no returning to them.

She stood and walked to the balcony door. Only one thing bothered her: Could she accept his love? "I don't know if I can decide that yet, Lord," she said aloud. She'd have to wait and see what the day would bring. A slow smile spread across her face and lit up the remaining tears in her eyes.


Christmas lunch was an informal gathering. Armand's holiday meant the whole family gathered in the kitchen, chopping lettuce, grilling steaks, and baking potatoes.

Mark's stomach growled as the aroma of juicy steak and spicy garlic filled the air. At just the right moment, he lifted the steak with a fork and turned it over. Perfect.

"Uncle George," Cally called through streams of onion-induced tears, "we've waited patiently since last night, and, frankly, I'm tired of the suspense. How'd you know what gifts to get those kids? Robert and I spent half of last night discussing—"

"Arguing," Robert teased.

"Discussing it." Cally thumped her husband's shoulder.

"Is that why you've been gone so much?" Luke asked Uncle George.

Uncle George chuckled and peered through his bushy eyebrows at the faces turned toward him. He looked like an old vet, eager to tell a war story. Mark's mind went on alert. Would his part in this come out, too?

"I guess I should tell you. It wasn't really a secret; I just didn't want to make a show out of it. You see, the people we help at the charity supper have been on my heart. We only see them once a year. I figured if we knew them, we'd be much better witnesses and we could help them more." He returned to his duty of washing the table.

"But how did you do it, Uncle George?" Luke asked.

George looked up and glanced around. "Oh, yes. Didn't explain that, did I? I went to their neighborhoods, made friends, made my list, checked it twice."

"You let him do that?" Cally turned on Aunt V., accusation in her tone. "That's dangerous! That is not a nice area of town."

Mark turned away and began to pepper a T-bone somewhat liberally.

"Of course she did." Uncle George said. "And now that it's over, Mark's out of a job."

# NINE

hat?" Mark and Aunt V. flung the word out in unison.

Uncle George tapped his head knowingly. "You think I'm getting a little slow.... Well, maybe I always have been. But I'm not addlebrained. Couldn't help but notice I had a baby-sitter."

"Oh, so that's the mystery!" Bridget said. "I've been so thick-skulled not to see it."

"Dear George," Victoria said, "I hope you're not too upset. I was worried for your safety."

Uncle George patted her hand when she came to stand beside him. "Yes, I know. And there were times I was glad to have him." His eyes saddened. "But I don't want to give up my new friends. Do you think you could accompany me there every so often, young fellow?"

"Of course. I'd be glad to," Mark said.

At lunch, Aunt V. declared they should have a family party before everyone left for home. The thought of returning home was a shock to Mark. If he didn't move quickly, Bridget would leave and he'd never see her again. Mark ran his hands through his hair. *Think, buddy! You've got half a day to change her mind.*

The party was set to kick off at three o'clock that afternoon. At five minutes till, Mark was pawing through his dresser drawers.

How did they dress for this kind of thing? He'd feel more comfortable in flannel and jeans, but what if everyone else dressed up?

He found a compromise in black jeans and a dress shirt, then hurried downstairs to the living room. He'd come last, as usual. Everyone was there waiting for him. The folding doors had been drawn back to open up the sitting room, where a buffet table was set up.

Cally called them all to order. "Does Mark know how to play the game?" she asked.

"I don't think so," Bridget said. "The boys made it up three or four years ago, didn't they?"

Mark looked at her. She was standing arm-in-arm with Uncle George. He hadn't seen much of her since they'd read the journal, but now she looked happy, even excited. His heart thudded hard.

For an instant, she looked up, and their eyes locked. A split second seemed like an eternity, and then she smiled. It was hardly a smile—more a softening of her features and a sparkle in her eyes. Then she looked away.

There was hope for him after all.

"Okay, here's what you do," Luke said. "It's like musical chairs, but the person who ends up without a seat has to answer a question—"

"No, Luke," Robby interrupted, "everyone gets to ask him a question—something embarrassing—and the loser has to answer all the questions without lying."

"Yeah, and if he lies or won't answer, he has to do the chicken walk," Luke said.

"One time around the group for every question he gets wrong—and then he's out. If he answers them all, he's not out. Got it?"

Mark cleared his throat. "So, how do you do this chicken walk?"

"Yes, boys, demonstrate," Cally said.

Robby hesitated, but Luke pulled him over to a clear space. "I double-dog dare ya, chicken lips."

"All right, monkey brain. I can do it."

The boys squatted and bent their arms until their thumbs touched their armpits. Then they strutted around, flapping their wings, with a *bawk-bawk* noise coming from their throats.

Mark laughed. "I'm up to the challenge. How about the rest of you?"

Robert and Mark gathered six side chairs and placed them in a circle in the sitting room. Uncle George searched the stereo cabinet for suitable music and came up with a collection of nursery rhymes.

"That'll do, unless some of you are stuffy," Aunt V. declared. "I think I'll run the music while the rest of you fight for chairs. After all, none of you has a chance if I play."

"Just because we wouldn't want to shove you out of a seat," Luke said.

"Some win by force and some by cunning." She smiled at him.

Aunt V. settled herself by the turntable, and the remaining seven players gathered inside the circle of chairs. With great fanfare, Aunt V. eased the needle onto the old record, and the game began.

Bridget struck out first. Mark was next, then George, and after the boys crashed and burned, the final round began with Cally and Robert facing it off. The family grouped around to watch the bitter end. Mark touched Bridget's shoulder.

"Would you like me to get a plate of food for you?"

Bridget chuckled. "You ask so nicely, how can I refuse?"

"I've learned my lesson. I'll only order you around when I want you to do the opposite thing."

"Hey! I'm not that bad."

Mark flashed a grin and headed for the food table. "I'll go get that plate before you change your mind."

He filled two plates with finger sandwiches and chips. Then he placed them on the same small table he'd used during the Christmas dance. He turned around to get the punch but saw Bridget walking his way, a crystal cup of the drink in each hand.

"Is this what you need?" she asked.

"Yes. That and a beautiful dinner companion."

"Oh. In that case, maybe I should call Cally over. But you'll have to wait until they finish the game, and then you'll have to fight Robert for her—"

"Okay, okay!" He laughed. "I meant you. You are beautiful."

Bridget bent down and put the cups on the table, her hair falling forward to hide her face. Mark leaned toward her to see if the color on the nape of her neck reached her cheeks. But she stood up then, controlled and only slightly pink.

He pulled up a couple of chairs, and they sat across from each other in the recess of the bay window. The open curtains revealed a breathtaking blue sky, with the bare limbs of winter trees etched along the horizon.

"What's next for you, Mark? I mean, after this vacation."

"You want my New Year's resolution?"

"Sure."

He paused for a minute. How would she take this? He knew he'd heard from God. Her reaction, good or bad, couldn't change that. Taking a shallow breath, he charged on.

"I told you about my relationship with God. That's my first goal. I want to know him better."

"I know what you're saying." Bridget nodded. "I want that, too. My writing and all my plans are worthless without him."

She understood! Mark's adrenaline started pumping. "Let me tell you about an idea I've had. I'm still going to get my master's degree and teach dance, but I can do both. You see, Uncle George got me thinking...." He told her about the café, the inexpensive food, the jobs board, and Robert's idea for classes. As he spoke, her face glowed with growing excitement.

"I wish I were in this area! I could teach a reading class for you. A lot of people need reading skills desperately."

Mark's eyes locked on hers. Would she mind living in Denton? Perhaps with a husband? Her gaze didn't falter. His heart begged him to ask the question he longed to have answered. But this was a once-in-a-lifetime shot. He had to be sure of her feelings before he risked it all.

"Hurray! Couldn't answer that one, could you?" Cally shouted in victory.

The moment interrupted, Mark and Bridget looked back to the game.

"It was a setup!" Robert said. "What was I supposed to say? 'Do you like my soufflé or Aunt V.'s better?' You should recant that question."

"No way! You have to do the chicken walk," Cally said.

Mark stood and took Bridget's hand to help her from her seat. He held on longer than he had to, then let it slide from his grip.

He steered toward the joyful group and forced his attention onto Robert's chicken waddle. The entire family whooped and cheered as Robert took another turn around the one remaining chair.

"The loser gets all the glory!" Robert gloated, and took a bow.

"Mark." Bridget's soft voice at his shoulder made his heartbeat go crazy.

"What is it?"

"I wanted you to know I've forgiven you. I'm sorry I didn't do it sooner."

Mark looked down into her soft brown eyes and found himself looking into her heart. A rush of emotion choked his throat. He squeezed her hand at his side, then forced his gaze back to the group in front of them. Hope surged through him like a flood. Now, what was he going to do about it?

# TEN

**B**ridget threw another folded sweater into her suitcase. Her stack of Christmas gifts sat bundled on the bed. She'd be ready to go in less than an hour.

The bleak mood closed in. "Oh, God, I want to be happy with you alone, but this is tearing my heart out. How can I go back home and never see Mark again?"

He wasn't cooperating, thick-skulled man that he was. Mark hadn't made a move toward her since she'd told him she'd forgiven him. If he intended to, he'd better hurry. After supper, she'd be gone.

She sighed. It would be easier to propose to him herself. Her mental gears ground to a stop. When did this change in thinking start? The last decision she'd consciously made was not to decide. But she had decided. And she couldn't revoke that decision if she tried.

Half an hour later, Bridget lugged her suitcase down the hall to the back staircase. She'd hoped to find help, but she'd seen only Luke, who bolted down the main stairs as soon as he saw her.

Well, maybe she could shove it down. She grabbed the pull strap, and the bag groaned into reluctant cooperation. At last, the huge suitcase thudded onto the kitchen linoleum. Once she'd shoved it out the door, getting to the garage was smooth sailing.

Bridget pulled her bag beside the red Miata. She inserted the key into the keyhole and stopped. How could she lift this monster into the car?

At that instant, the purr of a well-kept engine approached the garage. Bridget turned to look and saw the white Cadillac roll up the drive. Uncle George hopped out of the front passenger seat, his white hair standing out around his head like a bunch of electrified cotton balls. Bridget shook her head to clear away the *déjà vu* when he trotted off toward the wine cellar. Like the day of her arrival, Mr. Stout followed close behind him.

Not until the back passenger door began to open did she recognize the trend. A slow smile spread across her face, and anticipation trilled through her being. Two hands descended from the car's interior, followed by a head of gold-brown hair rounding the door.

Bridget folded her arms and sauntered toward the man facing her on bended knee.

"I'll find out what you're up to if it's the last thing I do," she said, smiling.

"You won't have to. I'll tell you." His emotion-filled voice caught her heart.

Mark stood up and walked to her. He stopped inches away, his eyes locking onto hers.

"Bridget Deans, will you marry me?"

Her heart thudded up into her throat, and tears welled up, then spilled, from her eyes. Love stared back at her from the familiar lines of his face.

"Yes, Mark, I will."

His arms wrapped around her, and he rained soft kisses on her eyelids, her wet cheeks, and finally, her mouth.

"You will?" he whispered. In response, she pulled his head back down to hers.

"I guess she said yes," came Cally's voice.

Bridget backed up a step and saw Cally, Robert, Aunt V., and the boys gathering around.

Uncle George opened the cellar door and blinked in the sunshine. "Are you finished, or should I go ahead and get comfortable?"

Bridget laughed, tears streaming down her face as her family surrounded her with hugs, laughter, and congratulations. Was there anyone as blessed as she was? Maybe Great-great-grandfather Rutledge.

"Come on inside, you two," Aunt V. said. "We've got a lot of planning to do."

Mark put his arm around her shoulders as they walked back into Rutledge Place. A few steps later, he planted a kiss on the top of her head. Bridget looked up into his shining eyes.

"I'll never let go of you again," he murmured in her ear.

Bridget slipped her arm around his waist. "I'm counting on it."

# THE
# BEST MAN
SHARI MACDONALD

# ONE

Can a girl forget her ornaments, or a bride her attire?

JEREMIAH 2:32

"S top squirming, Carrie!" Madison Pierce ordered as she continued to work several yards of stiff netting and smooth satin over her best friend's shoulders. With a sigh of exasperation, she blew away one unruly golden curl that had fallen over her blue eyes. "You're only making this worse."

"But it doesn't fit!" The cry was muffled by the mountain of fabric as Carrie struggled to get into her wedding finery.

"Don't be silly. It's going to fit," Madison assured her firmly.

"Maddie—"

"We took your measurements four times. It's going to fit." Her businesslike tone brooked no argument.

But after twenty years of friendship, she wasn't surprised when Carrie ignored her calm assurances. "Maddie, I tell you— it's not going to fit! Something's wrong. I've...I've just ballooned," she wailed dramatically, still wrestling to pull the dress over her head. "Will you look at me?"

Madison grinned. Under the circumstances, it was impossible to see Carrie's body at all.

Usually, even her most stressed-out clients didn't fail to be soothed by Madison's calm manner, particularly in the relaxed atmosphere of her shop. Warm and homey, the boutique was located in the heart of Portland's Nob Hill district. In the front room, a combination of trendy and classic furniture complemented the display of rack after rack stocked with original "Madison's Avenue" designs. But it was in the back room that Madison conducted her favorite side of the business: measuring clients, discussing styles, planning and implementing her newest designs. Since it was in this room that she spent most of her time, Madison had chosen to give it a comfortable, sitting-room feel.

Along the far wall, a sofa covered in a woven sage green fabric sat facing her desk. A matching chair and ottoman were tucked into one corner, and near the back of the room Madison had placed the table where she cut out most of her patterns. Beneath the women's feet, natural pine floors were covered with a lovely Chinese hook rug in shades of rose and cream. The effect was that of working in the comfort of her living room. Earlier in the week, Madison had even put up a Christmas tree, covering it with tinsel and a rainbow of colored lights. Unfortunately, neither her assurances nor the cheerful decor had been successful at comforting this particular bride.

"Why did I have to keep tasting all those wedding cakes? And all those catering samples? What was I thinking? I just knew I was getting fatter. And now the whole day is absolutely ruined. I can't afford to buy another dress—not that there'd be time to get one made, even if I did—and I'm going to look like an absolute hippo in this one—"

"Thanks for the vote of confidence," Madison said dryly. "It's good to see you're not overreacting."

"Come on, Maddie, you know that's not what I was saying. Your dress is gorgeous. It's *me* that's the problem. I'm…I'm just a little piggy. It's never going to fit. I mean it—" The squirming intensified as Carrie struggled with the dress.

"No, *I* mean it," Madison said and gripped Carrie solidly by the shoulders. Somehow she managed to sound serious, although it was hard to keep from laughing at the sight of her friend's pale arms flailing wildly in the air, the only parts of her body visible over the voluminous puffs of material that had become her prison. "You're going to be fine, but you've got to hold still or I can't help you. The netting's just stuck around your shoulders."

Carrie whimpered like a child but managed to remain motionless for a moment.

"There," Madison said approvingly. "That's better. Okay, I've got it now. Here you go." Triumphantly, Madison straightened the piece of offending fabric and pulled the dress down over Carrie's shoulders. "And...voila!"

A head of fiery red hair poked through the neck of the dress, and the bride-to-be smiled as the soft folds fell into place around her. Breathing a sigh of relief, she slipped her arms into the long satin sleeves while Madison straightened the crepe skirt and organza train. Finally, Carrie turned toward the full-length antique mirror that stood in the corner of the room.

Madison had chosen the fabric carefully, and it was a perfect match for Carrie's skin tone. Many whites simply accentuated her naturally pale coloring—a fact Carrie bemoaned when wearing her stark nursing uniform. This particular shade of white, however—*champagne*, the fabric catalogs called it—had just the faintest undertones of copper. Two bright spots of pink appeared on Carrie's cheeks as she smiled in delight.

"Oh, it's beautiful," she breathed. Her eyes filling with tears, she pirouetted in front of Madison. At five-foot-nine, she was tall enough to model, and certainly beautiful enough for it. The dress Madison had designed showcased her stately figure perfectly.

"No." Smiling softly, Madison reached out with gentle fingers and arranged Carrie's long red curls around her shoulders. "You're beautiful. You're a gorgeous bride, Carrie."

"Oh, Maddie!" Carrie turned and threw her arms around her friend, enveloping her in a cascade of white. "Thank you for doing all this. I never could have afforded anything this magnificent if it weren't for you. You're an angel. A miracle worker."

"Don't be silly." Madison squeezed her friend briefly in return, then pulled away, embarrassed. Since going into business for herself two years earlier, her designs had been praised not only by local clients here in Portland and in Seattle but by socialites from as far away as New York City. But even after all her struggles and hard work, it was still difficult to accept praise or to believe that she was truly talented. "The only miracle here is that you found such a great guy. You're a really lucky girl." She spun Carrie back around and began to fumble with the tiny hooks at the back of her dress. "Come on. Let's get you fastened up."

Obediently, Carrie made the one-hundred-eighty-degree turn. "I know," she said contentedly. Her expression was the blend of amazement and delight worn only by brides-to-be. "I am truly, truly blessed. Don't worry, Mads," she said over her shoulder. "You'll find a great guy, too, one of these days. You'll see."

Madison grunted and pulled at Carrie's seams. "What's that supposed to mean?" she said. "You know I already have." She steeled herself for the argument that was to come. It was one of the few things the two of them fought about.

"Sure you have." Carrie rolled her eyes. "*Sheldon*. He's nice enough for now, I suppose. But you know you're not going to actually marry him."

"I don't know any such thing." She wasn't sure how to respond. She was exhausted, and the last thing she wanted to do was get into the Sheldon issue tonight. She decided it would be wise to let the matter go. Besides, it was hard to tell which approach Carrie was taking this time around: tackling the subject of Sheldon's worthiness as a mate or the fact that after a year and a half of dating, he still had not proposed to Madison—and was giving her no indication that he ever would.

"Now, hold your breath for a minute." Madison's order was issued as much in desire to make her friend drop the current subject as it was to get the dress properly fitted.

Carrie complied but could keep silent for no more than five seconds before letting out her breath in one great rush of air. "Come on, Maddie. You know Sheldon's not the right guy for you."

"So you've been telling me for the past year and a half. But Shel's *my* boyfriend, and I don't see anything wrong with him. As far as I'm concerned," she said pointedly, "the only problem here is the fact that you won't accept him." For over a year, Carrie had been voicing her concerns about Madison's love life. The problem was, Madison herself had questions about her compatibility with Sheldon, questions she never dared to speak out loud—making it even more difficult to convince anyone else, especially Carrie, that she was happy with the way things were.

She'd tried to make it clear that the subject was not open to discussion. But Carrie had either missed the point or was ignoring it. "You see no problem in the fact that you're dating the most boring guy in the world?"

Madison shook her head disapprovingly. "Stop exaggerating."

"Okay, then. In the United States."

"Carrie…"

"All right." She shrugged. "The truth is, he's only mildly boring. But he's still boring. How can you live with that? Don't you want some…some excitement?"

"Actually, no," Madison said quietly. It may not have been what Carrie wanted to hear, but it was honest.

"Maddie!" Carrie's green eyes opened wide. She looked appalled. "Come on. I know what this is about."

"This isn't 'about' anything," Madison protested.

"Try telling that to someone who doesn't know you so well."

Madison fought the urge to take her head in her hands. Grateful Carrie was back on the shelf, and Bossy Carrie was on the loose.

"Remember," Carrie continued, "I was there. I saw how your parents' divorce hurt you. Your dad was fun and creative and exciting, and you loved him. And then he ran off. But that doesn't mean everyone with a little spunk is going to leave you. Take me, for example."

"My dad," Madison said evenly, refusing to toss Carrie the compliment she was obviously fishing for, "was exciting. You're right. But he was also an irresponsible flake. He left my mom with three kids to feed, and he broke her heart. That kind of excitement I don't need."

"Of course you don't," Carrie said reasonably. "But there are other kinds of excitement, you know. There's romance and mystery and, well, a passion for life." It was a word she used a lot; as a redhead, she considered herself an authority on passion.

Madison smiled, picturing Carrie's fiancé, Todd: twinkling brown eyes, thick brown hair, and an easy grin. He and Carrie had met taking hang-gliding lessons. Madison knew that he gave Carrie all the things she had just mentioned: romance, mystery, passion.

He had been her boyfriend, though, for nearly three years— long enough to show his true mettle. In that time, he had supported Carrie through the death of her father, two not-too-pleasant job changes, and one cross-country move. There was no doubt about it: Todd was exciting, but he was also the kind of guy a girl could depend on. A rare breed.

"Not everyone is like Todd." Madison was surprised to hear the hint of sadness in her own voice. She'd been feeling melancholy for months but had become pretty good at hiding her dissatisfaction. Was it getting worse, or was Carrie just digging too deep?

"No. There's no one else like Todd," Carrie agreed. "But there's someone else out there who's just as good for you. I just know it."

Madison worked with the folds of satin at Carrie's back. "I'm happy with things the way they are." She tried to sound convincing, but the words fell flat.

"Then why did you say it was a miracle that I found someone so great?" Carrie said triumphantly.

Madison glared at the smug-looking image in the mirror. "I was talking about how perfect you and Todd are for one another. That's pretty uncommon, you know. But it doesn't mean that couples who are any less perfect shouldn't get married. If everyone waited for a match like yours, the entire human race would be extinct."

"Hmm. Interesting. Very intriguing," Carrie said thoughtfully, scratching her chin. "I must have missed that *National Geographic* special, my anthropological friend. 'How "Settling" Has Contributed to the Propagation of the Species.'"

"Har har," Maddie said, managing to avoid Carrie's penetrating gaze in the mirror.

"I'm just saying," Carrie insisted, "that you could do better. Much better. I mean, let's start with the guy's name, for crying out loud—"

"Would you stop persecuting him for his name!" Madison said. "There's nothing wrong with 'Sheldon.' Nothing at all."

"I agree," Carrie said calmly. "It's his last name I have a problem with. Addison."

"I know, I know." Madison sighed.

"You would be Madison Addison." Carrie wriggled her eyebrows for emphasis. "Sheldon and Madison Addison. I get hives just saying it."

"We've already covered this," Madison said coolly. "I would just keep my maiden name. Besides, aren't you the girl who once dated a guy named Doug Barrie?"

"Yes." Carrie nodded. "I am. Thank you for proving my point. Doug's name was exactly the reason I broke up with him. He was a very nice boy, but I was not about to wind up Carrie Barrie. And look where I am now. You see? It was just as well. God had something better for me all along."

The corners of Madison's mouth twitched, foiling her attempt to appear aloof. Only Carrie could build an argument around both sarcasm and spirituality.

Seeing her reaction, her friend took the lead and ran with it. "In a way, it's a shame," she said, feigning disappointment. "It would have been perfect for The Name Game. Carrie, Carrie, bo-Bar-rie…"

Both women giggled like the schoolgirls they'd been when they first met. "Banana-fanna fo-far-rie, me-my mo-marry…*Car*-rie!" Soon the two were grinning from ear to ear.

"Okay, I'm sorry," Carrie said, when they finally became serious again. "It's just that I'm so happy, Maddie. Honestly, I am. I never knew real love could feel like this. I feel—" she searched for the right words— "I feel *safe* with Todd. Cherished. Respected. I want that for you, too. I—" She threw a glance over her shoulder. "What on earth are you doing back there? You've been trying to button me up for the last ten minutes."

"It's nothing," Madison lied. "Keep talking." She tried to keep a poker face as she examined the problem at hand. How was it possible? They'd finished the alterations just four weeks earlier. With only one week to go before the wedding, a final fitting was supposed to be nothing more than a formality.

"What's wrong?" Carrie spun around like a dog chasing its tail in an effort to see the back of her dress.

"Nothing." The word was intended as a reassurance but came out with a squeak, turning it into an admission of guilt. "Now will you stop it? You're winding the train all around your legs and getting your hair caught in the hooks."

"It's not nothing. You can't fool me," Carrie said, her voice rising in pitch. "You never tell me to keep talking. Especially when I'm lecturing you."

"Whatever. Talk, don't talk. It's up to you. I've just got to find a way to get these hooks fastened."

"See, I told you. I was right, wasn't I?" For a moment, Carrie almost sounded pleased to have been proven correct. Then the gravity of the situation hit her. "Wait a minute. You mean you really can't get the back closed? At all? How bad is it? Oh, *maaaaaan.*"

Madison's lips twisted in amusement as her friend resorted to using their old high school exclamation.

"I knew it. I just knew it! Everyone told me, 'Before the wedding, every bride loses weight. Make sure you eat. Don't forget to eat.' And so I ate. And ate—"

"And ate," Madison broke in.

Carrie scowled at her. "You are not helping."

"Sorry," Madison said innocently.

"And now look at me!"

"I'm looking."

"Tell me the truth. I'm a cow."

"You're not a cow."

"I am. A cow."

"Please. You're not even a calf."

"Then I'm a horse."

"You're not a horse." Madison continued to fiddle with her

195

tape measure and the material at Carrie's back. "I assure you, you don't resemble any kind of barnyard animal I've ever seen."

"What about a rhino? Or some other creature from the African jungle?"

"Carrie, give it a rest."

"All right, all right," she grumbled, frowning at her reflection in the mirror. "This is really bad, though. Isn't it?"

"Well, it's not good," Madison admitted. "But the damage isn't irreparable. Tell you what: you eat sensibly for the next week—"

"I promise," Carrie said brightly. "Nothing but carrot sticks and apples for this girl."

"Carrie, I said 'sensibly.' You can't starve yourself, or you'll pass out at the altar, and then what will Todd's mother say?" It was a low blow. Carrie was terrified of her future mother-in-law. But Madison was glad to see that bringing in the big guns seemed to work.

Carrie's face fell. "Good point."

"You just lay off the goodies for a while—no more cake—and I'll let out a couple of these seams."

"You can do that? Seriously?" Carrie's eyes searched hers, and Madison felt an overwhelming wave of compassion. Her friend was known for being overly dramatic; minor problems could be blown into major crises within a matter of minutes. But it was clear that this was different. Carrie had been looking forward to her wedding day since she was a little girl and was terrified that it would be ruined. "Is it really going to be okay, Mads?"

Madison took Carrie's hands between her strong fingers and squeezed them tightly. "Really," she said. "Cross my heart."

Carrie's expression brightened at that. "Hope to die? Stick a needle in your eye?"

"Good grief." Madison dropped her friend's hands and gathered up an armful of fabric as she prepared to lift the dress over Carrie's head. "I certainly hope not. I'd never finish your dress if that happened, and who knows what you'd wear to your wedding then...."

# Two

For she had a tongue with a tang,
Would cry to a sailor, "Go hang!"

WILLIAM SHAKESPEARE, JULIUS CAESAR

The dull thud of heavy rains hitting the roof shifted into the steady spatter of water against the pavement as Madison opened the door and peered out into the street.

"Ugh." Carrie wrinkled her nose and pulled her down-filled jacket together in front as the wind whipped the heavy drops against their faces. "I hate this."

"We shouldn't complain. It's the rain that makes everything so green," Madison said automatically. Not a "fair-weather" Oregonian, she was always quick to jump to the defense of her state, region...even her neighborhood. Although the area surrounding her boutique's location on Northwest Twenty-third Avenue was riddled with parking problems and car-stereo thefts, Madison remained charmed by Portland's Nob Hill district.

Once an elegant neighborhood inhabited by wealthy business tycoons, lumber barons, and shipping magnates, Nob Hill—or Northwest, as Portlanders commonly called it—was now home to an eclectic assortment of students, business professionals, and families. Many lived in apartments or row houses that had been carved out of French-style châteaux, Victorian gingerbread houses, and Georgian mansions. Madison's boutique was housed in the lower level of one of the lovely old Victorians.

As one of Portland's most popular shopping areas, Northwest Twenty-third was always packed with potential customers. Even in miserable weather like today, the streets were lined bumper-to-bumper with cars and scores of shoppers huddled under their umbrellas, dashing from shop to shop in their quest for the perfect Christmas gift.

Madison peered down the street in the direction she would have to walk. All the way down the sidewalk, the trees were draped with strings of golden lights—a year-round display that at Christmastime enhanced the displays in store windows. Despite the cheery decorations, Madison didn't relish the thought of walking home in this weather. She lived just a block and a half away, in one of the many old red-brick townhouses that lined the Northwest side streets. There was no need for her to drive to work; she couldn't park any closer than the garage of her home.

With one hand Madison switched off the lights in her shop while using the other to rummage in her pocket for her keys.

"All right, all right." Carrie was still complaining about the weather. "I love Portland as much as you do, and you know it. But does it really have to rain quite so much? I mean, if it's going to be wet, couldn't it at least snow? I can't remember the last time we had a white Christmas."

Madison shrugged. There wasn't any point in getting worked up about something she could never change. She and Carrie were very different that way. Take Sheldon, for example. She'd never admit it to Carrie, but it was true: Shel *was* boring. No one was more aware of that fact than she. Yet he was also so many other things she needed: dependable, solid, trustworthy, *dependable....* Why bother worrying about the qualities she couldn't change when there were so many commendable ones already?

While Carrie opened her designer umbrella against the downpour, Madison pulled her hood tightly over her head and tied it around her face.

"Come on, Maddie," Carrie shouted over the rain. She threw a disdainful look at the darkened sky as Madison locked the door behind them. "It's too gloomy to go straight home. Let me buy you some ice cream." She nodded to the left and pointed with her chin down the brightly lit street. "What do you say? Shall we hit Häagen-Dazs?"

"What? Are you crazy? It's thirty-nine degrees outside!"

"Oh, come on. Please? For me?"

"Carrie," Madison said, "didn't we just agree? No more sweets."

"Aw, Maddie. Have a heart," Carrie pleaded. "It's my last one, I promise. Let me go out with a bang."

Madison hesitated. "No, not tonight. But thanks." It had been a long day. Besides, as much as she loved Carrie, today her friend was being especially pushy. "All I want to do is light some candles, put on *Scheherezade,* and climb into a nice hot tub."

"You can do that later," Carrie insisted, grabbing her by the sleeve. "Come on. Just one scoop."

"It's too cold for ice cream."

"Well…maybe they have coffee, too. We can check."

"Carrie!" Madison protested, digging in her heels. "Really. No, thanks."

"But—"

"I said no."

For a moment, Carrie looked defeated. Then her lower lip trembled and her face fell, though Madison thought she saw a small twinkle in her deep green eyes before Carrie lowered them. "Fine," she said. "All I wanted to do was thank you for my dress. It was just a little gesture anyway. Not worth arguing over." She turned away, hanging her head heavily. "Maybe you'll let me take you some other time. Sometime when you can squeeze me into your schedule...."

"Gee," Madison said, raising an eyebrow at Carrie's dramatics, "throw in a steak and baked potato, and we'll have dinner theater."

Carrie's eyes flickered to Madison's face. "That's fine. Have a good laugh at my expense. I'm just trying to—"

Madison chuckled in spite of herself. "I know what you're 'just trying' to do, you little fink," she said fondly. "You want some company, and you're determined to get it. So you're using emotional blackmail, which doesn't work on me half as well as you think it does. I really should just walk away. But since you've amused me, as usual, I'll stay another half hour, as long as you supply the java. I think I'd rather go to Torrefazione, though—"

"No, no!" Carrie said quickly, grabbing her arm. "I tell you, I'm really craving something at Häagen-Dazs."

Madison narrowed her eyes. This sounded suspicious. "What are you craving?"

"Uh..." Carrie hesitated. "Just something. I haven't decided what yet. Humor me."

Madison shrugged and fell into step beside her friend on the rain-spattered sidewalk. Sometimes it just wasn't worth trying to figure out Carrie's idiosyncrasies. She'd learned to pick her battles...and this one wasn't worth the effort.

Once inside the store, Madison decided ice cream looked better than coffee, after all. They each ordered a sugar cone with one scoop—Madison, Cappuccino Commotion; Carrie, Coffee Fudge—and settled down at a table in the front of the shop.

"So…" Madison led off. Obviously Carrie had some sort of agenda. They might as well get right to it.

"So, what?" Green eyes blinked back at her innocently.

"So, what's on your mind, missy?"

"What makes you think there's something on my mind?"

"Some days I wonder.…"

"Hey!" But Carrie didn't look offended. Gentle barbs were par for the course in their long-standing friendship. "I'm *always* thinking. I'm a regular Einstein, I'll have you know. That doesn't mean, however, that I have anything in particular that I want to—"

"Oh, stop it!" Madison laughed. "You are so bad at this. Come on, spill it."

"Oh, all right," Carrie grumbled. "It's just this whole Sheldon thing—"

"Whoa," Madison cut in, frowning. "Stop right there. You know this subject isn't open to discussion."

"Fine," Carrie said pleasantly. "We won't discuss. You don't have to say a word. Just listen."

"Carrie." She waved her paper napkin in warning.

"Please. I just have one suggestion. If you don't like it, you'll say no, and I'll never bring it up again."

Madison raised one eyebrow.

"All right," Carrie said. "I'll bring it up again. But you owe it to me to hear me out at least once."

Madison just stared at her.

"Okay." Carrie sighed in exasperation. "You don't owe me anything. But would you please listen? Just for a minute?"

Madison squirmed in her seat. This was not a subject she wanted to discuss. Not tonight. Not with Carrie. Not with anyone. But it wasn't often her friend made such a simple, forthright request. "All right," she said reluctantly. "Just for a minute."

"Great!" Carrie looked enormously relieved. "All right, this is the thing: I've always said Shel wasn't the right guy for you."

"Yes. I know."

"And, you know, Todd agrees with me."

"Todd *what?*" Madison sputtered. "Why are you and Todd even discussing my love life?"

"He cares about you, too, Mad. He thinks of you as a sister."

"Well, fine. But that doesn't mean that he has to—"

"You promised you'd hear me out."

"Okay," she managed through clenched teeth. "Go ahead."

"Well, we both agree that you need someone who can make you laugh. You don't laugh enough, do you know that?"

"You make me laugh plenty."

"Yeah, but I'm not always around," Carrie said softly. "I've got Todd now. More of my time and energy is going into that relationship—"

"As it should."

"And you should have someone great, too. You're serious enough, Maddie. Dangerously serious. You don't need someone who's even more sedate than you."

"So what are you suggesting? That I hang out at comedy clubs, trying to meet stand-up comics?"

"No. Don't be silly," Carrie said. "You don't have to do that to meet someone fun. Todd and I have got the perfect guy for you. He's cute; he's nice; he's got a great sense of humor—"

"You and—? Oh, no." Madison's eyes opened wide. "I get it now. You're talking about Todd's roommate from college. Chip, wasn't it? Or Rip, or something like that. You guys tried to fix me up with him last year."

"It's Kip," Carrie said indignantly. "And you would have liked him, but you never gave him a chance. You never even met him."

"Carrie, the guy is a goofball."

"How do you—? I mean, he is not."

"Oh, no? Todd told me all about him. He earned extra money during college by working as a clown at children's birthday parties."

"I think that's cute."

"He wrote his master's thesis on the impact of balloon animals on a child's psyche."

"Very clever."

"He was the school mascot."

"So?"

"So, he was a beaver. A big, furry beaver."

"Well, it's not as if they were his real teeth."

"Carrie." Madison tried to sound reasonable, but the woman was really trying her patience.

"Besides," her friend said knowingly, "I'm beginning to think I might be onto something here. For someone who says she's not interested, you sure do remember an awful lot about Kip. You know, 'Methinks the lady doth protest too much,' and all that."

"Oh yeah?" Madison shifted uncomfortably. "Methinks a certain someone doth meddle too much."

"Spoilsport," said Carrie. But her eyes betrayed a flicker of victory.

"Give it up, Carrie. I only remember him because he sounds so…so weird. You know that's not the kind of guy I want. We've been over this a million times."

Madison had tried dating a few artistic types in college. Most of them had been as irresponsible as she'd feared. Even the few who were emotionally mature had made her nervous. She never could relax with creative men. They seemed too flighty, too unstable. And yet, as a creative person herself, she couldn't seem to connect with men who lacked an artistic flair. It was a lose-lose situation. No wonder she was still on her own.

"But, Maddie, you've been so depressed lately."

Madison stared at her hands. She had no answer. It was true. She'd hoped no one else would notice, but she was becoming increasingly melancholy as Christmas Day drew near. Although she was thrilled about the wedding on Carrie's behalf, thinking about it made her feel blue. Holidays were often hard for her, but she was afraid this would be the worst one yet.

"I'm fine. Besides, my emotional state has little or nothing to do with the absence or presence of men in my life. I think it's just the Christmastime blues," she said. "People get that way, you know. For some reason, emotions just seem to intensify at this time of year. Joyful feelings are even more joyful, and lo—" She stopped herself.

"What, Maddie? The loneliness is even worse? Is that what you were going to say?"

"I'm not lonely." Madison ignored the question. "Not really. I'm just—"

"Dissatisfied? Restless? Desolate?"

Madison blinked at her friend. "Well, I wasn't—" she tried to sound lighthearted—"until you just mentioned it."

"Oh, Maddie." Carrie reached out and patted her friend's hand comfortingly. "I'm sorry. I don't mean to make you feel worse. I'm just worried about you, honey."

"You don't need to be. I'm fine." Madison tried to shake off the feeling of unrest that was settling around her.

"If you say so. But I was just thinking that maybe it would do you some good to go out and have a little fun. You know, Kip's coming in a week early for the wedding, to spend some time with Todd. Why don't the two of you—"

"No, Carrie." Suddenly, Madison felt strangely panicky. "I can't do that. Sheldon would—"

"Sheldon wouldn't do anything, and you know it," Carrie said. "He's never made any kind of commitment to you."

"He's committed. We go out every week. At least twice."

"That's not the same thing as a commitment. I've never once heard him refer to you as his girlfriend."

"That's just semantics. I call him my boyfriend, and he doesn't seem to mind. He just doesn't feel comfortable using the word himself."

Carrie shook her head in amazement. "Do you hear yourself? You sound like you don't even care how he treats you."

"I care. I think Sheldon treats me just fine," Madison argued, but her face felt warm. She always blushed when she felt embarrassed…or when she lied.

"Well, then, why don't you do something about it? Leave, or make him offer you something more."

Madison glumly watched as her ice cream began to melt and drip down the side of her cone. "Maybe I don't want something more."

"Maybe." Carrie said amicably. "Then again, maybe that's what you keep telling yourself so you won't have to think about what else might be out there. Or *who* else."

Madison turned away, grateful for the distraction as about ten rowdy junior high school kids, accompanied by a jauntylooking Santa Claus, entered the ice-cream shop and approached the counter.

"I wanna large chocolate-chip cone," ordered the first kid, a grungy-looking boy in flannel.

"Mmm. Me, too!" said a slim young girl standing behind him. From the look on the child's heavily made-up face, it was clear that she adored the older boy and wanted to prove she liked the same things he liked. One by one, the kids crowded up to the counter and shouted out flavors.

Carrie threw the crowd a sidelong glance, looking a bit agitated by the interruption. Her eyes had grown round as saucers, as if something about their appearance bothered her, but she quickly turned her attention back to their conversation. "Look,

Maddie, there's something I need to tell you, and I don't think you're going to like it. Please don't get mad at me, but—"

"Hey! That's mine!" Two of the kids were now fighting over their orders.

"No, it's not!" one boy yelled at another. "You ordered chocolate fudge."

"Uh-uh. I ordered fudge brownie," the other insisted. As they argued, their voices grew increasingly louder.

"Hey, you guys." The kids' chaperon strolled over with a jaunty swagger, looking like a cross between jolly old Saint Nick and John Wayne. "What's the problem?"

Madison closed her eyes and shook her head. She didn't have patience for scenes like these. Why did people take kids places if they couldn't control them? She didn't remember being so unruly at that age.

"Um…Madison," Carrie began. "You should know that—"

"Give it!" The smaller boy yelled and grabbed for the cone, which was just beyond his reach.

"No way!" With the slightest twist of the wrist, the older teen swiped the other kid's face with the tip of the cone, leaving a long brown smear on his nose.

"Hey!" Tempers were raging now. "You did that on purpose! I'll show you, you big—" Arms and legs went flying as the younger boy leaped, tackling his nemesis and throwing him down—right onto the table between Madison and Carrie.

Both women leaned away from the struggle, too stunned to get up from their chairs, as the drama unfolded under their noses. Arms and legs flailed and ice cream flew as the two boys wrestled for their prize. Within seconds, both women were dripping as the two boys covered each other—and them—with the ice cream in question.

Before the shop's manager could step out from behind the counter, a grim-looking Santa Claus had gripped each boy firmly by the shirt collar and lifted them from the floor, where the two had fallen. The man looked at Carrie helplessly, then turned an apologetic gaze on Madison.

"I am so sorry about this," he said with a sincere look in his eyes.

"Well, you should be!" Madison spat out angrily. Suddenly, she felt like crying. She hated the way out-of-control situations always made her feel so emotional. Why did things like this have to happen? Why couldn't people be more calm and composed? Didn't they realize how their outrageous behavior hurt other people?

"What were you thinking?" She hoped that if she kept talking, no one would notice the sudden trembling of her lower lip. "If you can't keep those kids out of trouble, you shouldn't take so many of them out at a time."

By now, both boys had quieted considerably. After being lifted from the floor, they had begun to look slightly embarrassed. Madison's outburst seemed to be making an even greater impression. They looked up at Santa with stricken expressions on their faces. "We're sorry," the younger one whispered. The older boy nodded in agreement.

"Don't tell me," Santa said grimly. "Tell the lady."

"We're, um…" The smaller boy grew speechless as soon as his frightened eyes met Madison's angry ones.

"Go on," Santa urged gently.

"Sorry," the older teen said boldly.

"Yeah, sorry." The echo came as a whisper.

Madison swallowed hard. What was she supposed to say here? That it was okay? It wasn't. She wiped away a glob of ice cream that had landed on her cheek. Santa's eyes twinkled. He looked as if he might laugh at any moment. Somehow that made her feel even worse.

"Thanks for saying so," she told the boys coolly, then trained a disapproving eye on their chaperon—who still looked amused by the entire chain of events. Suddenly, she wished there were some ice cream left so she could smear it across his smirking face.

As Santa released the two offenders, Madison reached into her purse for a tissue and began a valiant effort to clean up the mess on her face and on her Italian leather coat. While she worked, she kept her gaze lowered and tried to put the image of the laughing Santa out of her mind. From the corner of her eye, she could see that he was still standing there, although the boys had wandered away. Why didn't the exasperating stranger leave?

"You know, they're really not bad kids," the man said finally, breaking the awkward silence. His smoky gray eyes sought out hers. Weren't Santa's eyes supposed to be blue? Madison thought absurdly. But somehow, these seemed perfect—gentle, kind, a bit crinkly around the corners. She forced herself to look away.

"They just don't have a lot of self-control," the man was saying quietly. "They count on adults like you and me to model qualities such as self-control, compassion, and forgiveness."

Madison looked at him sharply. Was that supposed to be some kind of reprimand?

"To teach them how to be responsible grown-ups," he explained.

The words cut like a dagger to Madison's heart. Somehow, this only added to her anger. She knew she was being unreasonable. But something about this ridiculous gray-eyed Santa Claus in his floppy red hat and crooked white beard was triggering an overwhelming emotional reaction in her. The words came out in a rush before she could stop them.

"Well, I feel sorry for them if you're the best role model they've got," Madison spat. Across from her, Carrie looked appalled. Santa himself looked a bit surprised at her outburst.

"Kids are a big responsibility. If you can't handle them, you shouldn't volunteer to take care of them. I hope you'll think about that the next time you try a little excursion like this, Mister..."

"Jones," the man said easily. "Kip Jones."

Madison's eyes grew wide and her head began to spin as Carrie's voice interjected, as if from a distance, "Uh, Maddie, I'd like you to meet Todd's old roommate, our best man, and the guy you'll be walking with at the wedding. Kip, uh...this is Maddie."

THREE

One never repents of having spoken too little,
but often of having spoken too much.

PHILIPPE DE COMMYNES, *MÉMOIRES*

How could you do that to me?" Madison wailed the
next morning. One hand cradled the telephone
receiver close to her ear while both elbows remained
firmly planted on the oak desktop. The night before, she'd
managed to make a quick, if awkward, escape from the ice-
cream shop soon after her little outburst. But her feelings of
shame had grown stronger as the hours passed. Fretting about
her behavior, she'd tossed and turned in her bed until finally
falling into a restless sleep around 3:00 A.M.

"What do you mean?" Carrie said in the tone of the unjustly
accused. "You did it to yourself, my friend. You're usually so
nonconfrontational. I don't know what came over you."

"Oh, I don't, either!" Maddie sighed. "It's like he just pushed
all my buttons or something. One minute I was fine. The next
minute—"

"You were not fine," Carrie said. "You were crabby before
they even got there."

Madison fidgeted with the phone cord, twisting it between
her long, slim fingers. "And whose fault was that?"

Carrie snorted derisively. "All I did was bring up a subject you didn't want to talk about. I never told you to yell at those kids."

Madison's cheeks flushed hot at the accusation. "I didn't yell at the kids, did I?" she said, dropping the phone cord. *Just the man.*

"No. Actually, you just glared at them."

"Oooh," she moaned and lowered her head, resting her cheek against the cool wood of the antique desk. "Why didn't you warn me they were going to be there?"

"I was trying to, but you weren't cooperating." She paused. "And honestly, I didn't know the kids would be such a...disruption."

"Hmph. What was he doing with those kids, anyway? And since when does Todd's friend dress like an escapee from the North Pole?"

"I explained this last night," Carrie said patiently, "but you weren't listening. You remember when I told you last year that Kip works with troubled teens?"

"Yes." Madison's voice was dull and heavy.

"Well, that's his full-time job. He's here visiting for a week. But he didn't want to just sit around while Todd's at work, so he volunteered to help out at the Portland division of the ministry he works with down in L.A. He told me earlier in the day that he was going to take some of the kids downtown to see the Christmas tree at Pioneer Courthouse Square. I suggested that he might bring them by Häagen-Dazs before taking them back, so I could introduce the two of you."

"Oh, no!" Madison cringed. "Carrie, tell me the truth. Did he know that was a setup?" Somehow that made the whole incident even more embarrassing.

"Well, that depends on your definition of setup." Carrie spoke slowly. "Let's just say he knows Todd and I think the two of you are...compatible."

"Oh?" Madison said. "And what did he say to that?"

"Well, he wanted to know what you're like. We told him that you're a Christian, like he is, and that you've got a great smile and a sweet personality."

"Wonderful. No problem then. There's no way he'd confuse the person he met last night with the woman you just described. We'll tell him it was a simple case of mistaken identity—"

"Hey, what's this?" Carrie asked playfully. "I thought you didn't care whether Kip liked you or not."

"Carrie." Madison spoke as if she were addressing a five-year-old. "This is not about Kip. I don't even know the man."

"So what's it about, then?"

"It's about me. I acted like a jerk. You told him that I'm a Christian, but I sure didn't behave like one." She found this more than a little disturbing. She and Carrie had both become believers when they were in high school. During college, Carrie's faith had grown tremendously. But Madison couldn't say the same. Every time she came to a point where she needed to trust anyone—even God—her father's abandonment came back to haunt her. It was as if she started to give control to God, but at the last minute, held it tightly within her own grasp.

"Well," Carrie said, "you're only human. I'm sure Kip has acted like a jerk before, too—at some time in his life." Carrie didn't have any trouble grasping the concept of grace. "If it bothers you, just go apologize. You know it's going to bug you until you do."

Madison winced. For some reason, the idea of seeing Kip Jones again made her extremely nervous. *It's those eyes.* Those penetrating gray eyes that seemed to see deep into her soul. Somehow they—even more than the boys' misbehavior—had made her feel uncomfortable the night before. She didn't relish the idea of facing them again.

But Carrie had a point. Madison knew she wouldn't be able to put the whole humiliating incident behind her until she had asked Kip for his forgiveness. Which, she thought wryly, could have been part of Carrie's plan from the very beginning.

"Did you mean for this to happen?" she asked suspiciously.

"I don't know what you're talking about." Carrie sounded genuinely indignant. But she was very good at that.

"Never mind." Madison sighed heavily. "Where can I reach Kip?"

A sound like a muffled giggle made its way over the phone line. "I thought you'd never ask...."


The strong, heady aroma of Black Tiger blend tickled Madison's nostrils. She breathed in deeply, filling her lungs with the rich, coffee-scented air, as she nervously scanned the crowded café, looking for Kip. Amid the throng of holiday shoppers, several men stood out. In the corner, a bohemian with a scruffy goatee sat poring over a thick leather-bound volume. At the next table, closer to Madison, a young businessman in an Armani suit was pecking at the keyboard of his laptop computer. A third man— an intellectual type, about thirty-five, with a slightly receding hairline—occupied a table just to her left.

Anxiously, she surveyed the crowd. How would she ever know this Kip Jones when she saw him? All she remembered of the man was penetrating gray eyes, peering out at her from under fake, bushy white eyebrows and a red felt hat. She could hardly go table to table, staring at each customer's face, looking for a resemblance.

"Ms. Pierce?" A hand gently fell upon her shoulder. Madison jumped.

When she turned, Madison found herself looking up into a friendly face that perfectly matched those gray eyes. The brow, cheekbones, and jawline were all strong and well-defined. Yet although his features were somewhat angular, they were softened by gentle laugh lines around his eyes and the naturally upturned corners of his lips. Kip Jones smiled at her then, which made his cheeks dimple adorably.

"Sorry," he said softly. "I didn't mean to frighten you."

Madison shook her head vigorously and forced a smile of her own. "No, no. Not your fault. I'm a little jumpy today," she admitted, automatically licking her unusually dry lips.

"Well, then," Kip said with a grin, "it's a good thing we met here. A little caffeine should calm you right down."

Madison just stared at him. She was used to such teasing coming from Carrie. She wasn't sure, however, how to handle it coming from this stranger. "Well," she said, wiping her clammy hands against the skirt of her lime green wool dress. "I think I'll risk it."

Kip continued to grin at her as if she had said something immensely clever. She lowered her eyes and made a point of opening her purse and digging for pocket money, just to have something to do. What was wrong with this guy? Couldn't he sense how uncomfortable she felt? Madison gave him a quick sidelong glance. Apparently unaware of her irritation, he looked around the coffeehouse and began to whistle "Joy to the World."

At last, the customer ahead of her in line stepped aside, and she turned to the counter with relief. After she had placed her order, Kip told her he'd wait at the counter while she found them a table. Madison sat near the window. She was glad he'd agreed to meet her at Coffee People, her favorite coffeehouse. Familiar ground. Her own territory. Gratefully, she gazed up at the orange-and-brown sponge-painted walls and the high ceilings she was sheltered by nearly every day. Even if the meeting went poorly, she could drown her sorrows in her favorite espresso drink. She looked up as Kip approached, carrying both their cups.

"Here you go," he said cheerfully. "For the lady: one skinny caramel latte." He set the cups down on the table, snatched up the chocolate-covered coffee bean nestled on the white plastic lid of his cup, and popped it into his mouth.

"And you?" Madison said brightly, trying desperately to keep the small talk going. She seized her own coffee bean and set it aside purposefully next to her wallet, before it could fall prey to her companion's reach.

"A Slammahamma," Kip said. "Espresso mocha with spicy Mexican chocolate, a double shot of espresso, plus whipped cream. It sounds like it's got more sugar and caffeine than anything else."

"It sounds awful," Madison said. "Way too rich for me. What's it taste like?"

"I'm not sure yet," Kip admitted. He pursed his lips and blew on the steaming liquid. "I've never had one before. But I had to give it a try."

"A risk taker, are you?" She tried to make it sound like a compliment, but her lips twisted around the words and it came out more like an accusation.

"I like to think so." Kip gave her an odd look, but he didn't sound defensive at all. "What about you?" he asked, his keen eyes trained upon her tense features.

"Oh, no," she said coolly. With great effort, she kept her attention focused on the drink in her hand. She leaned forward and breathed in deeply, absorbing the rich caramel aroma. "I like stability."

"I see." He nodded at her cup. "How often do you get a caramel latte?"

"Every day."

He grinned. "Since when?"

"I don't know. Ever since I've had my shop, I guess. About two years."

"Huh." Kip looked impressed. "Now that's what I call a solid routine."

Madison felt her hackles rise. It wasn't that she expected other people to agree with the way she lived her life. She was used to dissenting opinions. In fact, Sheldon challenged her choices on a regular basis. He didn't like the location of her shop; he didn't think she charged her customers enough money for her designs; he thought she should work fewer hours.

When Sheldon voiced his opinions, she usually remained silent. After the fact, she would either take his advice or continue on with the way she'd been doing things. She preferred not to argue with him. It was easier just to let it go. But something about Kip made her feel feisty, ready for a fight. And for some reason, that didn't seem so bad.

"It is not a routine," she said, her voice cool. "May I remind you, you don't know anything about the way I live my life?"

"That's true," Kip said cheerfully. "Sorry. I didn't mean to insult you. Actually, I think routines are great."

"You do?" Madison had a hard time believing that. "And what kind of routines do you follow?"

"Well..." He thought for a moment. "At least once a day, I have a bowl of Grape Nuts with bananas."

"The same breakfast every morning?" Madison stared. That seemed awfully conventional.

"Oh, no. Not for breakfast," he said. "For a snack. Before I go to bed."

"Don't you know that if you eat before you go to sleep, the food just sits in your stomach all night?"

"Really?" Kip looked unconcerned. "How 'bout that?"

"What else?"

"Well, I do a hundred push-ups every night, whether I need to or not." One lanky arm flew up into the air as Kip made a show of flexing his muscles, which were hidden by his heavy sweater of dark Shetland wool.

Madison's lips twitched. "It's kind of hard to see the results...if there are any."

Kip gave his sleeve a rueful glance. "Well, trust me," he said. "They're there, all right."

She tried hard not to grin. "Anything else?"

"Hmm. Let's see." He scratched thoughtfully at his chin. "Oh, yes. Every Sunday night, before starting another busy work week, I like to take a long, hot bubble bath."

Madison's eyes grew wide.

"Afterward, I dry my hair, turn down the lights, get myself a nice cup of tea, and paint my toenails—"

"Stop it!" she cried, sputtering with laughter. "Now you're making fun of me."

"Never," he said, straight-faced.

"Tyrant."

"It did break the ice, though," he said, smiling. "I think that's worth something." The gentle laugh lines on his face melted away as he grew serious. "Carrie and Todd were right. You've got a great smile, Madison."

"Well...thanks." Somehow, she didn't feel quite so feisty anymore. In fact, she felt less like fighting than she ever had in her life. Madison looked at Kip incredulously. Carrie was right. The guy had made her laugh. For the first time in a long while, she had actually relaxed in a man's presence. And, she thought with alarm, the feeling she was experiencing was quite pleasant. But that didn't mean anything, no matter what anyone else believed. She, and only she, would be the judge of who was right for her to date. Madison knew what she wanted. Kip Jones wasn't her type, even if he was witty and clever and—she

220

was beginning to notice—incredibly attractive.

"Madison?" Kip leaned forward and tried to catch her eye. "Did I lose you?"

"Hmm? Oh, no. Sorry." Madison felt her face flush bright pink. "I was just thinking about something Carrie told me about you. Uh, she said you were really funny."

"Oh." Now it was Kip's turn to look embarrassed, which had the effect of making him even more attractive.

"She told me you were very forgiving, as well," Madison said quietly. Her eyes flickered briefly to Kip's face, then she stared at her hands, unable to meet his gaze. "Look, Kip, thanks for meeting me like this. I wouldn't have blamed you if you'd just hung up on me after what I did. I just have to say...I behaved horribly last night. I have no excuse. But I hope you'll forgive me." As a rule, Madison had a hard time speaking to people she didn't know well. But with Kip, the words spilled out in a rush. And she didn't even attempt to stop or screen them.

"I don't know if this helps any, but I can tell you that I was out of sorts before you even came in with the kids. The way I reacted didn't really have anything to do with you."

"I see," Kip said. Then, after a moment's thought, "Actually, I don't. But we don't have to talk about it, unless you want to." He sounded as if he was truly interested, but unlike Carrie, he seemed unwilling to push.

Madison stared out the window as a young woman pushing a stroller walked past. She wished there were a simple way to explain her feelings to Kip. She hardly understood them herself. "Let's just say I don't like getting out of my comfort zone," she said finally. "But 'out of my comfort zone' was where Carrie and I had been most of the night. What happened at Häagen-Dazs was just the straw that broke the camel's back."

"Oh." Kip sat quietly, processing this new bit of information. Then he continued, speaking slowly, as if chewing over each thought. "The truth is, I'm not sure that you really need my forgiveness. I don't know that there's anything to forgive. But if you want it," he said graciously, "I'll give it.

"You need to know, though, that I never judged you last night. As far as I'm concerned, you had every right to react the way you did. I might have gotten just as mad if I had been in your shoes. I'll admit I was a bit surprised that you responded as—well, as strongly as you did. But everything you said was true. As the group leader, I had a responsibility to keep those kids under control, and I failed at my job. I believe I need to ask your forgiveness, too."

Madison looked at him in surprise. This wasn't the reaction she had been expecting at all. Could anyone really be this charitable? She breathed a sigh of relief. "You're very kind. Shall we make a trade, then?"

"I'll forgive you; you'll forgive me?" He grinned.

"Deal."

Kip reached out one strong hand to shake on the agreement, and Madison allowed him to take her smooth fingers in his rough ones. For a moment longer than necessary, he held her hand firmly in his grasp, then gently released her from his grip. Madison felt something like sadness as his hand slipped away.

She watched as Kip drank a long draught from his cup, then smacked his lips appreciatively. "Eeoww! Mmm. This is *good.*" His gray eyes danced as she threw a disparaging look heavenward—obviously the reaction he was going for. She'd been right in her initial assessment to Carrie. The guy was a goofball. But such an adorable goofball she'd never seen before.

Kip looked at her curiously, and Madison's stomach turned a small flip. Did he know what she was thinking? Was it written all over her face? What on earth was she doing here with him, anyway? Her apology was delivered. It was time to leave.

"Um...I've really got to get going," she said abruptly, reaching down to gather the pocketbook and umbrella she had deposited at her feet. "I've got someone covering the shop, but she has to leave at two for a doctor's appointment."

"You're working even on a Saturday?"

"That's the way things go when you own your own business," Madison said. "I have a high school girl who usually helps out on the weekends, but she and her parents went down to Medford for the weekend to visit her grandparents."

Kip nodded, apparently unconcerned by her sudden mood shift. "Yeah. I really ought to get going, too," he said matter-of-factly. "Thanks for calling. This was nice."

"Yes." Madison spoke as if in a daze. She was still surprised at how nice it had been. "Yes, it was. Thanks again." A feeling of regret filled her heart as she stood and walked away.

"Hey, Madison?" Kip called after her.

"Yes?" She stopped at the door and looked over her shoulder. Her heart seemed to skip a beat.

"What time does your shop close?"

"Six o'clock. Why?"

"Well, I was just thinking, since you're so fond of coffee, maybe we could go grab another cup later?" As he spoke, he walked over and stood beside her. "Maybe we could grab a bite to eat at McMenamins or Pizzicato. We can even get dessert at Haagen-Dazs, if you dare."

"Oh." Madison stared at him, unable to think of what else to say. Her mind focused on the last words Kip had spoken. All she could think was, Sheldon never took her out for ice cream. He considered it too decadent.

Kip's face fell as she remained silent. "Or...not," he said and shifted his weight from one foot to another, looking uncomfortable for the first time since they'd met. "Please, don't feel obligated. I'm sure you have other things you'd rather do."

"Oh, no." Madison reached out impulsively, grabbed his hand, and gave it a warm squeeze. "It's nothing like that. Actually, I'd like very much to get ice cream with you, Kip. Or dinner." And it struck her, as she said it, how much she meant it. "It's just that I'm…uh…" He eyed her curiously. "Well, you see…" Why was this so difficult to say? "I'm sort of…seeing someone right now."

"Oh. You are." For a moment, Kip seemed to be at a loss for words. "Sorry," he said at last. "I'm just surprised. Carrie and Todd made you sound very…single."

Madison's eyes flashed. "'Very single'? What does that mean? Do you mean desperate? Is that what they implied?"

Kip laughed heartily at that. "You? Madison, you're gorgeous. And successful and charming. And very intelligent, that's clear. I can't think of anyone I see as less desperate."

His compliment warmed her right down to her winter-wet toes.

"It's just that they made a point of telling me—several times—that they thought you and I might hit it off. And," he said hopefully, "I'd like to think we have, even though we had a bit of a rough start. They brought it up so often, I just naturally assumed that you were available."

"I'm sorry about that." Madison sighed, realizing with surprise that she was feeling sorrier all the time. "Carrie's never approved of Sheldon. He and I aren't actually engaged, but we've been together for a long time. I've always had a thing about stability and commitment. Carrie thinks that if she can convince me that Sheldon isn't going to work out, I'll let her find a better guy for me."

"I see." Kip nodded soberly. "It sounds like our Carrie missed her calling when she went into nursing. In another century, she'd be the town matchmaker."

"Please." Madison made a face. "Don't give her any ideas."

She fumbled for her keys. Was the conversation over? It seemed a bad time to go, such an awkward way to end things.

"So," Kip said casually, "does that mean you aren't allowed to associate with anyone of the opposite sex? Under any conditions?"

"Why? What do you have in mind?" Madison tried to sound discouraging, but she couldn't manage to keep the grin from her face.

"Well, I realize you can't go out with me tonight. But Todd asked me to run some errands tomorrow after church. Last-minute wedding stuff. Since you know the city so well, I thought you might be willing to help me out."

"Um, sure. I mean, if you don't know the city…"

"Well, uh, I didn't say that exactly," Kip said, looking uncomfortable.

"Hey, what is this?" Madison's eyes narrowed. "Where'd you grow up, anyway?"

"Parkrose," he said sheepishly, referring to one of Portland's east-side suburbs. "That's where Todd and I first met."

"What?" She slapped him playfully on the arm. "You rat! You probably know the city better than I do."

Kip raised both arms in a gesture of surrender. "Hey, I never said I didn't know the city," he said. "I merely observed that with your knowledge of the town, you might be of assistance to me. One situation does not preclude the other."

"Oh, really?" Madison gazed levelly back into his innocent face.

"Come on, Madison. Do it for Todd and Carrie. For the sake of the wedding." .

"Well…," she said, pretending to consider, although she had already made her mind up to agree. It wasn't a tough decision; she knew she wanted to go. "All right."

"Great. How about meeting here tomorrow after church, about one o'clock?"

"Okay." She nodded slowly. "For the sake of the wedding. I mean, someone's got to keep an eye on you, right? Otherwise we're liable to end up with balloon animals for centerpieces at the reception."

"Hey, who told you about that?" he said, feigning disappointment. "That was supposed to be a surprise."

"Goon." She grinned as Kip pushed open the door and stepped out under the stormy Northwest skies.

"That's my name," he called over his shoulder. "Don't wear it out."

# FOUR

There is no disguise which can hide love for long
where it exists, or simulate it where it does not.

LA ROCHEFOUCAULD, MAXIM

"Are you sure you don't mind?" Madison plucked at the gossamer-soft threads of her pale green cashmere sweater. One quick, nervous glance revealed that Sheldon was settled comfortably against the cushions of her navy-and-maroon plaid couch—still scanning the newspaper, despite the bomb she had just dropped.

"Mind? Why should I mind?" Sheldon did, in fact, look completely unconcerned by her announcement. "Carrie's your best friend. Of course you should help out. Go; run your errands. I've got plenty to do myself tomorrow. I don't think it'll hurt us to have time away from each other."

"I'm not going with Carrie, though," Madison said carefully. "I'm going with Kip." Her voice sounded strange to her own ears. Why did she sound—and feel—so guilty? "You know, Todd's best man."

"I know. That's what you said. So?"

"So, that doesn't bother you at all?" *It should, you know. Because he's really attractive, and he seems to like me. Which is more than I can say for you, some days.*

"Of course it doesn't bother me." Sheldon sounded miffed

that she would consider such a notion. "Do you really believe I'm going to go into some kind of jealous rage just because you're going to run around town picking up tuxedoes and party favors with a guy you don't even know? Really, Madison." His voice dripped with disappointment. "Surely you know me better than that by now."

Madison stared at the blue-eyed stranger with the white-blond hair and the dark tan, even in midwinter. How well did she know Sheldon, really? She'd been so convinced that he loved her, despite the fact that he rarely spoke the words. But would a man in love really let her go so easily? Was it because he trusted her—a good thing, she reminded herself—that he didn't worry? Or did he simply not care about the possibility of losing her?

"You're not concerned that he might like me or that I might begin to like him?" She grabbed one of the overstuffed accent pillows from the chair beside her and held it tightly, as a makeshift security blanket.

"No." Sheldon finally lowered the paper and looked at her with a steady eye. "Should I be?"

Madison felt herself weakening under his penetrating gaze. "Well, it's not such a far-fetched idea," she said glumly, managing to avoid giving an answer—either to him or to herself.

"I don't believe you're going to run off with some stranger, if that's what you're suggesting."

Madison just stared. The extent of his confidence was irritating, almost nauseating. How could this not have bothered her before?

Then a tiny voice inside reminded her that Sheldon's overbearing attitude had, in fact, troubled her more often than she cared to admit. She simply hadn't wanted to acknowledge her dissatisfaction, even to herself. The thought caught her off-guard. Was she trying to force a relationship that wasn't truly meant to be? Startled, Madison tried to push the idea away, even as the image of Kip Jones's laughing, boyish face flashed through her mind.

"Why don't you think I'd run off with someone else?" Her voice sounded half-whiny, half-rebellious. "I mean, it's possible, isn't it?"

"Of course it's possible," Sheldon said patiently. "I just don't think it's likely."

"Because?"

"Because I know you too well," he said. "You're a creature of habit, Madison. You like things the way they are, and so do I. Neither one of us is about to stir things up now."

"So what, exactly, are you saying, Shel?" Madison pressed. "You sound like you don't want us to break up—"

"Break up?" Sheldon looked at her, shock written across his face. "Don't be ridiculous. Why on earth would we want to do that?"

Madison couldn't help but notice the note of alarm in his voice. Was he feeling the same apprehension about their future as she was? "So should I take that to mean you want us to be together for, shall we say, a long time?" Despite her misgivings, she wasn't about to let him take the easy way out.

"Now, Maddie." Sheldon's voice softened as he changed his approach. "Let's not get into this now."

"Why not now?" Madison refused to be calmed. "It's nearly Christmas. Everyone is out celebrating with the people they love. And here I am, wondering: Do I love Sheldon? Does he love me? Am I in a relationship that's actually going to last this time, or am I really alone? Should I be out there—looking, meeting people, going out on dates with other guys? Because I really don't want to be on my own forever."

"Maddie," he said in the same low, soothing voice. "Forever? Be reasonable. Come on. Tell me, what's this about? Is this a woman thing? Because sometimes women can get so emotional, for no reason, and I don't—"

"That's not funny, Shel. And it isn't fair." Madison glared at him. "Besides, this has nothing to do with my being a woman. And it isn't for no reason." She stopped. Her palms were sweaty, and her heart was racing. She took a deep breath. Things were getting out of control, which was something she always hated. *Be cool about this, Madison,* she told herself. *Just state your case. Tell Sheldon what you need.*

With dignity, she rose and went to sit beside him on the couch. After taking another long breath, she offered a weak smile and began again. "We've been going out for a while now, Shel. And you know I love you. I just don't think I can keep going like this. I need to know, once and for all, what it is you want from this relationship. I need to know what it is you want from me." Even as she spoke, Madison was uncertain about what kind of response she hoped to hear.

Sheldon reached out and pulled her into the warm, comfortable crook of his arm. "I'll tell you what I want, Madison." He played with her fingers, exuding charm. "*This* is what I want. You. Just like this. You and me, together." He gazed into her eyes and pulled her close. Madison felt her body relax slightly as he wrapped his arms around her...and planted a friendly kiss on her forehead. "All right, Madison? Are we okay?"

She pulled back gently and nestled against his side. It wasn't what she would call a passionate relationship, exactly. But it was easy, familiar. And it didn't look as if Sheldon was in any hurry to get away from her. There was no reason to overreact.

No, things were fine this way. Just as they had been for a long time. She didn't need Carrie—or some goofy friend of Todd's—to distract her from what she really wanted.

"Yes, Sheldon," she said softly, snuggling in at his side. "We're just fine."

I think she's just fine where she is." Kip pushed his spinach linguine around the plate with his fork. "She basically said she's not interested in seeing anyone else but this guy."

"Well, did you tell her you were interested in her?"

"Carrie!" Kip protested. "I just met the woman. What was I supposed to say? Hey, Madison, I know we're perfect strangers, but have I mentioned yet that you've got the most beautiful name I've ever heard? And that it's perfect for you, because you're the most beautiful woman I've ever seen?" As he spoke, he waved his fork, drawing large circles in the air. "Oh, and by the way, would you mind smiling for me one more time? Because I love how it makes your little nose crinkle up and your blue eyes sparkle, kind of like the sea. And while we're at it, could we maybe bottle that laugh of yours? I'll bet we could use it to heal people who have depression. The sound of it certainly makes *me* want to get up and dance and to grin from ear to ear, like the complete fool I'm sure I must become in your presence.…"

Carrie beamed and nudged Todd under the table.

"What?" Kip asked, trying to sound innocent. He swallowed hard. Oops. He might as well have taken out his heart and sewn it onto his sleeve. Ordinarily, he didn't lose his cool like this over a woman. But then, for some strange reason Madison Pierce was affecting him as no other woman had before.

"Well, I'd suggest you say those things only if they represent the way you actually feel," Carrie said. Her elbows hit the kitchen table with a thump as she leaned forward and studied him, the way he imagined a spider would survey a fly struggling against the sticky trappings of its web. "Is it?"

"Is it wh-what?" Kip stuttered.

"Is what you just said," Carrie said pointedly, "the way you really feel about Madison?"

"Well, uh—" Kip looked quickly from Carrie to Todd, who was watching the entire scene with an air of detached amusement. "Well, maybe. Sort of. But get that crazy look off your face, Carrie. It's nothing. I'll admit, I've got a little crush on her. But she's as good as married, so forget about it."

But Carrie refused to be denied her triumph. "You see, I told you!" she crowed to no one in particular.

"Sweetheart, I never doubted you," Todd told her.

"I know, honey," she said. "But poor little Kip here doesn't understand the extent of my powers yet."

Kip looked pleadingly at his old roommate. Todd just shook his head. "Don't even try to fight it," he advised. "Carrie knows what she's talking about when it comes to men and women. After all," he said, giving Kip a mock serious look, "she's the only one who ever figured *me* out."

"Well, that's all fine and good," Kip grumbled, "but I'm not so sure you all have got Madison figured out. She as much as said she's not interested."

"Were those her exact words?" Carrie asked.

"Well, no," Kip said. "I think she said she's 'seeing someone' at the moment."

"Please," Carrie said, making a rude noise. "'Seeing someone'? What is that supposed to mean? Either you're serious about someone or you're not. I don't think Sheldon's interested in making a commitment to Madison. Wait—" Her face lit up. "That's it! If you want to win her over, you've got to convince Madison that you're the kind of guy who can make a commitment to her. Oh, this is going to be the best Christmas."

"Whoa, now. Hold on." Kip waved his hands frantically. "What makes you think I even want to make a commitment to Madison? How come you're so sure I even like her?"

"Honey," Carrie said with a twinkle in her eye, "it's written all over your face. It might as well be in red ink. But that's up to you to figure out. I think I've made my point. The ball is rolling, I can see that. All I have to do now is sit back and watch." She leaned back in her chair and folded her arms across her chest, looking more than satisfied. "My work here is done. From now on, I won't say another thing." And to Kip's surprise, she kept her word.

At least through dinner.

# FIVE

Kindness it is that brings forth kindness always.

SOPHOCLES, AJAX

W e've got to stop meeting like this."

Madison laid her book down on the coffee-shop table and looked up into a pair of laughing gray eyes. A lock of thick brown hair had slipped out of place and fallen down over Kip's forehead, giving him a boyish, devil-may-care appearance. This morning, he had gone for the layered look: a navy wool sweater over a white waffle henley, and at his neck, she could see the edge of the gray T-shirt that covered the strong muscles of his chest. A beige parka, faded jeans, and battered black work boots rounded out his attire.

Madison tried to squelch the warm feelings that stirred inside her at the sight of him. She'd determined just yesterday that there could be no romantic interest between them. With her level of self-control, she would have thought this decision would keep her from noticing how attractive the man was.

Kip smiled at her then, and Madison felt herself blush. Why did he always seem to know what she was thinking? Her reaction seemed to please Kip even further—and the more he grinned, the redder she became. "You look great," he said appreciatively. She sat silently, wanting to speak but frozen by shyness, as his eyes surveyed the pale ivory silk-knit shirt she had designed herself, paired today with relaxed-fit jeans and smart, stacked-heel loafers. "Very stylish."

Madison bit back the words of thanks that rose to her tongue. "Nice try, but you can't sweet-talk your way out of this one, Mr. Jones," she chided instead. "You're fifteen minutes late." It was their third meeting in as many days, and Madison oddly found herself liking the familiarity of it. How much more interesting her daily trip to Coffee People would be if he were always with her, she thought, then firmly pushed the idea from her mind. She couldn't allow herself to think such things.

Kip dropped his day planner on the table with a thump and took a seat opposite her. "Fifteen? That's impossible. My watch says— Oh." He scowled as he consulted the timepiece on his arm. "Sorry about that. I could have sworn I was on time for once. It was twelve-thirty when I left the church. Then I stopped at Todd's to change—"

"Wh-what is that?" Madison broke in, recoiling in horror at the sight of his exposed forearm. It was hard to see what, exactly, was on his skin, but it appeared to be a picture of something big and black. A bird of some kind. A vulture, perhaps?

"Oh, that?" Kip puffed out his chest proudly. "It's my tattoo."

"Your *tattoo*?" Madison felt ill. "Since when have you had a tattoo?" She was sure she hadn't seen it the day before. Had both his arms been covered by shirtsleeves? Of all the details to miss...

"Since last night," Kip said easily.

"Last night?" It was more than she could take. "Was this before or after Häagen-Dazs? I hope you weren't expecting me to get a tattoo with you. Was that part of the invitation?"

Kip looked startled by the shock on her face. Madison knew she must look thoroughly appalled, and she hated to be judgmental, but...a tattoo? Several of her clients had gotten them recently. It had been all the rage last summer. But something like that was just a little too wild, too rebellious for her. Obviously, she had made the right decision concerning Kip Jones, she told herself. Suddenly, he didn't seem quite as attractive to her after all. Or did he? It was hard to tell with him sitting just a few feet away, chuckling and looking at her with those bright, laughing gray eyes.

"As much as I hate to disappoint you, I'm afraid getting a tattoo was never on the agenda." He spoke with an exaggerated tone of regret. "Actually, after you turned me down for ice cream, I went to the park and played basketball instead—"

"In the rain?" The downpour had been constant over the past few days. The man really was insane.

"Why not? I play in the rain all the time. But if it makes you feel better, these were covered hoops. Anyway," he said in an obvious effort to bring her attention back to the subject at hand, "I caught a pick-up game with a group of teenagers, and we ended up making a bet. As you can see, I lost."

"A bet? Are you sure you're a fitting role model for these kids?"

Kip shrugged, apparently not offended. "I wonder that myself sometimes. But don't worry; I never bet money. We were just playing Horse. You know: 'I'll bet you can't make this shot....'"

"So you lost a bet and had to get a tattoo," Madison said dryly. "And if you had won?"

"They would have had to come to church with me next week."

"To church." She regarded him with amazement. "To church? Seriously?"

"Yep," he said, looking very serious indeed. "I never kid about church."

Madison shook her head and stared at him in confusion. He

had done it again. Again. The man had drawn her out of herself, gotten her all riled up, and pulled her completely out of her comfort zone, while at the same time somehow making her like him even more than before. It was uncanny. It was bizarre. It was…it was downright dangerous, and she needed to keep her guard up. Obviously, she was even more drawn to the man than she had originally realized.

"And the tattoo?"

"Alas, a fake." He did a pretty good job of pretending to be disappointed, but Madison wasn't fooled. "I'll stop by tonight and show the guys I really did it."

"You didn't really do anything."

"Hey, I did exactly what I promised I'd do," he said. "I got a tattoo. They never specified what kind, or how long it had to last."

"Well, just don't let Carrie see it before the wedding," Madison warned. "She might hyperventilate."

"Actually," Kip said calmly, "that's exactly what she said about you. She suggested you get one, too, so we can match. I've got Daffy Duck. You could get Bugs."

Every muscle in Madison's face itched to smile. So much for the horrible big black vulture. "Not in this lifetime," she said as firmly as she could. Her heart skipped a beat. She was enjoying the battle.

"Maybe in the next one?" Kip asked. He sounded hopeful.

"You're incorrigible," she said, smiling, her eyes locked on his.

Kip grinned back at her. "And you're adorable." Even as the words escaped his lips, a look of dismay crossed his features. It was clear he instantly regretted what he'd said.

Madison froze. The color drained from Kip's face as he rushed to apologize. "Oh…oops. Sorry. I didn't mean that. I mean, I did, but I didn't mean to say it." He stumbled over his words. "It…uh, *adorable* rhymed with *incorrigible,*" he offered lamely, raising one hand in the air before Madison could open her mouth to speak. "I know, I know. You have a boyfriend," he said, waving her unspoken protest away. "I forgot for a moment. It won't happen again."

"Well, good," Madison said carefully, even though something inside her whispered that she wished it would. What if she hadn't been dating Sheldon after all? How might she have responded? Where would the conversation have led then?

"Okay," Kip said brightly, turning his attention to his day planner—a beat-up old leather-bound book with pages marked by runny, rain-doused ink sticking out of every side. Messy and disorganized and interesting looking, just like its owner, Madison noted. "Enough of that. Let me tell you what's on the agenda. Apparently Carrie gave Todd a list of things to do—"

"Let me guess. And Todd gave the list to you." It was not a question.

"Yep. So here we go. I've got the final guest count, which we need to give to the caterer. I've got a check I need to drop off at the rental company. There's something here about birdseed and little paper cups. I suppose that's instead of rice? We also need to ship two of Todd and Carrie's suitcases to the secret honeymoon location."

Madison nudged his arm gently. "Which is?"

"I am sorry to disappoint you," Kip said with dignity, "but I am a man of my word. Torture me if you want; I'll never disclose that the newlyweds will be traveling to Puerto Vallar— oops!" He covered his mouth like a small child who had just given away a precious secret.

"Ha, ha." Madison raised a brow. "I'm not fooled. I'm sure you know that I already know—"

"—what I know, and I know that you know it," he finished for her. "Whew! So, are you ready to go?" He peered into the depths of her cup. "What? You're not even halfway done. And you call yourself a coffee fiend? That's embarrassing."

"This is my second latte. I had time to kill," she reminded him.

"Oh. Right." Kip nodded vigorously. "Gotcha. You wanna stay and finish it?"

Madison stood, plucked the white lid from the tabletop, and secured it to her cup with a snap. "No. I'll just take it with me." She gathered her belongings and cinched her coat and hood up tight, tucking her short blond curls behind her ears to protect them from the elements. She pitied anyone who got caught out in weather like this. Why would anyone choose to play basketball in it? Kip really *was* a loon....

Moments later, they were standing in what appeared to be the makings of a full-blown storm. Despite her efforts to keep dry, Madison was chilled to the bone the instant she stepped outdoors. Winter rains in Oregon ranged anywhere from a drizzle to a gale, and today's weather was definitely on the rough side. Hardly the kind of day to put one in a holiday mood. The wind was strong, the rain heavy. Although she hadn't seen any hail yet, Madison half expected to at any moment.

"Where are you parked?" Kip shouted over the deluge.

Madison jerked her head to the right. "Around the corner and to the right. About three blocks away." Streams of rain ran down her face, making it difficult to talk or even breathe without swallowing water.

"Come on." Kip slipped his hand around her soggy mittened one and pulled her after him in a half-run, half-walk. "I've got Todd's car," he threw over his shoulder. "It's about a block and a half down." Madison fell into step behind him without resisting. Her handbag had been slung over her shoulder, and it bounced against her back as they ran. With her free hand, she tried to keep her coffee from sloshing out of the cup and onto her glove.

When they reached the corner, Kip paused to look for traffic. In that brief instant, a figure emerged from the shadows of a nearby doorway, where it had taken refuge from the storm.

"Excuse me, miss?"

Madison jumped as the strange-looking man approached. His clothes were covered in filth and grime. His hair was long and white and hung plastered to his face. And when he spoke, broken, stained teeth showed through his lips.

"Excuse me, do you got an extra quarter or a dollar you could spare? I'm a few bucks short, see?" he said. Madison tightened her grip on Kip's hand. "Actually...a hundred bucks short." The man grinned a toothy, yellow grin.

Madison felt emotionally torn. Certainly she could spare a few dollars. But she had always heard it was a bad idea to give street people money. What if he wanted to spend it for drugs or booze? She didn't want to have any part of that.

She looked up to find Kip studying her face. He gave her a gentle smile that seemed to say, "It's all right." He then turned back to the man, opened his mouth to speak, then quickly shut it again. Kip seemed as unsure how to respond as she was.

"It's mighty cold out," the man said. Madison nodded. Only her hands were somewhat warm: her left because it was held by Kip; her right because it gripped her steaming cup of coffee. She looked down at the drink, then reached out and offered it to the stranger.

"This might help," she said and smiled. Then, as an afterthought, she dug deep into her jacket pocket and pulled out the orange she had brought along for a snack, then offered that as well.

For a second, she thought the man might not take the items. He hesitated, then grinned ear-to-ear as he reached out and took the cup and the piece of fruit into his own grimy, bare hands.

"Thank you, ma'am," he said as heartily and happily as if she'd given him the hundred dollars he had spoken of. It wasn't what he'd hoped for, but he didn't seem to mind. "An' God bless you, miss."

"God bless you, too," she said with feeling. Then Kip put one strong arm around her shoulders, and they made a mad dash for the car.

Once inside, they sat—red-nosed and dripping—and stared at one another. Within the confines of the Honda's small front compartment, Madison felt even more aware of Kip's strong physical presence. She watched, fascinated, as the rain trickled down his face and ran off the hard angles of his chin.

Both refrained from speaking as they struggled to catch their breath in the wake of their sprint. During those first few moments of silence, Kip broke the tension by starting the car and turning on the heater. He was the first to speak.

"That was a nice thing you did back there," he said with a touch of wonder. "Most people turn and walk away as quickly as they can when they see a street person approach."

"I very nearly did," Madison admitted. "It's not that I was afraid of him, exactly—although I think I was, just a little bit. I see guys like that all the time, and I do try to go around them. I just don't know what to do. How to help. What do *you* do? You work with people on the streets, don't you? What's the best way to handle it?"

"Well, no matter what they say, it isn't usually a good idea to give them money. Actually—" Kip leaned back against the vinyl seat. "Let me take that back. That's a decision that's between you and God. I don't really believe there's a formula. If you feel led to give—and I mean really led and not just a feeling of guilt that you want to alleviate by giving the guy a few bucks—then by all means give."

Madison thought back to Kip's reaction. "You looked torn about what to do just now yourself."

"True." Kip warmed his hands by one of the tiny heater vents. "That's because you were there. I wasn't sure what you wanted to do. Especially after what you said yesterday about staying in your comfort zone. I wanted to respect where you're at. If I'd been alone, I probably would have stopped and talked to the guy...found out where he lived, what he thought he needed that hundred dollars for. I might have tried to set him up with one of the relief organizations in town. A lot of these folks already know where they can go, but I usually like to check. Not that I'd recommend that approach to you," he said, sounding oddly protective, "as a woman alone. But there are other ways you can help out, ways that are generally safer. Ways in which you can have a better idea of where the money you give is going."

"Like what?"

"Oh, most communities have shelters and outreach programs to help these folks. There's a great program here in Portland called Blanket Coverage that focuses on meeting physical needs first, although the ultimate goal is to feed their souls and bring about life change. And there are other groups, like the Red Cross and the Salvation Army, that do good work with the homeless. You can get some good leads at church," he told her. "But I'm sure you know that.

"The thing is, most of us just walk away when we see someone in need. We're a pretty cynical society—and often for good reason. We see a guy asking for a handout, and we think, *I know what he wants money for.* If we thought the money we gave him or her would be spent on food or clothing or housing, a lot more of us would be willing to shell out a few bucks. We think it's smarter to give some other way, but then we never do."

"I know that's true for me." Madison felt embarrassed. She thought back to all the times she, too, had simply walked away. "I just wish I could do more for that guy back there."

"Well…" Kip thought for a moment. "Maybe you can."

"How? You said we shouldn't give him money."

"Right. Probably not. But you did give him something," he pointed out. "What if you just did more of the same?"

"You mean what if I gave him—? Hey, this could be fun." A grin spread across Madison's face as she began to catch the vision. "Come on," she said eagerly, opening the car door to step back out into the rain shower. "There's a market down on Lovejoy. We can get some more food down there, buy some bagels at Noah's, then stop and pick up a thermos of coffee. Whatever he doesn't use, we'll tell him to pass on to someone else. Maybe you can talk to him, too, like you said, and see if there's something else he really needs."

Kip grinned and ducked out into the rain after her.


Fifteen minutes later, they were back at the same street corner, looking for the stranger.

"He's not here!" Madison cried in disappointment. If anything, the rain was coming down even harder. But this time she didn't care. "And after all that work! We did this for nothing."

"Oh, I wouldn't say that. Whether you find this guy or not, you've accomplished something important."

"What, gotten soaked to the bone?" she grumbled, finally noticing her bedraggled state.

"No," he said with a laugh. "I think you changed a heart. *Your* heart. You decided to do something this time, instead of just walking away. And that decision was worth the effort you put into it, no matter what happens next. The one who's getting the most out of this isn't this guy, anyway. It's you."

Madison looked at him skeptically. Was he kidding? He didn't look like it.

"Besides, you know what else you did today?" Kip asked cheerfully.

"No," she said, throwing him a teasing look. "But I'll bet you're going to tell me."

Kip grinned back at her. "You took a risk. I know that's not something you're comfortable with. And I have to say, I'm really proud of you."

Madison shook her head and looked at him in amazement. For a moment, there was nothing between them but the sound and the sight and the sweet smell of the rain. "How do you do that?" she asked in amazement.

Kip blinked at her. "Do what?"

"Make me feel as though you like me more than anyone else you've ever met." Madison felt the need to reach out and slip her hands into his. It was a good thing she carried a bag of food in each. "Is that something they teach you when you go into social work?" she wondered aloud. "Some kind of communication skill? What's the trick?"

Kip gave her a knowing look. "Oh, I'll never tell. I don't want to give up the mystery," he teased. "Then I'll lose my charm and you won't like me anymore."

"Oh, I don't think there's any chance of that." Madison realized too late how that sounded. She threw Kip a sideways glance to see if he'd noticed.

"Oh, really?" Kip said, his voice low.

He'd noticed.

"Yeah." Madison's heart began to race within her chest. "Really." She was about to say more when, across the street and over Kip's shoulder, her eyes caught a glimpse of a brown-clad figure, scurrying from one doorway to another.

"Hey, there he is!" she cried. "Come on!"

As she moved past him to cross the street, she thought she heard Kip mutter under his breath an echo of what the homeless man had said earlier: "God bless you, Madison."

And as her feet slapped the wet pavement, it struck her that, in a way she never would have expected, he already had.

# SIX

Love is a tyrant,
Resisted.

JOHN FORD, *THE LOVER'S MELANCHOLY*

T he lively melodies of Tchaikovsky's *Nutcracker* floated from two tiny speakers in the corner of the bedroom, weaving a joyful holiday serenade as Madison made herself ready for Todd and Carrie's rehearsal dinner.

With her hands resting on the gentle slope of her hips, she stared into the deep recesses of her closet and considered her dilemma. It wasn't a matter of not having anything to wear. Her walk-in was overflowing with the best and worst of her design creations: silk blouses, corduroy jackets, and twill pants with tiny flaws, which she couldn't justify selling for top dollar at the shop, hung next to flawlessly-made high-fashion items that she couldn't bear to part with after all the work she'd put into them.

No, the question wasn't whether she'd find anything to wear but how formal should she be? Madison knew both Carrie's and Todd's families fairly well and was certain that neither group would treat the event like a fashion show. The women would be dressed comfortably, probably in pantsuits or simple dresses. Madison had countless knit dresses, casual skirts, and colorful blouses that would do. Yet she couldn't resist the urge to reach into the back and pull out a dramatic sheath in an ice blue silk that she knew set off her eyes. It wasn't like her to wear something so alluring. But tonight she just couldn't help herself.

She held up her arms, slid the dress over her head, then turned to survey her image in the mirror. Without shoes or nylons, the knee-length sleeveless shift resembled nothing so much as a slip. Madison frowned at her reflection. She wanted to look beautiful and, well, sexy, but not immodest. After a moment's thought, she dug back into her closet and emerged with a soft, angora wraparound sweater of the same cool blue. The long sleeves seemed to caress her arms, and the V neckline exposed the top of the dress without revealing any cleavage. She quickly added a single strand of pearls, pale ivory stockings, and cream-colored heels, making the outfit complete.

*There,* she thought, surveying with satisfaction the picture she made. *We'll just see what Kip thinks of this! I mean, um, Sheldon....* She ran her fingers absently over the pearls and averted her eyes from her image in the glass, trying to turn her attention to something else, anything else that would push the renegade thought from her mind. How nice it was that Sheldon would be joining them after the rehearsal, for the dinner part of the evening. In a flash, she realized sadly that she probably wouldn't be able to sit next to Kip for the meal as she had hoped.

Madison found it disturbing that her musings turned so often to the man who had entered her life only seven days before. But, as she reasoned with herself during the nights when she lay awake thinking of him, it really was only natural. Kip Jones was an attractive stranger who had showered her with attention. She was only human. Of course she was drawn to him. That didn't change the fact that he'd be going back to his own life in just two days...something she'd tried hard not to think about all week during their fun-filled, wedding-related excursions.

Somehow, every day that week, Carrie, Kip, or Todd—even Madison herself—had come up with some task or detail that the best man and maid of honor simply had to handle together. It had begun with the bride, who insisted Kip and Madison become co-coordinators for the reception. "That means you'll need to meet with the caterer, the florist, the photographer, the videographer...."

At first, Madison refused. But her resolve wasn't anywhere near as solid as that of the strong-willed bride.

"Come on, Madison," Carrie pleaded, batting her eyes. "I just can't do it all myself. I really need you and Kip."

Madison wasn't fooled. She knew the tasks were choreographed attempts to make her spend time with Kip. Carrie's opinion of Sheldon hadn't changed since the beginning of the week; she had simply stopped voicing it outright. Only an idiot would fail to see that she was determined to get Madison and Kip paired up.

Madison had been all too happy to go along with a plan that called for her to spend time with Kip. She talked him into driving her to the airport to pick up Todd's parents, who were flying in from Arizona. "Since you know the city so well," she teased. And Kip had been more than willing to join in on the game, inviting her to join him for visits to the tuxedo shop, reception hall, and travel agent.

But as for a romantic pairing...that was an expectation Madison just couldn't fulfill. She was taken, and Kip Jones still wasn't her type. Period. End of story. The decision wasn't entirely up to her, anyway. He hadn't even asked her out since the day she told him about Sheldon. Of course, Kip did continue to give her offhand compliments, but they were of a different sort; none as forthright as the day he had called her adorable.

These days, most of Kip's praises focused on Madison's character: her sweet spirit, her kind heart, her generosity. Though none of the comments would generally be considered romantic, Madison was stirred to the depths of her soul when he delivered each one. Somehow, his words seemed more intimate, more tender, than any he could have uttered about her outward appearance.

These quiet moments between them were precious but rare. For the most part, she and Kip spent their time joking with one another and coordinating whatever task was at hand. At first, Madison had been hesitant to let herself become too familiar with him and had kept her guard up. But Kip continued to tease her—first gently, then mercilessly—until she began to tease back...in spades.

Madison hated to admit it, but Carrie was right. She had missed spending time with a man who could make her laugh. Usually she opened herself up only with her female friends. That didn't seem quite as threatening, since she wasn't worried about their disappearing from her life. In her experience, women were fundamentally relational. Even if they lost contact for a period of time, eventually most of them came back around and the friendships were ultimately renewed.

Men, Madison had decided, were different. She had seen her father—a creative, fun-loving, spirited man, much like Kip—slip out of her life and never come back. As if to confirm her suspicions, every man before Sheldon had broken up with her—or done something to make her break up with him—within a mere six months of dating. Although, Madison suspected, it was likely that her own lack of trust had largely impacted those relationships, making it difficult for either of them to stick it out. And now it was hard for her not to expect the same thing to happen should she get involved with Kip.

She mentally batted the thought away. *It doesn't matter what*

*Kip does,* Madison reminded herself. *He's not my boyfriend; Shel is. Solid, dependable Shel. He's not going anywhere. In fact, it looks like he might finally be coming around, after all.*

Sheldon, the man who was so reliable in the present yet so uncertain about the future. Over the past week, however, something had changed, although Madison wasn't exactly sure what that something was. She suspected it had something to do with all the time she'd been spending with Kip. Before, she had always known when to expect Sheldon's calls: every other evening at ten o'clock—just before bedtime. And one day a week, before she went to the shop in the morning, he would phone to ask her out for lunch. Just like clockwork.

But this week he had called every day and at irregular times…wanting to know how her day was going, how she was feeling, what was on her mind. Once he had even asked if she was planning on doing any more wedding errands. His change in behavior was inexplicable, although Madison suspected it was a result of hearing her laughing Monday-night report about the time she'd spent with Kip. Sheldon hadn't come right out and asked her about her feelings for the man, which was a relief. She didn't want to lie. She thought Kip was wonderful, and she was enjoying every minute with him. But at the same time, there didn't seem to be any point in bringing up something that would no longer be an issue once Carrie and Todd's wedding was over. Kip would be gone, and her life—with Sheldon—would go back to the way it had always been. The only thing she could do was enjoy things the way they were, while they lasted.

Madison gave one last little spin in front of the floor-length mirror. Then she stopped at her dressing table to apply a final coat of pale pink lipstick and to dab a touch of Sunflowers perfume at her wrists and ears. Then, with a nod of satisfaction, she headed for the door.

Kip Jones might be going home in two days. But Madison felt a perverse, unexplainable sense of pleasure at the prospect of making the man realize just what he was leaving behind.

"And so," the pastor told the wedding party, "after the exchange of rings, the blessing will be given. And following the blessing, the declaration…"

From her position next to Carrie, Madison tried to focus as the minister explained—one more time—what would happen during the ceremony the next day. But, as if of their own volition, her eyes kept drifting back to Kip…and that ridiculous hair of his.

What was that color, anyway? Azure? Indigo? Some dark shade of royal blue? His neat khaki pants and carefully pressed shirt made the outrageous shock of hair appear even more out of place. Kip caught Madison's eye and gave her a jaunty wink.

With great effort, she managed to remain poker-faced, which of course only intensified his determination to make her laugh. A series of hideous face contortions followed on his part. Madison tried to avert her gaze, but it was impossible not to see him out of the corner of her eye. Soon she was giggling like a little girl.

"Is something wrong, Madison?" The balding minister adopted the tone of a disapproving schoolmaster, but she grinned back at him, unconcerned. His fierceness was all an act, and she knew it. She and Carrie had known the man since he'd first been hired as the church's youth pastor, ten years earlier. He'd always put on the 'tough guy' act when trying to get the kids under control, but all the teens knew he was really just a teddy bear.

"No. Sorry, Paul." She smiled, looking completely unrepentant.

Until a few hours earlier, she might have felt a bit more sensitive about being singled out. When she'd first arrived at the church, which she visited about every third Sunday, she had been embarrassed. Her attendance at Sunday-morning services had dropped off considerably over the past few years, and she knew the pastor was aware of it. This might have affected her mood all evening, but just before the rehearsal began, Paul had pulled Madison aside and asked her how things were going.

"Actually, I'm doing really well. Lots of sales, lots of interest in my designs," she told him brightly, even though she knew he wasn't asking about her work.

"And outside of the design realm?" he asked. "You know, we haven't seen you around the church much lately." The words were spoken without accusation, but he cut quickly to the heart of the issue Madison had been hoping to avoid.

"Oh, I'm here," she said. Paul raised one eyebrow. "Well, not every Sunday, but I do come. Remember? I said hi to you and Alice just a few weeks ago." Madison knew she was getting defensive, but she couldn't help herself. She'd been feeling guilty about her hit-and-miss church attendance for months. Even though the pastor's inquiry was anything but judgmental, she felt as if she were on the hot seat.

To her surprise, Paul did not berate her. "Well, I just wanted to make sure you know we love you," he said in a mild tone. "It's true, we don't see you as much as we'd like. But you come whenever you can, Madison. We enjoy having you." He turned then, and Madison was getting ready to slink away in relief when he turned back to her and said softly, almost as an afterthought, "You know, you don't have to feel embarrassed to come back, no matter how much time passes. God's arms are always open wide. You're always welcome."

The words were more than a little comforting to Madison. She'd been feeling guilty over the fact that her spiritual life had suffered greatly since her college days. She couldn't blame Sheldon for the problem. He was a Christian, too. He was happy to attend church with her when time allowed, but time didn't allow every week. He was a busy man, Madison knew, and he hated to tie up his schedule with more commitments than he could handle. Sheldon liked to focus on the things he knew he could follow through on. That's what made him so solid. That was one of the things she liked best about him—wasn't it?

"And after the declaration, the bride's father will deliver a prayer," Paul was saying. "Then there will be the affirmation of the community...."

Madison looked over at Kip. He was still watching her, smiling. She narrowed her eyes and gave him a speaking glance, as if to say: "You got me into trouble, mister. I hope you're happy."

Kip did, in fact, look happy. Madison liked the way his whole face expressed joy, not just the eyes or lips or cheeks, but all of his features. In particular, she liked the way his eyes crinkled up with little crow's-feet when he smiled.

"Ms. Pierce," Paul broke into her thoughts, "I believe it's your turn."

"What?" Madison spun around. Everyone was looking at her. Carrie and Paul had begun the recessional and were already at the back of the church. The flower girl and ring bearer were right on their heels. Thoroughly mortified, Madison took the arm Kip offered and allowed him to lead her back to the narthex.

"Sorry to bother you back there," Carrie said.

"Guess my mind was wandering," Madison explained unnecessarily, trying to hide her embarrassment. She suspected that Carrie had a good idea of exactly where her mind had been. How aggravating that her best friend knew her so well! Even better, it seemed, than she knew herself.

"I guess so," Kip said innocently. "You completely spaced out."

Madison grabbed his arm and shook it, hoping that her reddening face did not give her away. "Look who's talking, you troublemaker. The least you could do is 'fess up to your crimes. Making faces in church like that. You should be ashamed of yourself."

"Oh, no." Carrie wagged her head in disapproval. "Forget about that. He's got enough trouble explaining that hair."

"Another bet?" Madison guessed.

"How'd you know?"

She gave him a look of pity. "Wow. You must be a really bad basketball player. You're never going to get those kids into church if you don't practice."

"What do you think I'm doing, if not practicing?"

"Oh, is *that* what you call it? Well then, that's okay. But don't you think it might be a good idea to hold off on the betting part until you get a little better at the game?"

"And what would be the fun in that?" he said amiably. "Besides, there's more motivation this way. Anyway, I've just about convinced these kids I'm a total loser. Pretty soon, they'll think they can bet me anything and be sure to win."

"What, do you mean you're losing on purpose?" At his bland look, Madison raised her brows. "I think you're having entirely too much fun with this."

"Yeah. At our expense," Carrie grumbled. She took a lock of his hair between her fingers and examined it closely. "Are you absolutely certain this stuff is going to wash out by tomorrow?"

"I promise," Kip said solemnly. "Would I do that to you? Really, Carrie, it'll come right out. And if it doesn't…" He scratched his chin and thought for a moment. "I can always cut it all off."

"Please." Carrie rolled her eyes. "I am not going to have a bald man in my wedding."

"Hey!" Just then, their semihairless pastor walked by, assuming the most injured-looking expression he could muster.

"Sorry." Carried patted his arm comfortingly. "I didn't mean that. I meant only *naturally* bald men are allowed. Everyone with hair is responsible for showing up with it in presentable condition tomorrow."

"Man," Kip sighed. "Weddings. If it isn't one rule, it's another."

By this time, the entire wedding party had made its way to the back of the church. Carrie left the two of them then so she could circulate through the crowd, making sure everyone had directions to the nearby restaurant where the dinner would be held.

Almost immediately, the mood between Kip and Madison changed. He looked at her timidly, then stared down at his shoes like a nervous schoolboy.

"Well, looks like Todd and Carrie are gonna make it," he said awkwardly.

"Yeah. I guess they are." Madison realized with dismay that now that the week was at an end, their easy camaraderie had disappeared. "Less than twenty-four hours to go. By this time tomorrow, they'll be gone." *And so will you.* A feeling of agitation began to grow within her.

"You, uh…" Loudly, Kip cleared his throat, then tried again. "You look incredible tonight, Madison."

"Thanks," she said, trying to sound lighthearted. There was no reason to let Kip know how she felt. That would only make things more difficult for everyone. Out in the lobby, the soft rumble of the small crowd diminished as, one by one, people left for the restaurant. Madison and Kip were the only two left in the sanctuary now. Pretty soon, they'd be the only two left at the church. Madison knew she should leave; Sheldon would be waiting for her at the restaurant. But she could not make herself move.

"Hey, Maddie?" Carrie poked her head in through the door that led to the hallway. "I think I left all my notes and schedules and lists down front. My planning books should be down there, too. Could you and Kip pull those things together and meet us at the restaurant?"

Earlier in the week, Madison would have readily agreed. But she wasn't amused by Carrie's cute little setup any longer. In fact, a distinct feeling of resentment was beginning to surface.

"Oh, I don't—"

"Sure," Kip said, speaking at the same time. The two of them looked at each other in embarrassment.

"Great," Carrie said, ignoring Madison's response. "I'll see you both in a little while." Then the door swung shut behind her, and she was gone.

Without a word, Madison made her way to the front of the church and began to collect Carrie's belongings. Kip followed on her heels and made himself busy gathering up loose schedule sheets while Madison stacked two wedding planners, a calendar, a clipboard, and a date book. Silence hung between them.

Finally Kip approached Madison and said simply, "Something just doesn't feel right here. Is it me? Have I said or done something wrong? If I have, I don't know what it is. But I'd like to make it right."

Madison tried desperately to gather her thoughts. It would have been so easy to walk out without discussing the problem. That was the way Sheldon would have handled it. How could she stay angry with Kip when he was clearly, so thoughtfully, concerned about her feelings?

"No...yes. Actually, I don't know," she admitted. "I guess I feel strange. About this. About being here with you. About this being the end."

"Me, too," Kip said quietly.

"Isn't that silly? I mean, we're friends and all." She forced a laugh, and it came out sounding stiff.

Kip didn't seem to notice. "I don't think it's silly at all," he told her softly. "This is an emotional time, and not just for Carrie and Todd."

Madison wasn't sure what he meant by that, but she braced herself for the questions that were sure to come: *"What's the matter? Why are you so sad? Does it have anything to do with me?"*

But Kip did not ask any of those things. Instead, he gently lifted the stack from Madison's grasp and laid it on the first pew. Then he led her around the twinkling Christmas tree filling one corner of the sanctuary to the altar, where Carrie and Todd had stood minutes earlier, where the couple would stand the next day to pledge themselves to one another for the rest of their lives.

"You know what I'd like to do?" Kip whispered in a husky voice.

Madison shook her head, unable to speak.

"I'd like us to say a prayer together for Todd and Carrie. A prayer of blessing." Then he took her hands, as if she were the bride and he the groom. When their fingers touched, a feeling of fundamental rightness filled her heart. The two friends they loved most in the world were about to start their lives together. What greater gift could she and Kip give them than to lay their marriage at the Father's feet?

As she stared at their joined hands, a tiny voice inside her whispered that she was not good enough to make such a request. She hadn't been attending church regularly, it insisted. She hadn't been saying her prayers. Why should God listen to her? But before the thoughts had even been fully formed, a stronger, more powerful sense of belonging overwhelmed her. What was it Paul had said to her earlier? *"You know, you don't have to feel embarrassed to come back, no matter how much time passes. God's arms are always open wide. You're always welcome."*

At the time, she'd thought he was talking about their specific church family. But now she knew that what he'd really been talking about was the open, loving nature of God's heart. Something stirred inside Madison. She closed her eyes for a moment and felt an overwhelming wave of love. And she knew God was welcoming her back home.

She opened her eyes and lifted them to meet Kip's. This, too, was what she had been missing. It wasn't just Kip's laughter she needed. It was the way he challenged her, the way he brought out the best in her, the way he cared not just for her heart but about the well-being of her soul. And in that moment, she realized that no matter what happened, Kip had changed her life forever. She would never again be the same.

The moment passed between them, and then they bowed their heads. Together they stood, his cheek lightly touching her hair, as they silently approached the throne of God.

"Dear heavenly Father," Kip began. "Thank you for our friends Todd and Carrie. Thank you for the blessing they have been in our lives. We recognize that nothing is a coincidence with you; all that happens to us is a part of your plan. We are so grateful that out of all the times and all the places in which we might have been born, you have brought us here and allowed the paths of our lives to cross."

As he spoke, he caressed Madison's fingers with his own, not in a sensual way, but in a manner that communicated comfort, friendship, and...love.

Madison opened her mouth to speak, hesitated, then began again as she drew strength from Kip's touch. "Lord, you are the God of love," she said simply. "Give Todd and Carrie love. For you, and from you, and for one another." The words were simple but heartfelt. And although she was out of practice in turning her deepest wishes and concerns over to God, she felt the truth of Paul's words. It felt as though she were coming home. There was no guilt; simply a wondrous sense of peace.

Kip squeezed her hands. "May you—Father God, Jesus, and Holy Spirit—bless, protect, and keep Todd and Carrie in your care. Bless them with health and wisdom, joy and peace, and a family that is devoted to you. Most of all, may you be with them every day of their lives. Help them to love you and each other more and more with each passing day." Kip paused and cleared his throat. "And God," he said in a clear, strong voice, "about this dear woman now before me…"

Madison began to tremble. Kip's grip tightened ever so slightly, steadying her. "I want to take this opportunity, Lord, to thank you not only for Todd and Carrie but also for the influence they have had on my life. Specifically, I thank you for using them to introduce me to this wonderful, beautiful woman. She is so incredible, so precious, Lord. Help her to know what a delight she is to you…and to me. And help me, Lord, to lay our relationship in your hands when I leave on Sunday. For I will miss her more than I can say."

Madison's eyes flew open, and she found Kip gazing back at her, looking every bit as startled as she felt. Without a word, he leaned forward, ever so slowly, until his lips were hovering just above hers. His hand gently traced the slope of her cheek, and as she stared deeply into his eyes, she felt as though she were sinking into their warm, gray depths. With one rough thumb, he traced the outline of her jawbone and moved to cover her soft mouth with his lips.

"No…Kip!" Madison pulled away abruptly.

"Madison?" He stood, blinking, as if trying to catch his bearings.

"I can't do this," she blurted. "I just can't. I'm sorry." Her arms felt bereft without his touch. Her eyes pleaded with him to understand.

"Oh. I see. Is it…Sheldon?" Kip looked pale, almost as though he were feeling sick.

"No, no," she said, feeling rather nauseated herself. "It's us. It's this. You just said it, Kip: You're leaving the day after tomorrow. Don't you see?"

As Kip stared back at her, his eyes filled with hurt and confusion, Madison knew she'd never felt anything this painful, not even the loss of her father. "I can't love you; I can't lose you. You know you need to leave. And I have to let you go." She started to withdraw her hand, but he would not release it.

"Please." With a quick tug, she extricated herself from his grip. "This is too hard. Let's not make it any harder." Madison tore her eyes away. She knew she could not look at him. If she stayed one moment longer, her heart would be lost for good…if it wasn't already.

Through her tears, she managed to grab her coat and gather up her belongings before stumbling toward the door.

"Madison—" Kip tried one last time. She looked back at him with tear-blurred eyes. He looked as though he had been punched in the stomach.

"Please. I have to go. Just tell Carrie, tell Shel—" Her voice broke. "Tell everyone I wasn't feeling well, so I headed home. I'll…I'll see you tomorrow." Then she turned her back on him and ran outside, where the rain streaming down her face mixed with her tears.

*Tomorrow.* Never before had the word held such weight. It was a day she wished would never have to come.

Or if it did, would never end.

# SEVEN

The man who has never made a fool of himself in love
will never be wise in love.

THEODOR REIK, *OF LOVE AND LUST*

**D**early beloved, we are gathered together here in the
sight of God, and in the presence of these witnesses,
to join together this man and this woman in holy
matrimony...."

Madison kept her eyes trained carefully on Carrie. Her
friend was a beautiful bride. Her rich red hair stood out against
the wedding's dark green color scheme, which included three
forest green velvet bridesmaid dresses—designed by
Madison—and the enormous Christmas tree in the corner. The
wedding gown had turned out perfectly. Whether it was due to
Madison's skills as a seamstress or Carrie's willpower at staying
away from sweets—or a combination of the two—in the end,
the dress was a perfect fit.

"...which is an honorable estate, instituted of God, and sig-
nifying unto us a mystical union which exists between Christ
and his church...."

It had taken nearly superhuman effort, but by remaining
hidden away with the bride while she dressed, Madison had
managed to avoid Kip before the ceremony. She simply could
not face him. *Christ and his church...Christ and his church.* She

focused on the minister's words. *Think about that, Madison,* she told herself. *God's the one who will see you through now. Not the man standing across from you, nor the one who asked you last night to become his wife....*

It was unbelievable. An absolute nightmare. After years of longing for the security, the stability, of a long-term relationship, Madison had at last found herself on the receiving end of a marriage proposal...from a man she no longer loved. The offer had come less than two hours after she had left Kip standing at the altar.

"What are you doing here?" Sheldon had asked petulantly after she let him into her apartment. "I was waiting for you at the restaurant."

Madison settled back against the deep cushions of her comfortable plaid couch. "I know. Didn't Kip tell you?" It pained her just to say his name. "I wasn't feeling well." That was the understatement of the year. She'd never felt so horrible in her life. She pulled a soft Adirondack throw over her legs, hoping the prop would help convince him.

"Yeah?" Sheldon wandered aimlessly around the apartment. "He didn't look like he was feeling too well, either. You guys were together today, weren't you?"

Madison nodded but deliberately remained silent.

He continued to pace, finally offering: "Maybe it was food poisoning. Did you eat the same thing at lunch?"

"Sheldon," she said firmly, "it was not food poisoning. Now would you sit down? You're making me nervous."

"Oh. Not food poisoning, huh?" He sounded disappointed. The request to be seated had fallen on deaf ears. "Maybe it's just a bug going around."

Again, Madison said nothing.

"You know, your eyes are kind of red—"

"It's nothing." Since when had Sheldon become so observant?

"Right." That seemed to satisfy him for the moment. "Is there anything I can get you?" he asked, wandering toward the kitchen. "Juice? Soup? Antacids?"

"No, I'm fine. Really. I just want to rest, that's all."

"Are you sure? Because I can—"

"Sheldon."

He laughed nervously and gave her a sheepish grin. "Sorry. I guess I'm just trying to make up a little bit for what we missed tonight."

"What we—huh?" Madison gave him a blank stare. "I'm sorry. You lost me."

"And you," Sheldon said, theatrically bending down on one knee, "have found…me."

Madison gave him a look of confusion that she hoped did not communicate the irritation she felt. "Sorry," she said dully. "I'm afraid I don't understand."

Sheldon popped back up again. Madison wondered what was with him tonight; all of a sudden, he was one big bundle of nervous energy. Thankfully he did not resume his pacing but instead planted himself on the couch beside her. "What I'm trying to say, Maddie, is that I've been thinking about everything you've said. You know, about not going on like this forever?"

A feeling of dread began to dawn upon Madison as he spoke. But, like the sensation of being unable to move just before a collision, she was unable to take any action to stop what was about to happen.

"It actually makes sense," Sheldon said. "I mean, we've said for a while now that we don't want things to change between us, right? So what could be more stable than promising to keep things the same from now on?" Sheldon took Madison's hand, looking at her with pleading eyes. She suspected that he knew, deep down inside, what her response would be.

"I know I haven't been exactly what you've wanted, Maddie,"

he said. "But I honestly don't want to lose you. Please. Say you'll be my wife." When she didn't answer right away, he rushed to fill the empty silence with more words. "I was going to ask you tonight, in front of everybody at the rehearsal dinner. I thought you'd like that. Wouldn't that have been nice? It would have been like a double celebration."

"Sheldon, I…I don't know what to say." It was clear that he had sensed the changes that had been happening over the past week. "You know, if you had asked me a week ago, I would have said yes." He nodded, but the look dawning on his features made it clear that he saw what was coming. "I think you're a great guy, really, I do. It's just that—"

"It's just that this wasn't meant to be," he finished for her. "Isn't that it, Madison?" He shook his head slowly. "I guess I knew it all along. All week I felt there was something wrong. But—" He stopped and thought for a moment. "It wasn't just this week, was it? We've both known it for a while. Isn't that true, Maddie? Or am I crazy?"

Madison took his hand and held it tightly. She knew that what he was saying was true. And yet it was still so hard to let go. "You're not crazy, Shel," she whispered, her voice threatening to fail her.

"It was Carrie's wedding that made you see it, huh? It just took me awhile to catch on. But you've known it all week. Ever since—" His eyes searched hers. "It's that Kip guy, isn't it?"

She nodded mutely, unable to speak. It was Kip. It was always Kip, from the moment she first saw him. But this wasn't just about him. It was about her, too. About the fact that she was finally beginning to know who she was. About the way she finally understood what she needed most of all and was willing to walk away from someone who, as much as he wanted to, could not give her those things. And it was about the fact that she had found someone at last who truly, deeply, wanted to know her. Or at least *had* wanted to. She had no reason to expect he would give her another chance after her scene in the church.

"Does he love you?"

At his softly voiced question, Madison fell, sobbing, into Sheldon's arms. How could she answer? How could she know what Kip felt? She had walked away, without giving either of them a chance to explain, without making any kind of effort to work things through. After all these years, the truth was clear: Madison was her father's daughter. Dad had taught her only one lesson, but she'd learned it well—walk away. How could Kip ever forgive her?

"If anyone can show just cause why they may not lawfully be joined together, let them now speak, or else hereafter forever hold their peace...."

The more Madison avoided looking directly at Kip, the more his presence consumed every shred of her attention. She stole a quick glance, only to find that he was looking straight at her, just as she had feared...and hoped. She searched his face with fearful eyes but saw no anger in his expression, only compassion and understanding, and perhaps, still, a hint of love. Or was she simply imagining it? Her heart beat rapidly in her chest as her thoughts raced. Maybe she wasn't as bad as her father, after all. Maybe Kip could forgive her and love her, even with all her weaknesses. Perhaps there was hope, beyond hope.

"I require and charge you both, as you stand in the presence of God, before whom the secrets of all hearts are disclosed, that, having duly considered the holy covenant you are about to make, you do now declare before this company your pledge of faith, each to the other."

Paul took Todd's and Carrie's hands and laid them one over the other. Madison watched, mesmerized, as the two intertwined their fingers, an unconscious illustration of the bond they were creating. With a look of adoration unlike any Madison had ever seen, Todd gazed tenderly into the eyes of his lovely bride. In all the years the two women had known one another, Madison had never seen Carrie look so radiant, so content, so joyful.

"In the name of God, I, Todd Arthur Andrews, take thee, Carrie Leigh Phelps, to be my wedded wife, to have and to hold, from this day forward, for better, for worse, for richer, for poorer, in sickness and in health, to love and to cherish, till death us do part, according to God's holy ordinance; and thereto I pledge thee my faith."

"In the name of God, I, Carrie Leigh Phelps, take thee, Todd Arthur Andrews, to be my wedded husband, to have and to hold, from this day forward, for better, for worse, for richer, for poorer, in sickness and in health, to love and to cherish, till death us do part, according to God's holy ordinance; and thereto I pledge thee my faith."

As the loving couple looked longingly into each other's eyes, Paul concluded the ceremony. "Forasmuch as Todd and Carrie have consented together in holy wedlock, and have witnessed the same before God and this company, and thereto have pledged their faith each to the other, and have declared the same by joining hands and by giving and receiving rings; I pronounce that they are husband and wife together, in the name of the Father, and of the Son, and of the Holy Spirit. Those whom God hath joined together, let no one put asunder. Amen."

Kip looked directly at Madison and spoke the word like a covenant.

*"Amen."*

A warm rumble of laughter and murmurs of affirmation rose from the crowd as Todd and Carrie embraced for the first time as man and wife. Yet Madison could not tear her eyes from the man who would soon escort her back down the aisle. Kip's bright-eyed gaze flickered from the happy couple to Madison's face, and when he grinned at her, she felt her heart surge with an assurance and joy so great that if she'd wanted to at that moment, she would not have doubted her ability to fly.

Time stretched on endlessly as she waited for Kip to reach out for her hand. At last, Carrie and Todd passed them in a blur, and Kip's fingers were on hers. Warm. Strong. Reassuring. Madison smiled at the crowd, sharing her joy with everyone. But all too soon they were in the narthex, and as the other attendants joined them, Kip was pulled from her side.

The moments following the ceremony were filled with shouts of celebration as friends and family gathered around to join the bride and groom in their happiness. Madison tried to catch Kip's eye, but their gazes caught and held for only an instant before he was dragged away by the groomsmen, friends from college, for some sort of postceremony male bonding. Madison wondered with a sense of dread why Kip didn't just tell his friends no. Was this an omen? Why didn't he take the time to pull her aside and talk to her, if he still cared? But the message she saw in his eyes was, *Later. When the time is right.* Madison wondered if she was reading his expression correctly, if her imagination was running wild, or if those words were being spoken by God directly to her own heart.

At the reception, she quickly worked her way through the crowded room to claim her spot at the head table. Nearly fifteen minutes passed before Kip finally returned to join the rest of the party. According to custom, he and the other male attendants sat at the long head table to the right of the groom, while Madison sat to Carrie's left with the other women. Kip's eyes were bright, and he wore a goofy, I've-been-struck-by-lightning look on his face. Several of the guys mumbled comments to him, making him grin even wider than before.

*Men,* Madison thought fondly. *They're so crazy.* She'd

believed it for most of her life; always before the connotation had been negative. But "crazy" didn't seem like such a bad thing anymore.

She watched with great anticipation as Kip stood with a flute of sparkling cider in hand, to raise a toast to the bride and groom. In his other hand, he held a small leather Bible, which he began to read from, starting with a passage from Ecclesiastes.

"'I saw emptiness under the sun,'" he began in his steady, clear voice. "'A lonely man without a friend, without son or brother, toiling endlessly yet never satisfied with his wealth—"For whom," he asks, "am I toiling and denying myself the good things of life?" This too is emptiness, a sorry business. Two are better than one; they receive a good reward for their toil, because, if one fails, the other can help his companion up again; but alas for the man who falls alone with no partner to help him up. And, if two lie side by side, they keep each other warm; but how can one keep warm by himself? If a man is alone, an assailant may overpower him, but two can resist; and a cord of three strands is not quickly snapped.'" Solemnly, Kip lay the worn little book on the banquet table and turned to the bridal couple, raising his glass high.

"To my dear friend Todd and his wife, Carrie. You are truly my inspiration," he said with feeling. "This passage is my prayer for you. May your emptiness today be ended. I pray that your stumbles will be few and far between, and yet when you do fall, that it will be into each other's arms. May you keep each other warm and protect one another from life's assailants. And may the cords of your new bond never snap or fray.

"Todd, you are my closest friend. And, Carrie, now a sister. Protect and cherish your love for one another; it is the greatest gift you will ever receive. Today, and always, you are in my prayers. May God keep your marriage under his protection and grant it with his blessings. And may this, your first Christmas together, be the first of many to come." The room erupted in applause as the toast ended. But Kip remained standing.

"And now, on a personal note," he said over the murmur of voices. "Since I have the permission of the bride and groom, I'd like to tell you what I meant when I said they were my inspiration." Most of the crowd watched with an air of amused curiosity; for some reason she could not explain, Madison found herself holding her breath.

"Thanks for bearing with me, folks," Kip continued. "You see, I've known Todd since we were in tenth grade. I always knew he was a great guy, but I never expected he'd be lucky enough to find such a beautiful, wonderful bride." This drew a small burst of cheers. "But he did. And you know what? I realized this week that it wasn't luck at all. It was God. The reason I know this is because this week I met the most incredible woman I've ever known in my life. All along, I've been praying, 'God, is this what I think it is?' And God said to me, 'Yes, Kip. It's a woman.'"

Kip turned to face Madison, giving her a broad wink. The crowd broke into laughter. Kip grinned. "No, seriously. I've felt that God has been telling me what I've waited my whole life to hear. Those of you who know me won't be surprised at what I'm about to say. You've seen me do crazy things before. But I'm afraid this particular woman is just getting used to my quirks."

Madison wanted to leap up and shout, "I *love* your quirks!" but she forced herself to sit on her hands and hear what he had to say.

"I suppose it's a little early to ask her to marry me," Kip said, "since we haven't gone out on a real date yet, and I don't actually have a ring." A few catcalls and boos erupted from the crowd. Everyone was getting into the little drama. "And there's a very real chance that she'll refuse me and that I'm up here making a complete fool of myself. But I'm willing to make a fool of myself...especially for love. For *this* love."

With that, he extended his hand to her, and Madison stood to a chorus of cheers, the loudest of which came from Carrie's lips. Moments later, Madison's hand was secure in Kip's, where it belonged.

"And so, without further ado," Kip said, smiling, "I would like to announce my intentions.

"Madison Pierce, you are the one I have dreamed of, waited for, and prayed about. I believe that God is leading us to be together. I pledge before God and these witnesses to love you, to support you, and to help you become the woman God wants you to be. What do you say, Madison? Make me the happiest man in the world. Will you agree to date me, with the understanding that I have every intention in the world of one day making you my bride?"

For a split second, Madison paused to consider. What she was about to promise certainly took her out of her comfort zone. But being comfortable didn't seem so important anymore. Because she was finally learning to accept the truth that her life was in God's hands.

"I will," she said with conviction and a confidence born of a deepening faith. With those words as his cue, Kip took her in his arms and smiled down into the eyes of his wife-to-be.

"Hey!" someone shouted over the enthusiastic roar of the crowd. "Somebody kiss the bride!"

Kip and Todd threw each other a broad-faced grin.

And then they did.

Blanket Coverage is an incredible, real-life ministry in Portland, Oregon. To find out more about Blanket Coverage or to send contributions, you can reach them at:

Blanket Coverage
Post Office Box 3603
Portland, Oregon 97208
1-888-BE WARM 1

# PALISADES...PURE ROMANCE

## ⟨ PALISADES ⟩

*Reunion*, Karen Ball
*Refuge*, Lisa Tawn Bergren
*Torchlight*, Lisa Tawn Bergren
*Treasure*, Lisa Tawn Bergren
*Chosen*, Lisa Tawn Bergren
*Firestorm*, Lisa Tawn Bergren
*Surrender*, Lynn Bulock
*Wise Man's House*, Melody Carlson
*Arabian Winds*, Linda Chaikin
*Lions of the Desert*, Linda Chaikin
*Cherish*, Constance Colson
*Chase the Dream*, Constance Colson
*Angel Valley*, Peggy Darty
*Sundance*, Peggy Darty
*Moonglow*, Peggy Darty
*Promises*, Peggy Darty
*Love Song*, Sharon Gillenwater
*Antiques*, Sharon Gillenwater
*Song of the Highlands*, Sharon Gillenwater
*Texas Tender*, Sharon Gillenwater
*Secrets*, Robin Jones Gunn
*Whispers*, Robin Jones Gunn
*Echoes*, Robin Jones Gunn
*Sunsets*, Robin Jones Gunn
*Clouds*, Robin Jones Gunn
*Coming Home*, Barbara Jean Hicks
*Snow Swan*, Barbara Jean Hicks
*Irish Eyes*, Annie Jones
*Father by Faith*, Annie Jones

*Glory,* Marilyn Kok
*Sierra,* Shari MacDonald
*Forget-Me-Not,* Shari MacDonald
*Diamonds,* Shari MacDonald
*Stardust,* Shari MacDonald
*Westward,* Amanda MacLean
*Stonehaven,* Amanda MacLean
*Everlasting,* Amanda MacLean
*Promise Me the Dawn,* Amanda MacLean
*Kingdom Come,* Amanda MacLean
*Betrayed,* Lorena McCourtney
*Escape,* Lorena McCourtney
*Dear Silver,* Lorena McCourtney
*Enough!* Gayle Roper
*Voyage,* Elaine Schulte

## ⌒ ANTHOLOGIES ⌒

*A Christmas Joy,* Darty, Gillenwater, MacLean
*Mistletoe,* Ball, Hicks, McCourtney
*A Mother's Love,* Bergren, Colson, MacLean
*Silver Bells,* Bergren, Krause, MacDonald

# THE PALISADES LINE

*Look for these new releases at your local bookstore. If the title you seek is not in stock, the store may order you a copy using the ISBN listed.*

### *Surrender,* **Lynn Bulock**
ISBN 1-57673-104-9
As a single mom, Cassie Neel works hard to give her children the best she can. This year, young Sarah and Zach want to show their appreciation for what she does by giving her a date with handsome police officer Lee Winter as a birthday present! Surprised and flattered, Cassie accepts. But little does she know where that one date will lead....

### *Wise Man's House,* **Melody Carlson**
ISBN 1-57673-070-0
Kestra McKenzie, a young widow trying to make a new life for herself, thinks she has found the solidity she longs for when she purchases her childhood dream house—a stone mansion on the Oregon Coast. Just as renovations begin, a mysterious stranger moves into her caretaker's cottage—and into her heart.

### *Moonglow,* **Peggy Darty**
ISBN 1-57673-112-X
During the Summer Olympics set in Atlanta, Tracy Kosell comes back to her hometown of Moonglow, Georgia, to investigate the disappearance of a wealthy socialite. She meets up with former schoolmate Jay Calloway, who's one of the detectives assigned to the case. As their attraction grows and the mercury rises, they unwrap a case that isn't as simple as it seemed.

### *Promises,* **Peggy Darty**
ISBN 1-57673-149-9
Elizabeth Calloway, a Christian psychologist, finds herself in over her head when a client tells her about a dangerous twin sister. Elizabeth turns to her detective husband, Michael, asking him to find the woman. Unexpected events plunge the couple into danger, where they rediscover the joy of falling in love.

### *Texas Tender,* Sharon Gillenwater
ISBN 1-57673-111-1
When Shelby Nolan inherits a watermelon farm, she moves from Houston to a small West Texas town. Spotting two elderly men digging holes in her field each night, she turns to neighbor Deputy Sheriff Logan Slade to figure out what's going on. Together they uncover a long-buried robbery and discover the fulfillment of their own dreams.

### *Clouds,* Robin Jones Gunn
ISBN 1-57673-113-8
On a trip to Germany, flight attendant Shelly Graham unexpectedly runs into her old boyfriend, Jonathan Renfield. Since she still cares for him, it's hard for Shelly to hide her hurt when she learns he's engaged. It isn't until she goes to meet friends in Glenbrooke, Oregon, that they meet again—and this time, they're both ready to be honest.

### *Sunsets,* Robin Jones Gunn
ISBN 1-57673-103-0
Alissa Benson loves her job as a travel agent. But when the agency has computer problems, they call in expert Brad Phillips. Alissa can't wait for Brad to fix the computers and leave—he's too blunt for her comfort. So she's more than a little upset when she moves into a duplex and finds out he's her neighbor!

### *Snow Swan,* Barbara Jean Hicks
ISBN 1-57673-107-3
Life hasn't been easy for Toni Ferrier. As an unwed mother and a recovering alcoholic, she doesn't feel worthy of anyone's love. Then she meets Clark McConaughey, who helps her launch her business aboard the sternwheeler Snow Swan. Sparks fly between them, but if Clark finds out the truth about Toni's past, will he still love her?

### *Irish Eyes,* Annie Jones
ISBN 1-57673-108-1
When Julia Reed finds a young boy, who claims to be a leprechaun, camped out under a billboard, she gets drawn into a century-old crime involving a real pot of gold. Interpol agent Cameron O'Dea is trying to solve the crime. In the process, he takes over the homeless shelter that Julia runs, camps out in her neighbor's RV, and generally turns her life upside down!

### *Father by Faith,* **Annie Jones**
ISBN 1-57673-117-0
Nina Jackson may not know much about ranching, but she knows business. So when she buys a dude ranch and hires recuperating cowboy Clint Cooper as her foreman, she figures she's set. But her son, Alex, doesn't think so. He's been praying for a father, and the moment he sees Clint, he tells everyone that God has answered his prayers and sent him a daddy!

### *Stardust,* **Shari MacDonald**
ISBN 1-57673-109-X
As a teenager, Gillian Spencer fell in love with astronomy...and with Max Bishop. But after he leaves her heartbroken, she learns to keep her feelings guarded. Now that she's a graduate student studying astronomy, she thinks she has left the past far behind. So when she gets an exciting assignment, she's shocked to learn she's been paired with the now-famous Dr. Maxwell Bishop.

### *Kingdom Come,* **Amanda MacLean**
ISBN 1-57673-120-0
In 1902, feisty Ivy Rose Clayborne, M.D., returns to her hometown of Kingdom Come to fight the coal mining company that is ravaging the land. She meets an unexpected ally, a man who claims to be a drifter but in reality is Harrison MacKenzie, grandson of the coal mining baron. Together they face the aftermath of betrayal, the fight for justice...and the price of love.

### *Dear Silver,* **Lorena McCourtney**
ISBN 1-57673-110-3
When Silver Sinclair receives a polite but cold letter from Chris Bentley ending their relationship, she's shocked, since she's never met the man! She confronts Chris about his insensitive attitude toward this other Silver Sinclair, and finds herself becoming friends with a man who's unlike anyone she's ever met.

### *Enough!* **Gayle Roper**
ISBN 1-57673-185-5
When Molly Gregory gets fed up with her three teenaged children, she announces that she's going on strike. She and her husband Pete stand back and watch as chaos results in their household, in a hilarious experiment that teaches their children how to honor their parents.

### *A Mother's Love,* **Bergren, Colson, MacLean**
ISBN 1-57673-106-5
*By Lisa Tawn Bergren:* A widower and his young daughter go to Southern California for vacation, and return with much more than they expected.
*By Constance Colson:* Cassie Jenson wants her old sweetheart to stay in her memories. But Bruce Foster has other plans.

*By Amanda MacLean:* A couple is expecting their first baby, and each plans a surprise for the other that doesn't quite turn out as it should.

### Silver Bells, Bergren, Krause, MacDonald
ISBN 1-57673-119-7

*By Lisa Tawn Bergren:* Noel Stevens has to work up the ranks in her new job, but being assigned to Santa's workshop is too much. Until she gets to know Santa....

*By Laura Krause:* Writer Bridger Deans goes home for a family Christmas and finds her ex-fiancé there.

*By Shari MacDonald:* Madison Pierce feels lonely at the thought of her best friend's wedding...until she meets the best man.

# ALABASTER BOOKS
*Romance, mystery, comedy....Real life.*

### Homeward, Melody Carlson
ISBN 1-57673-029-8

When Meg Lancaster learns that her grandmother is dying, she returns to the small town on the Oregon coast where she spent vacations as a child. After being away for twenty years, the town hasn't changed...but her family has. Meg struggles with her memories of the past and what is now reality, until tragedy strikes the family and she must learn to face the future.

### Arabian Winds, Linda Chaikin
ISBN 1-57673-3-105-7

World War I is breaking upon the deserts of Arabia in 1914. Young nurse Allison Wescott is on holiday with an archaeological club, but a murder interrupts her plans, and a mysterious officer keeps turning up wherever she goes!

### Lions of the Desert, Linda Chaikin
ISBN 1-57673-114-6

In 1915, Allison Wescott arrives in Cairo to serve the British military and once again encounters the mysterious Bret Holden. And to mix things up even further, the chaplain she is thinking of marrying comes to Cairo as well.

*Watch for the final book in the trilogy, coming in spring 1998!*

### *Chase the Dream,* Constance Colson
ISBN 0-88070-928-6

After years apart, four friends are reunited through the competitive world of professional rodeo, where they seek fame, fortune, faith...and love.

### *Song of the Highlands,* Sharon Gillenwater
ISBN 1-57673-946-4

Kiernan returns from the Napoleonic wars to find out he's inherited a title. At his run-down estate, he meets the beautiful Mariah, and finds himself swept up in the romance and deception of a London Season.

*Watch for more books in Sharon Gillenwater's Scottish series!*

### *Promise Me the Dawn,* Amanda MacLean
ISBN 0-88070-955-3

Molly Quinn and Zach MacAlister come from very different backgrounds, but both seek to overcome the past. Enduring hardship and prosperity, the promise of a meeting at dawn brings them through it all.

### *Redeeming Love,* Francine Rivers
ISBN 1-57673-186-3

The only men Angel has ever known have betrayed her. When she meets Michael Hosea in the gold country of California, she has no reason to believe he's any different. But Michael is different. And through him Angel learns what love really means—the kind of love that can wipe away the shame of her past.